HARVEST AMERICAN
Writing

MARBLES

MARBLES

Oxford Stroud

A Harvest/HBJ Book

Harcourt Brace Jovanovich, Publishers

San Diego New York London

HBJ

Some material previously appeared in *NATIONAL FORUM: The Phi Kappa Phi Journal* under the title "Baptism."

Library of Congress Cataloging-in-Publication Data
Stroud, Oxford S.
Marbles: a novel/by Oxford S. Stroud.
p. cm.
ISBN 0-15-157055-8
ISBN 0-15-657200-1 (pbk.)
I. Title.
PS3569.T733M37 1991
813'.54—dc20 91-21512

Designed by Trina Stahl

Printed in the United States of America

First Harvest/HBJ edition 1992

A B C D E

For my mother,
Viola Goode Liddell;
and my wife,
Mary Anne Stroud

MARBLES

Chapter One

I was ten and unbaptized when Aunt Rebecca discovered my fatal flaw, after which she put the verbal lash to Mother, and I was scheduled for sprinkling the following Sunday in Deen Presbyterian Church.

I loved Aunt Rebecca because I was afraid not to. Our family roots and her influence spread everywhere in the church. She had graduated from Calvin Bible Institute, where she struggled mightily with the divine enigmas, and afterward her judgments on the here and the hereafter were like steel shafts driven into the rock of God. No church elder dared cross unbidden the wake of her doctrine. No pastor, young or old, fared well without her favor. Once, directly before she went to the institute, a country gentleman, one John Decker, had forsaken her for another, and thereafter she had closed the door of matrimony forevermore.

Every Sunday morning after song and prayer, Aunt Rebecca marched me and seven others into the anteroom behind the pulpit, closed the heavy white door upon us, and taught us Sunday school. She sat us alphabetized in a horseshoe facing the back door, over which hung a large picture of Jesus reaching from a small boat to lift Simon Peter from the waves. Aunt Rebecca sat in the mouth of the arc and called our full names, to which we responded with memorized Bible verses. Then she prayed. Seldom did she pray for God's mercy or love. She prayed for retribution and divine justice for those who had beheld God imperfectly. After the prayer, Aunt Rebecca opened her Bible and read in clipped phrases, pausing to warn, to caution, to forewarn, and to admonish. She lectured in exacting tones, and the vivid images of Hell and Satan she created in our minds sent me many times screaming out of my dreams into the hallway. If ever I see a piece of Heaven, I believe that it will be not because of my own godly virtues but because Aunt Rebecca frightened me upward from the horrors down under. She drove a hard bargain. "We are all sinners," she nailed into us Sunday after Sunday, "and the wages of sin is death." It didn't take me long to figure out where we were all headed. My sins were manifold, and the greatest of them, according to Aunt Rebecca, was shooting marbles for keeps. I was a crack shot. I had a quart fruit jar full of "keepers," every one a mortal sin.

Then, the Sunday before baptism, the Sunday before I was to be sprinkled, something happened that would become nearly the end of me. Aunt Rebecca seated us in our predestined pattern facing the terrified disciple and the angry waves. She called the roll: "Alice Jane Adams . . . , Carl Hooper Barnett . . . , Sylvia Anne Grayson . . . , Harvey Michael Johnson . . . , Janis Ellen Roberts . . ." and down to "Shelly Leopold Webster." It wasn't hard to learn a new Bible verse, but it was next to impossible to remember it in Aunt Rebecca's presence. For fun, Harvey Johnson and I once used "Jesus wept" on the same Sunday, and Aunt Rebecca mashed my toe against the floor with her Sunday slipper. "Brevity is not the soul of wit," she admonished. The next week Harvey started in on Genesis, and he had worked himself into the third verse.

Harvey spoke up: " 'God said Let there be light,' " and stopped.

" 'And there was light,' " Aunt Rebecca prompted. "Genesis one:three. Say it all again, correctly." Harvey did.

When she called, "Silas O'Riley Simeon," I was ready.

" 'Study to show thyself approved unto God . . . ,' " I began, and said the entire verse correctly, adding: "Second Timothy two:fifteen."

Shelly had an amazing brain and had memorized the whole thirty-eighth chapter of Job. Aunt Rebecca had to stop him when he got down to "Have the gates of death been opened unto thee?"

The lesson was about Noah and the flood and the destruction of the world. Then Aunt Rebecca made her astonishing announcement: we were all to "Find God this week and bring Him with you to Sunday school next Sunday."

There was small twittering among the girls. Shelly smiled down into his Bible. Sylvia opened her beautiful eyes in amazement. Aunt Rebecca explained that there were but three ways that led into the company of God: Duty, Dedication, and Self-Denial—any of which could lead us into the holy center of His Presence. She stood up and held the Holy Scripture straight out in one hand and put the other on top, making a Bible sandwich. Through our imperfect means and by His own miraculous power, she said, God would show us the pathway to Him; then He would, for a moment, pull back the veil through which we see darkly, so that each of us might get a glimpse of Him and then, however briefly, take hold of His Divine Being.

"Find Him!" Aunt Rebecca instructed. She held

out her Bible in one hand like a cleaver and chopped the air. "Secure Him in your own way, and bring Him with you next Sunday. Remember," she said at last, "ye shall know the truth, and the truth shall make you free, for the Lord moves in strange and mysterious ways."

That was it.

I was stunned with the gravity of the charge. God gave saints their entire lives to find Him. Aunt Rebecca gave us a week.

As we passed through the door and into the body of the church, Aunt Rebecca said, "Silas, you are to pump the organ this morning for church services." The organ was an old colossus with a windbag in the middle and a pump handle in the side. Harvey's mother, who played when Aunt Rebecca was ill, had legs like a Roman and could keep the machine ablast by the pedals alone. Not so Aunt Rebecca. Her calf muscles were small and tight like a grasshopper's. When I pumped, I was sealed off from the congregation and choir by a right-angled mahogany tomb but had a full view of my aunt. She perched herself on the organ stool like Queen Elizabeth, her feet poised to follow the rhythm of the pedals. Her dress tightened at the waist as she soared to the high notes. In profile her face was gray steel, sharp as a woodman's hatchet.

"Glad she ain't my aunt," Harvey said after

church. For Harvey, finding God was a joke. For Shelly, it was a problem, a mystery. For Sylvia, it would entail a performance. For me, it was an imperative: Aunt Rebecca was family. With her, God was the one fact in all creation; and my not finding Him, not laying even one little finger on the tiniest speck of Him, would amount not only to failure but to denial and damnation.

Harvey grinned. "Where you going to find God at?"

On Monday I was worried. By Wednesday I had lost my appetite. On Thursday I dreamed a scary dream: I was the only marble in my jar of keepers—a lone, sinful agate rattling about. But it was *my* jar and *my* marble. And so was born my private Jar of Marbles, an involuntary habit of collecting souls, a personal game I played right up to the beginning of my part in World War II.

On Friday I climbed up in Uncle George's hay barn and asked God to show Himself, to give me a sign—something from His divine Everywhere that I could lay before Aunt Rebecca on Sunday morning.

God started answering my prayer the next day, with the remote aid of Blue. Blue was our Negro cook's boy. In our running dialogue on the location of the human soul, Blue had decided that the "Big Ghost," God, could be anywhere He wanted to, but for convenience, Blue kept *his* "little ghost," his soul, in a snuff can on the mantel over the fireplace.

My prayer was not fulfilled before I had suffered. Friday night, before tucking the covers under my chin, Mother put her hand on my brow and wondered aloud about my health. Father said from downstairs if I didn't have any fever, to hush. It was deep in the night before I tumbled off to sleep. In a nightmare, Aunt Rebecca was transformed into a giant wasp. On waves of overwhelming music she arose on her stool from a smoking organ pit, charioting a flaming organ across a dark void and wielding lightning bolts that flashed from both hands. It never occurred to me in the dream that perhaps *she* had risen from the regions below. I knew only that if the organ was a devil, Aunt Rebecca was in the coachman's seat and the sounding bellows was nothing more than an infernal instrument completely at her command.

"You were having a bad dream," Mother said, steadying me from arm's length.

"What's the matter with him now?" Father said from downstairs.

"He had a nightmare about Rebecca and something about God."

"Silas," my father said.

"Sir."

"You want to come sleep downstairs?"

"No, sir," I said.

"Silas said Rebecca was flying a flaming organ and dealing out lightning."

"That's no dream," my father said.

Mother said, "Now you forget about Becky and go back to sleep."

The part of my prayer that was answered started happening Saturday afternoon, when I was alone in the house. I stood in the doorway of my room, looking at my stuffed animals on the mantelpiece. Uncle George had mounted them and given them to me. There was a crow and raccoon on one side and a hawk and an abused screech owl on the other. One of Mother's cats had found dispute with the owl and left the hapless bird partially defeathered and cross-eyed. In the middle, between two clumps of dried broom sage, was the red Prince Albert smoking tobacco can I kept matches and rabbit tobacco in. Every once in a while, Shelly and Blue and I slipped off and sinned; we smoked the rabbitweed rolled in brown sack paper out behind the barn or down at Tucker's Spring below the church.

Through the open sash of my window I could see Judge Webster's observatory, and rain clouds festering. The low rumblings in the distance brought to my mind the image of Aunt Rebecca charioting the flaming organ and dispensing thunderous authority. It was then that God started answering my prayer. My eye was drawn to the middle of the mantel, where my rabbit tobacco can was, and then to the oval spot where the prince stood. The red can began acting upon me like a magnet, extracting my fears, pulling them straight out of me like iron filings across a sheet of paper.

God was moving, burning open the way.

Then I knew exactly what I must do. It wasn't anything I thought up. It was simply that, at that given moment, a curtain was drawn and the way was there: *I would pray God into the Prince Albert can.*

I rushed the can to the bathroom, shook the rabbit tobacco leaves into the commode, scooped slivers of Mother's best hand soap into the cavity, watered it down, capped it tight and sloshed it around until suds oozed from the lid, then dumped water and foam into the commode and flushed it down, rabbit tobacco and all, in one gulp. I rinsed the Prince Albert can clean, dried it with a clean cloth, and laid it purified at the head of my bed.

In the prayer business I had been a complete failure. Except for once. That was the time Blue and Shelly and I set out to find the chest of Civil War gold buried somewhere on a fork of Uncle George's land, where Snake Creek runs into the river. The raft we made was too big for the creek; so Blue and I, in the sanctuary of our hayloft, fell to our knees, praying fervently for rain, and it did rain. It had rained solid for a week when we hopped aboard, cut loose, and went swirling away. Downstream around the first bend, we piled into a beaver dam and jammed fast. We hopped off and hitched a ride home on a cotton wagon. The waters rose treacherously and washed our raft afloat again, I'm sure, and swept the small craft downcreek into the river and away forever. It was the worst flood in Alabama history.

This prayer would have to be different.

This time I wouldn't be asking God to move a part of His creation in my favor, like the rain or like trying to pray a .22 rifle out of the Sears Roebuck catalogue and under our Christmas tree. I would be asking God to move the whole Everywhereness of Himself, His whole everlasting Godself in one piece.

With God all things are possible, Aunt Rebecca had said. And so it was. I was surprised at the simplicity of it all. I lugged up from downstairs our voluminous family Bible and Mother's candelabrum. I placed the Bible, open, on the edge of my bed and the brass candleholder on the side bureau, in the middle of the mirror and in line with the Bible. Flush against the top seam of the Bible and in line with the center candle in the candelabrum, I set the Prince Albert can. Then I went to open the window. The clouds were bundling up in windrows. I could smell it was going to rain. I loosed the tiebacks, and the side curtains fell together and turned the room blue. I used one of my rabbit tobacco matches to light the candles and then knelt down on the Bible side of my bed to pray. I knitted my fingers, closed my eyes, and put my knuckles under my chin.

Across the back pasture, Uncle George was revving up his airplane motor. He'd throttle the De Havilland up a couple of times and let her idle. Uncle George had been a hero in the First World War and secretly hoped there would be a second, so he could get in it. Numerous times, secure between Uncle George's knees, I had flown in the wonderful ship and, holding the magic stick, had guided the De Havilland with my own hands. I wondered if finding God for Aunt Rebecca could be as exciting and dangerous as war. Blue would have understood my kneeling down in prayer. We had prayed together for just about everything. But the thought of Uncle George or Shelly walking in on me all hunkered down like a scared monkey sent a little shower of shame over me.

Now was the time.

"God . . . ," I said into the empty room. Uncle George throttled the De Havilland wide open. I opened my eyes.

I had forgotten to open the lid on the can so God could get in. I pressed open the lid—then squawked when I saw myself in the mirror. The candelabrum on the bureau had cast itself in the mirror behind me and multiplied itself a million times, and in the middle of the two avenues of light my severed head hovered over the Bible.

I clamped my eyes shut.

"God."

I waited for the message to reach Him.

"God."

It was not working. I opened my eyes and thumbed back a clump of Bible pages and pointed down for some magic help from God's word.

It said:

"And his concubine, whose name was Reumah, she bare also Tebah, and Gaham, and Thahash, and Maachah."

This was not it. I moved my finger across to the opposite page. It said: "And the angel of the Lord called unto him out of heaven, and said, Abraham, Abraham: and he said, Here am I."

This was it.

I closed my eyes again and prayed aloud.

"God, here I am too, and Aunt Rebecca's not going to wait on you or nobody."

I kept my eyes closed and held on to both sides of the huge Bible and swayed back and forth.

"Will you please . . ."

The way was opening up.

"Please . . ." I swayed.

It was like darkness making way for the sun.

"Please . . ."

My prayer was being answered.

"Will you get in the can?"

There was a holy silence. I waited. The clock downstairs struck the half hour, held its breath, swallowed, then resumed its tocking. Then God said, matter-of-factly:

"Yes." His voice filled the room.

Uncle George throttled the airplane up again and let her die with a pop.

"When?" I asked God.

"Now, if you like," God said pleasantly.

"Will you say *'Now'* when you get all the way inside?" I asked.

"Yes, of course," God answered. "Are you ready?"

"Yes," I breathed. A drop of sweat ruptured and ran down my forehead and off the end of my nose. Then God said:

"Now."

That was it.

I opened my eyes and slapped the Prince Albert can shut. I hurried to the window, pulled back the curtains for more light, and got some slingshot rubbers—narrow bands I'd scissored from an old inner tube—and wrapped God tightly around and around. Then I blew out the candles and put God in my pocket.

Granny, what a feeling! I was amazed at my power of release. It felt like the time Shelly and I got into Mother's sherry. Leaving the Bible on my bed, I went downstairs and ate a breast of cold chicken, a drumstick, two biscuits, a bowl of greens, and a glob of peach cobbler, and drank a glass of iced tea.

When Mother drove into the backyard, I ran upstairs for the Bible and candelabrum and put them in their places. Then I tipped back up to my room, closed the door, and took God out of my pocket and held Him in my hands. I smiled at the thought of Aunt Rebecca charioting her flaming organ. The next day, upon my pronouncement, her face would rise in wonder and fall in praise.

I pulled aside the rubber bands on the tin can and looked at the grand prince: his bald head and groomed beard, his high collar and bunched tie, his black frock coat with militant buttons on both sides, carnation in lapel, his gloved hands and royal stance.

That night at supper, Aunt Rebecca phoned and said I was to wear a white shirt, black tie, and black shoes for my baptism the next day and that after I had been sprinkled I was to pump the organ for church services. And what difference, Mother wanted to know, would it make what color I wore if God looked on the heart and not on the outward appearance and if, after I was baptized, I'd be sealed off from sight in the organ pit? To which Aunt Rebecca said that black *was* the proper color for a soul as yet unclaimed by God and that whether I was seen or unseen by the congregation or whether I was sealed away or unsealed, *she* could see me from her organ stool. Then she asked Mother if I was "ready" for Sunday school.

"What does Becky mean, did you find him?"

"It's just something I had to do," I said.

"Just you?"

"No, ma'am. We all had to. Shelly too."

"Well," Mother said philosophically, "I hope *you're* ready for *Becky*, or God help you."

"Aunt Rebecca said we shall know the truth and the truth will make us free."

"Yes," Mother said, "but she didn't say it would make you happy."

I got up from the supper table. The lightning outdoors glowed softly, then darkened. I could count to seven before the thunder came.

"And your Aunt Rebecca said that you had just about worn out Second Timothy two:fifteen and to get you a new verse for tomorrow."

That was easy. I'd use the verse that had triggered all my good luck with God.

But it was not easy. It took the better part of an hour to even find the verse in my small Bible. But once I had taken a picture of the words with my eyes and set them up in my head, I could say them out pat.

I propped up the Prince Albert can against my Bible, clicked off the bed lamp, and lay back in the darkness to savor God, to tumble Him over in my soul. To think of it—God, all of Him, at my right hand!

It was a long time before I dropped off to sleep. I kept seeing myself, to the amazement of all, presenting God to Aunt Rebecca. Then I got to thinking how, with God in the can, I could improve my fishing. It was all mighty fine for Aunt Rebecca to pronounce God as Everywhere, but I had all of Him hemmed up in one spot. By my own asking and by His own permission, I had made God available. I could travel down the bank of Snake Creek holding God in my hand and spread the moccasins the way Moses parted the sea, and when the fish refused to bite, I could thump God awake and have the best bream and bass transfixed on my hook in an instant.

Outside the window, the lightning was making crooked stitches in the clouds. I could see the glass eyes of my stuffed screech owl on the end of the mantelpiece. Then I fell to thinking about the flood that smashed the raft Shelly and Blue and I made when we started down the creek to find the gold. . . .

Holding God aloft in the can like a water witcher with his magic branch, I was swept up at a roaring speed into the night, above the trees and across eagle distances of space below, then was pulled down and down, tumbling through a tunnel of soft curling vines and brambles onto the very spot where the chest was buried. When I picked myself up out of the leaves,

Prince Albert and Shelly and Blue were there. The prince was dressed in red overalls and sat bareheaded under an oak. I was standing over the open chest. Just as I imagined: it was full of small loaves of gold. The prince was rolling a cigarette out of the tobacco from his own Prince Albert can. There was no way to know whether he had seen us or not. He paid us no attention whatever. The prince lit his cigarette, pulled the smoke deep inside him, and let it out in a cool blue line. When I looked back, Shelly and Blue had vanished. The gold bars would not come out of the casket. They slipped through my fingers like warm honey. When I looked up, the prince was gone too, except for a little whip tail of smoke under the oak tree. . . .

It was still cloudy and rumbling outside when I woke up. The dream had created a problem. To expose God abruptly in Sunday school would break the spell; the bond between us could be broken. I had not given God a chance to prove Himself. And what a glory it would be to God and to them all for me to lay a couple of gold bars before Aunt Rebecca and then lay one on the pulpit before Reverend Grayson and the whole congregation.

When Mother started up the stairs, I covered up God with my Bible. She dropped the white shirt, black tie, and black shoes on the foot of the bed and said I looked "sheepish." Was I ill? No. But I wasn't hungry again. For breakfast I ate one biscuit, which didn't go all the way down. I went upstairs to get God.

"It's time for Sunday school," my father called. "Now hurry. It's going to rain."

I put the Prince Albert can in my coat pocket and went downstairs and crawled into the back seat of the car and waited for God to move in one of His mysterious ways.

"Silas," Mother wanted to know as we drove along, "did you learn a new Bible verse for Rebecca?"

I did. I propped up the words in my mind and said them back to myself. The biscuit had stopped at the bottom of my throat. When we got to the church, Aunt Rebecca, dressed in gray and gold, was stepping out of her black coupe. Her slightly silver hair was stacked in a cathedral on her head, and her collar flared out like eagle wings. I could hear—all the way across the churchyard—her crisp dress swish in the damp air. The gentlemen at the top of the steps tipped their hats as Aunt Rebecca entered the church.

Shelly was beside himself with my flying dream about the prince and the gold and said we could fly to the creek at night again in his own dream and seek out the elusive treasure.

After a song and a prayer, the congregation split up and went to separate places in the church for Sunday school lessons. The silver bowl with holy water for my baptism sat on the pulpit, and Aunt Rebecca stood beside it, holding her Bible to her breast with one hand and beckoning to us with the other. For some reason, the silver bowl of holy water reminded me of Aunt Rebecca's goldfish. I followed behind Harvey. Aunt Rebecca opened the big door and marched us through. When we were closed in and seated in our semicircle, she motioned our heads down with her finger and prayed. I put my hand in my coat pocket and took ahold of God. My hand was dry. I could feel God. His power flowed up my arm like electricity. Aunt Rebecca was praying for the kind of rain that would purify all the earth with God's righteousness. I wondered in what silly way Harvey had found God.

". . . Amen," Aunt Rebecca said.

"Alice Jane Adams." Jane said her verse. Had she found God and brought Him with her this morning? She had. She helped her mama wash dishes and made her bed every day and knew God was with her all the time. Carl said something equally unamazing. Pretty Sylvia read her Bible every night and saw God in a cloud. And so it went. It was dull just listening to them. Harvey was the worst of all. He helped his daddy work on the farm and said the word "God" was in the Bible, and he brought his Bible with him, so he reckoned that amounted to bringing God to Sunday school. How dumb can you get?

Shelly was a genius, and Lord knows what verses he had memorized this time. But as for bringing God to Sunday school that morning, he was going to play on the piano a vigorous flourish from the German composer Wagner, maintaining, as his musical mother had often declared, that God was in all grand sound. Aunt Rebecca's face would be worth seeing when Shelly got up to play. I was ready with my Bible verse when Aunt Rebecca got to me.

"Silas O'Riley Simeon."

" 'And the angel of the Lord called unto him out of heaven, and said, Abraham, Abraham: and he said, Here am I.' Genesis twenty-two:eleven." The sound of the verse soaked into the walls.

Then Aunt Rebecca said, almost secretly, "Silas, this is an important day for you. Are you ready?"

"Yes, ma'am."

"Now," she said, leaning forward and pressing her Bible tightly between her palms, "did you find God last week?"

"Yes, ma'am," I said. I was holding on to Him firmly in my pocket.

"Do you have Him with you this morning?"

"Yes, ma'am." God's power was strengthening into me.

"And, Silas, what did *you* do?"

"I prayed."

Aunt Rebecca pulled in her chin with the slightest wisp of a smile and arched her neck in surprise.

"You prayed?"

"Yes, ma'am."

"Then," Aunt Rebecca assured me, "you have brought God to us this morning in your heart."

"No, ma'am," I announced. Then I pulled God out of my coat pocket, rubber bands and all, and held Him up before her eyes. "I've got Him right here in this Prince Albert can."

A terrible change came over Aunt Rebecca. She neither spoke nor stirred, and yet her every feature had altered. It was as if she had been shot and her eyes were awaiting the fatal message that her body had already received.

"He's inside the can," I explained. "I prayed Him right in there."

"You what?" she wailed.

"I got down on my knees and prayed Him in." I held God out closer toward her. "I swear, Aunt Rebecca. God told me in His own voice—"

"Enough!"

The girls stopped their twittering. Shelly was hiding behind his Bible. Consternation showed in Sylvia's eyes. My hands were sweating.

"Do you know what this is?" Aunt Rebecca wagged her finger at God.

"It's a Prince Albert can."

"I don't mean that," she said, shaking her head. "I mean do you know what you have *done?*" Her breast swelled. "And"—she paused—"on the very day of your baptism!"

"It's not just a plain can," I pled. "God's inside. God told me—"

"Enough!" Aunt Rebecca said. It was like chopping a worm in two with an ax.

I lowered God a little. Aunt Rebecca rose.

"You other children move out into the church—at once," she instructed. "Swiftly!" She snapped her fingers three times behind them. Sylvia's lips said to me, *You better be careful*. Shelly lingered, and the last thing I saw of him before he closed the door was his eyeballs. Aunt Rebecca turned to me.

"This," she said, pointing down at God, "is sacrilege," and, with added intensity, "blasphemy," then, sounding alarm on every syllable, *"i-dol-a-try."* I had only the dimmest notion of what these words meant, but the gravity of them fell heavily upon me and their essence seeped through my pores like liniment. I started to put God back in my pocket.

"Silas O'Riley Simeon, don't you dare put that thing back in your pocket." I held God down and let Him swing in my hand like a pendulum. "So God is in the can?" she asked.

"Yes, ma'am." I could feel myself coming undone. My strength was going back into the can, and my fingers were slick against the rubber bands.

"Well, then," Aunt Rebecca said, "we'll just have to get Him out." She was looking at the Prince Albert can.

"I can't. God promised—"

"Silas," she said, laying a cluster of fingers on my shoulder. She looked at the big door leading to the pulpit, then back to me. "Don't go getting God mixed up with your silly notions, do you hear—certainly not on the day of your baptism." I was coming apart quickly now, like a spool of yarn spinning backward. Then, completely undone, I released myself toward Aunt Rebecca and cast my head upon her bosom.

"Who can say God can't be in the can if God said He could?" I sobbed. Her heart was knocking firmly against her chest bone like a small damp mallet.

"I can," she whispered in my ear.

My feet started moving away before I did. I was running toward the back door of the anteroom and under the picture of Jesus with Simon Peter sinking down into the waves. Then I was out the door and running through the moist air and down the clay path and into the woods. The path was hard, and my cheeks shimmied as my feet came down and came down. I ran on downhill through Tucker's Hollow, where the old tomato-can water dipper hung on the limb over the box spring and where Shelly and Blue and I smoked rabbit tobacco, and on up the hill and out into a field and sat down in the middle of the freshly plowed ground to breathe.

Thunder was jarring the horizon and making the earth rattle, and I sat listening to the sound bumbling around the edges of the world.

Sunday school was over; church had started.

. . . *but the master of the sea* . . .

The first hymn floated over Tucker's Spring and through the pines.

. . . *heard my despairing cry* . . .

I wondered if Harvey was hand-pumping the organ for Aunt Rebecca in my stead. I wondered if Mother had missed me in church.

. . . *from the waters lifted me* . . .

It had sprinkled some already. Between my feet was a saucer-sized puddle, where a few dirt daubers were rolling up little balls of mud. One dauber landed on the toe of my shoe. He flicked down to inspect the wet edge of a clod, adjusted his wings delicately, and dug in with a scurrying motion of front legs until he had shaped a tat of mortar. Then, surveying his canyon, he took off like a bomber.

. . . *love lifted me* . . .

I still had God in my hand. I slipped off the rubber bands and flipped open the lid. Down in the bottom was PRINCE ALBERT.

. . . *when nothing else would help* . . .

I held the lid of the can between my forefinger

and the heel of my palm and, brushing away the dirt daubers, scooped the Prince Albert can full of mud and mashed the top shut.

A trickle of muddy water ran down my arm. I felt a kind of dizzy sickness as God rushed out. It was like seeing myself through the wrong end of a telescope, being drawn out into a smallness, miles and miles away from the hillside I'd just run up. I knew then that it would take me longer to go back than it had to get there.

. . . *love lifted me* . . .

I decided to walk back home a different way, alone.

Nerves of lightning crackled above the clouds.

. . . *when nothing else would help* . . .

I walked to the middle of the field and kicked a hole in a furrow and threw the can in, buried it, stamped it down, mud and all, tight in the ground, and stood over it. I wondered what would become of my holy water in the silver basin on the pulpit.

It started sprinkling again. Then, while I was standing there, the rain started coming down in earnest.

Chapter Two

It had taken Aunt Rebecca but a glance, a groan, and a scant five minutes to blast God out of my Prince Albert can forever. My utopia lasted exactly eighteen and one half hours. Not even a whole day. Adam and Eve were barely dry when they were booted out of their garden. Tarzan, in his already flawed paradise, made out a speck better, but not much. He and Cheeta alone might have made it to some happy end; but with the intrusion of fair, genteel Jane, there must have arisen an agonizing lament from the primal heart of the old jungle. Then, with the arrival of Boy, the innocent family was doomed. Thereafter poured in the ever-engorging stream of ivory hunters and all manner of other evils.

Yes, I know. The tenderest shoot that cracks the earth must cast its shadow. Be it so. But oh, that sweet moment of first love while I still had one toe in paradise—a love so pure, so particular and absolute, that it transcended sex and sin, Satan and all God's angels. Falling in love with Sylvia Grayson was like jumping off the barn and getting the world jerked out from under you and then floating down forever in one big sigh of fear and ecstasy. Every boy in our school, within reasonable age and range, whether he admitted it or not, was in love with Sylvia. She was the blithe spirit that soared nimbly out of reach and above us all.

I fell in love with Sylvia in the fourth grade; and thereafter, soon and later, she was a trouble to my dreams. Scorn those who stamp young love as frivolous; crack their old bones and turn your back upon them.

Sweet Sylvia, at times your face looms up before me out of a chalky blackboard classroom of long ago. . . . From a dim dance floor before the war, in a hectic blast of strings and clarinets and old big-band sounds and in the swish of skirts and the twirl of other cheeks and hair and other eyes, your face appears. . . . You skip in and out of my present dreams, tucked into that thigh-high parasol dress, swinging and singing like a silver bell.

❖

Sylvia and I were standing in the cloakroom when Clayton hacked his way through the split curtain to get his lunch. He brought his lunch each day in a brown paper sack.

"You don't let anybody ride the Red Flyer, do you?" That's what I called my bicycle. Sylvia said this *to* me, but she said it *for* Clayton. She emphasized "anybody."

"No," I said. The truth was, Clayton rode my bicycle whenever he pleased, and I tried not to look.

"Not ever?"

"Not ever," I said. Dear God, how I worshiped her—her soft presence, her bare arms, her fingers, her knuckles, her elbows, her closeness, her little-girl smell. I was in love with her shoes.

I was standing between Sylvia and Clayton. Miss Gibbons, chalk in hand, was in the classroom, contemplating our afternoon's arithmetic lesson. A distant relative of the Graysons, Miss Gibbons lived in a bungalow in the Graysons' backyard. For two weeks she had been prodding and dragging us into long division. From the cloakroom we could hear her chalking out problems on the blackboard.

"Clayton, you ought to quit being so ugly to Miss Gibbons," Sylvia said.

"I ain't ugly. She's just all the time pecking at me."

"She doesn't peck at anybody, does she, Silas?"

"She's all the time squinting me over with them eyes of hers. She's a crookbill old hawk," Clayton said, almost loud enough for Miss Gibbons to hear. Clayton was partly right, especially about the hawk look. Miss Gibbons was lean and keen-jawed. She had narrow-spaced, sharp brown eyes that could drop a spider off the wall.

"No she's not," Sylvia said. "She's as sweet as she can be, if—"

"She hates me hair and hide because of Papa," Clayton said, louder.

"She does *not*," Sylvia protested, holding a clinched white fist toward Clayton's chest.

"She's a skinny old bitch dog," Clayton said, speaking straight down into Sylvia's knuckles.

"Clayton Slaughter!"

Sylvia swished against my arm and flipped through the split curtain. Her pink electricity passed into my body and stayed there through lunchtime and all the way into long division.

Sylvia rode home in a black Ford coupe with Reverend Grayson for lunch. Shelly and I ate outside, behind the coalbin. Shelly was large for his age. In his metal lunch box, with a clipped-in thermos of milk, were two pineapple sandwiches, an apple, and a piece of chocolate cake. Mother had wrapped my lunch in white paper tied up with a string. I had a ham sandwich and a boiled egg. Between the top two planks of the coalbin we could see Clayton riding my bicycle. He had one leg of his overalls rolled up to keep it out of the sprocket teeth and had turned the handlebars and front wheel around backward, showing off to a cluster of admiring kids. "He's doing it again," Shelly said. After lunch, Miss Gibbons came to the rear of the school building with her desk bell and rang us in.

Before we were settled in our seats, Sylvia snuggled a note in my hand: *Meet me at recess by the Red Flyer—Sylvia.* At the bottom, she had penciled a love heart with an arrow sticking in one side and out the other. Clayton was the last one to come back into the classroom and the last one to sit down. After which Miss Gibbons held out her long fingers and snapped us to attention.

Nobody knew where Clayton's papa or his tribe came from. Cale Slaughter arrived in Deen, Alabama, during the Depression in a crumbling 1928 Chevrolet, top-loaded, side-strapped, and crammed full of family and everything he had: a half-Cherokee wife, a mammy cat with kittens and sandbox, a kerosene stove, a beagle hound, a mop, bundles, bedstead, slats, tied-on mattress, two extra tires wired to the rear spare, a little boy, Robin, a pretty daughter, Queeny, and rawbone Clayton. Mother said later they looked like Pa Joad and his family on the road in *The Grapes of Wrath.*

Clayton was a loner. Tight-jawed, barefooted, mean, and malnourished, he followed nobody. The smaller children were afraid when he appeared. He climbed the schoolyard pecan trees as adroitly as a chimp, not because he liked climbing but because he was hungry. He gathered the nuts from way up and far out from the trunk, cracked them with his jaw teeth, and ate the meats, poised on the limb like a squirrel. Once a limb snapped under him and he dropped thirty feet to earth, so violently that he bounced upright. When I ran to help, he snatched away, grimacing. "Don't go layin' yo hands on me," he said, and went right on chewing. Then, on solid ground, he put two pecans in the cups of his hands and popped them between his knees, never taking his eyes off me.

Nobody could stare Clayton down, not even the teachers. Thinking back now, I believe our principal, Mr. Winters, as well as the teachers, was intimidated by Clayton's fearless standoffishness and lonely arrogance. He never avoided your eyes. He'd grin, bare his gray teeth, and look you down. He smoked hand-rolled Bull Durham cigarettes, wore washed-out overalls, cussed like a pulpwooder, and carried a pearl-handle switchblade. At night I felt sorry for Clayton. In daylight I wished him dead. I dreamed one night that Clayton fell out of a schoolyard pecan tree and killed himself. As a gesture of kindness, I happily dragged his crumpled body up behind the auditorium stage curtain so, at the proper moment,

I could reveal my sad discovery to the assembly. When I pulled the curtain for all to see, Clayton was crouched on top of the piano, grinning and shucking pecans in his nimble paws like a squirrel.

When Clayton's papa spent a week in the second story of the county jail on a moonshining charge, Clayton had gone there each day with a newspaper, which his father fingered up to the bars with a string. Clayton swore openly and bitterly on his father's behalf and dared any of us to breathe a word of the dishonor in his presence. I sensed something dangerous in Clayton the first day he stepped off the school bus. "It's in his blood," my father said.

Maybe so. These were the anemic Depression days. Clayton had thin blood and sores. The slightest scratch or bruise festered on him and made a rising. When a sore got ripe in class, he would pluck the scab from his flesh like a mashed blackberry and drop it down the neck of a screeching girl. Miss Gibbons once barely saved Sylvia from this fate. Afterward Miss Gibbons sent Clayton—scab and all, with a smack across his jaw—into the cloakroom for the rest of the morning. "And destroy that ghastly thing at once," she cried.

"It ain't gonna bite her," Clayton said.

Another thing, to my mortification: Clayton was smarter than I was, smarter than anybody in our class except Shelly. "Brilliant," one teacher was heard to say. "But," she added, "brilliance oft is brittle and seldom doth endure." The only thing I could do better than Clayton was shoot marbles. I could beat anybody in school. I always played for keeps and never lost. When I was within range, knelt on one knee, and took dead aim, I seldom missed. Once after school, before his bus came, I killed Clayton off in one game, took his six marbles, shooter too, and left him standing alone beside the coalbin.

Clayton never studied that I knew of and rarely listened. He made two kinds of grades: F's and A's—the F's to frustrate the teachers and the A's to get by, to humiliate me, and to baffle Shelly. Shelly, even with his unique and magnificent brain, progressed from month to month and grade to grade on the influence of his family and the kindness—the awe—of his teachers. Day or night, Shelly felt sorry for Clayton. I made my skimpy A's the hard way, and jealously. Clayton made his, when he made them, effortlessly and arrogantly, and he made them at the very last of each month to buoy up his other, abysmal marks to the brink of passing. "I ain't giving nothing away," he'd say, then he'd grin and stare you down. My hate for Clayton was unbounded.

Recess was at two o'clock. I reread Sylvia's note and penciled heart. When Miss Gibbons tapped her class bell for recess, I put the note in my shirt pocket and went to the bathroom. Standing at the toilet, I fetched out the note again and marveled at the shape of Sylvia's words, the texture of her letters, and how close they had been to her fingers.

Shelly was in the bathroom.

"Sylvia says come on out right now," he said. "She says hurry," and after a moment, "I saw her hand you a note."

"Well?"

"Let me read it, Silas," Shelly said.

"No."

"Can I see it?" I held the note up in the air so he could see it and stuck it back in my shirt pocket. "You are in love with Sylvia," Shelly said fatally. It was true. I had dreamed of flying with Sylvia in the De Havilland and soaring into ecstasy.

"Oh, Shelly, for cat's sake," I said, following him out the bathroom door.

According to Milton's gospel, citing another glorious but fatal day of long ago, Milton's Adam said to his new Eve:

I from the influence of thy looks receive
Access in every Virtue, in thy sight
More wise, more watchful, stronger, if need were
Of outward strength; while shame, thou looking on,
Shame to be overcome or over-reacht
Would utmost Vigor raise, and rais'd unite.

Which means: Lovely Eve, in this big Garden, let me hang around near you just in case this unknown monster jumps us. Merely by casting your eyes upon me you will give me the strength of ten Adams.

Adam, how right you were. Hallowed be thy name.

Shelly knew where I parked the Red Flyer and was holding open the side hall door that looked out on the playground.

"Don't let him hurt the Red Flyer," Shelly said. "Don't let him do it again." Shelly felt sorry for the bicycle.

Sylvia was standing on the small teachers' observation platform that overlooked the playing field, where a bunch of kids had gathered to watch Clayton's antics. He was riding backward on my bicycle—sitting on the handlebars, facing the rear wheel, and pumping the pedals like crazy. He had the handlebars shoved down in a hurt, defeated angle. There was no way now for me not to see Clayton "doing it." Clayton caught a glimpse of me out of the slant of his eye. Then came his grin and the gray teeth.

"He's doing it again," Shelly whispered in my ear.

Above the scramble of kids was Sylvia. She more than looked at me: her presence was command awaiting utterance, energy awaiting action. A messenger of power, she swayed in her white dress, paused, stabbed her hands down resolutely on her waist, cocked one hip at a girly angle, and said:

"Silas O'Riley Simeon, are you going to let Clayton Slaughter ride your Red Flyer that way?"

O, Milton! O, Adam! I, with Sylvia's eyes upon me, had the strength of ten Silases. With Sylvia's divine assistance, Clayton hadn't a chance. He never knew what hit him. To be sure, even with God's help, Clayton could not have defended himself very well while riding backward on my bicycle. No matter. I drove into him with all my force, cracking my knuckles against his gray teeth. On the way down I could see nothing but bicycle pedals, spokes, patches of bare legs and knees crowding around, and heard cries calling out our names. Sylvia's voice was above them all, pumping more rage into me. One side of the handlebars had Clayton pinned to the ground. Good luck and thank God. I flailed into him again. There was red on Clayton's lip. His eyes were shocked, astonished, but not afraid. There was in Clayton a kind of calm acceptance in our going down together, a forbearing composure in his absorbing my blows. Shelly began crying and repeating, "Stop, here comes Miss Gibbons." Clayton and I wobbled to our feet, Clayton in disbelief.

Sylvia in her white dress was still aboard the platform, now bouncing up and down in her black shoes, calling out in cadence, "Kill 'im. Kill 'im. Kill 'im." That did it. I flew back into Clayton with added fury. Poor Clayton; how I hated him. In going down our last time, he seemed like a shrunken old man surprised by a calamity not of his making. All the kids had now chimed in, Sylvia leading the chorus: "Kill 'im. Kill 'im. Kill 'im."

Then there were arms about us. Miss Gibbons and the thick-legged sixth-grade teacher were pulling us apart. Across my forearm was a thin smear of Clayton's blood. God, the glory of it all! Shelly was on his hands and knees, looking up into my face. "Silas, come on now, get up, stop." He started pulling my bicycle lovingly from the fracas. Sylvia's shoes and legs were beside me—her heavenly, mysterious legs, which went all the way up into her dress, somewhere.

When I stood up, Clayton, dumbfounded, was sitting on the ground. And there was Sylvia, beholding me, beaming.

Immediately after my conquest at recess, Miss Gibbons sat Clayton in the first desk on the right aisle and me in the last desk on the left. There were four rows and five desks to a row. Sylvia sat in the head desk on the left aisle and Shelly, being tall, sat in the back. Margie Cash was sitting in front of me. When Clayton dared turn his eyes back toward me, Miss Gibbons snapped her fingers and motioned his face to the front. This was the last class for the day, our reading hour. We read silently for half an hour, then, as called upon, orally for half an hour. Today the narrative was about King Arthur almost getting slain by the secret King Pellinore and being saved at the last moment by Merlin with his magic powers.

Sylvia, her silken hair flowing in front of her cheek, was looking back, trying to get my attention. Could she, she indicated, pass something down the aisle to me? Yes, yes, yes, I nodded. Magic powers? I wondered. What was going on behind Clayton's eyes? What had I started there? After school, Clayton had to ride the school bus home. I wondered what Clayton would do tomorrow. Tomorrow?

Sylvia's note came carefully, hand by hand, down the outside aisle. Margie slipped it to me below the desk without looking back. "It's from Sylvia," she whispered.

How girls did it—how they folded a sheet of paper up and down, this way and that, back and forth, then tucked in the ends so that it held together like a tiny accordion—I never learned. It was a trick they used for special news. I arranged the note inside my open reader, over a picture of the strange knight about to cut off Arthur's head, and began to unfold its mysteries. I didn't look at its contents directly, even after I had it open. I laid it facedown and turned it back slowly from the top so I could savor the words one line at a time:

Dear Silas,

I love, love, love,
love, love, love,
love (a whole page of loves)—YOU!

Sylvia
XXXXXXXXX

P.S. Meet me after school in front
of my house under the chinaberry tree.

On either side of her name she had inscribed the love heart and arrow. What were the X's for?

Oh, holy moment! In the beginning was the word, and the word was *with* Sylvia, and the word *was* Sylvia. Sylvia was in my Jar of Marbles before I was born; as for Clayton, there was no way to keep him out. The poet hath said, Never seek to tell thy love. Very well, but each "love" and heart she had penciled down was like a shot of helium to my soul. And so it was, and so I soared, above King Arthur, above Excalibur, above the lonely Maiden of the Lake, and, for an instant, above even Clayton Slaughter.

Christine was reading: *Who is he? asked the Knight. He is King Arthur, Merlin replied. . . .*

I decided that after the last bell I would go and sit on the commode behind the stall door and wait for the school bus to carry Clayton away.

Then Shelly was reading, very slowly and with

great elocution: *Who is the Knight? asked Arthur. It is King Pellinore; and he shall . . .*

I had my books stacked and ready for the last bell. Sylvia was the first one out the door. I hurried to the bathroom but did not sit down on the commode. I looked at myself in the cracked mirror over the lavatory. After the last rattle of the old school bus was gone, I eased out of hiding, tucked Sylvia's note back into my pocket, and walked from the schoolhouse into the soft April afternoon.

II

The handlebars of the Red Flyer were not bent, just forced down. But the back fender was injured, and a spoke was popped loose. Damn. So what. I took out Sylvia's note again and let my eyes luxuriate over each "love" and symbol. My ecstasy was near perfection.

Some say Adam's Fall was inevitable because, long before the apple deal, Adam had already been so smitten by his lovely partner that he gradually, but surely, weakened, lost control, authority. Nonsense. So perfect a love a weakness? A flaw? God forbid.

My way home took me directly past the Graysons'. Riding around the bend in the road, I could see Sylvia a great way off, a tiny bud against the background of her picket fence. She was in her promised place, under the chinaberry tree, which can hardly be called a tree; for although a chinaberry grows to sizable and lush proportions, it is mainly a weed. Its fruit is stinky and inedible except to jaybirds. Its branches get brittle in a freeze and crack in a gale. But it is pretty, short-trunked, and fun to climb. I wondered if Clayton had ever climbed a chinaberry tree for fun. Certainly not to eat the berries. I was getting real leg power in my bicycle strokes now, drawing nearer.

Sylvia was waving her hand over her head: *Here I am right here.* And so she was. Gliding along nicely, lightly, I could see plainly at this distance Sylvia's features, the golden S of hair across her cheek, her eyes, her Shirley Temple innocence. Oh, love, love, love, love, love . . .

Something was not quite right. My balance was a bit off. The front wheel of the Red Flyer had veered a tat off the hardroad, popped slightly sideways under a single piece of gravel, and I was slicing through a stinging fuzz of ditch weeds. Then abruptly came the picket fence: bicycleless through the air I sailed, toward a vague blob of green, and piled into the middle of Mrs. Grayson's japonica bush, hauling down with me both limb and flower. A month of Clayton's mistreatment could not have embarrassed a bike more. The Red Flyer was lodged upright between two fence pickets. My strapped books had flown partway with me, then departed and scooted separately across the yard like a deck of playing cards. There was a red scratch up my right arm. I was disengaging myself from the japonica bush, the bookstrap dangling sadly about my neck, when Sylvia trotted over, thoroughly untroubled with my distress.

"Don't let Mother see us," she whispered, gathering up my books. What could this mean?

"Why?" I asked.

"Just *because*," she said with irrefutable logic, and held out my books.

I unwound the bookstrap from my neck and bound the volumes together again. She took hold of my arm and pulled me into the walkway under the chinaberry tree. There was a red-cushioned footstool beside the trunk.

"You got Clayton real good," she said. "For both of us." I had forgotten her plea to Clayton concerning Miss Gibbons.

"He ought to *ask* if he wants to ride my bike," I said.

"You knocked off one of his dirty old sores," she said. So that was it. I hadn't hurt Clayton after all, just raked a scab off, something that would have dried and sloughed off anyway. Clayton's pale blood on my arm became less heroic. Or was it my own blood from the collision with the bush?

"I didn't want to hurt him," I said.

"You did, though. You hurt him good," Sylvia said. "You made him bleed. See?" She touched her finger triumphantly to the red smear on my arm.

"What did Clayton say after school?" It was important that I hear of this.

"Nothing," she said. "You busted his ugly mouth shut." With a tinge of pity and fear, I could imagine Clayton in his overalls, with his lunch sack balled up in his hip pocket and one of his pants legs rolled up, climbing into the ratty old school bus and sitting stoically among the others and taking the long journey home in silent humiliation.

"Did he cry?" I wanted to know.

"Clayton Slaughter can't cry. He never learned how to," Sylvia said.

Maybe so, I thought. But I remembered Clayton's eyes. I wondered what the fancy footstool was doing under the chinaberry tree.

Something was about to happen, because of the way Sylvia was looking at me. I could feel it as surely as you can smell springtime a month away. Then it happened. Sylvia took ahold of my shoulders, looked me squarely in the face, and said:

"Silas Simeon, do you want to kiss me?"

Oh, sweet thought! Eternal Jesus, yes, yes, yes, yes. Love, love, love, love. But what? There could be no answer to this from me, no utterance whatsoever to the utterly unknown and unexpected, to the absolutely inexplicable. How could I, confronting such sweet immensity, breathe a response or dare interrupt a spell of such holy suspense? Sylvia read my eyes. She said:

"We'll have to climb up in the tree to do it."

Up in the tree? I wondered. Mrs. Grayson? Why not kiss right here on the ground? Right now? No matter. To dream of being airborne with Sylvia in the De Havilland was sweet. This was sweeter; albeit this new tingling was now laced with a trace of danger. I need not have *climbed* the tree at all. On celestial energy alone I could have floated up to the topmost branches.

The climb was easy. The footstool—so that was it. Up Sylvia went: off the spongy red stool, one foot atop the picket rail, a handclimb, a foothold halfway up, another handclimb—oh, divine ascent, her pink body flowing and swaying upward in the snowy parachute of her dress—another pull, a swing, a turn, and she alighted in the crotch of the tree. Lord Almighty, love, love, love . . . In a moment I was up in the tree beside her.

But wait. First there was something else—a gift, a toad-sized brass chest on the arch of a limb, as if it had grown there. Sylvia lifted the little vault toward me, clicked it open with a tiny key so I could catch a glance of its contents, snapped it shut at once, then dropped the key in her dress pocket.

The chest, Sylvia explained, was mine to keep forever but to keep secretly closed until such time as she at last would give up the key to me, so that we might then have a mutual and future brass-chest opening and forever afterward live in the soft light of eternal happiness, in the flower of all forevers, her other treasures to disclose. Yes, yes, yes. I slipped the trophy deep into my pants pocket.

I had no gift or trophy to bestow in complement. "I'll give you a ride in the De Havilland," I offered. Sylvia looked at me with rapture. "Will you fly with me? Please?" I pursued.

"Yes, yes," she said.

"Promise?" I asked.

"Oh, ye-e-es," she breathed.

John Milton, poet divine, your Adam—having the misfortune of being created grown—knew no such bliss. Here, right here, not a handspan away, in the smooth dichotomy of this green chinaberry tree, was my tender Sylvia breathing her precious breath on me. The whole sky stopped, and I was spinning head over toes into delicious infinity.

This was it.

"You can do it now," Sylvia said, drawing away the last earthly curtain between us. Her words were moist and two-dimensional, like those spoken down into the darkness of a well. She closed her eyes and held her face in readiness.

Now, oh, God, a problem.

I once had a dream in which I was required to pick up a bodyless head. The problem: How does one do so? Who has written the manual on picking up severed heads? Who knows how much a head weighs? How do you go about picking it up? Do you go for the hair? the neck? the ear? Certainly not the nose. Do you slip your thumb into the esophagus, a finger into an eye socket, and your little finger into an ear, as you would a bowling ball, or roll the head into the open mouth of a sack with your foot? Who is to say?

"Silas Simeon!" Sylvia was impatient and opened her eyes. "Here," she said, pointing to her lips.

Sylvia closed her eyes again. I could see the steeple of the Presbyterian church sticking up behind her head like a spiked diadem and wondered what Aunt Rebecca would say to see me perched like a silly jaybird in the fork of a chinaberry tree with Sylvia all puckered up to kiss. It is true, without discussion, that the female of our species is enormously more resourceful and expedient than the male. Contrary to Aunt Rebecca's theology, it is doubtful if God exercised free will at all when He created Eve; He was compelled to do so when He saw what a botched-up job He had done on Adam. Poor Adam alone in his orchard would have pined himself away in sordid inactivity and grown fat on dates and daydreams.

"Like *this!*" Sylvia said, falling suddenly upon me. She seized me in a clasp, pinning my arms helplessly to my ribs, then stamped on my mouth a long, hard, wetsmacking kiss.

So this was it. But now what? Sylvia's impassioned embrace had been, for me, less an experience of endearment than an entrapment and a balancing act. With Sylvia glued around me, I had neither equilibrium nor grasp; and her forward motion had accelerated my backward motion. Claiming more of the tree than I in this position, Sylvia was able to latch onto a houseward limb; but gravity was getting the best of me. My faltering inertia and that bottomless tingling in my groin told me I was headed for the ground again, this time not from the Red Flyer, horizontally in a smooth arc, but straight down to sudden earth. In my descent I recalled lovely Sylvia receding into the chinaberry green like a little white cloud, my arms groping upward for what few branches and leaves and sky I could grasp. . . .

I didn't bounce up from the ground the way Clayton did when he fell out of the pecan tree. Maybe my landing was softened by the bundle of limbs and branches I brought down with me. I felt no pain, but the world was jarred sideways.

"Sylvia Grayson!" It was Sylvia's mother, on the front porch. An ample woman, standing with hands on hips, elbows flared, and feet apart, Mrs. Grayson looked like an arrested Dutch windmill. "What on earth are you doing up in that tree with Silas?" I was certainly, now, not *up* in any tree. In a moment Mrs. Grayson was standing over me. "Are you hurt?" she asked. Reaching down with her hefty arm, she lifted me, like a puppy, by the nape of my shirt collar.

"No, ma'am," I said. But I was not sure. I felt warped.

Sylvia was out of the tree now, dangling in one hand the forlorn footstool. There was a little scar of chinaberry green down the belly of her dress and a tiny rip in its hem. Why do women, from maid to matron, put their hands on their hips when they prepare to make solemn proclamations? Sylvia mounted the front steps and, before swishing her lovely self into the house, posed with flared elbows, precisely as her mother had done a moment before.

"I'm going to tell Mother *everything!*" she announced.

Oh, merciful Jesus, no, I thought. Not *everything*.

Then Mrs. Grayson shut the door.

It took some struggling before I could dislodge the Red Flyer from the picket fence and ride home. Our place was but a sprint and a puff from the Graysons'. The dirt road ahead spun a crooked country six miles to Jackson's Bluff and across the river where Clayton lived.

In the pale sunlight it was hard to tell the difference between Clayton's blood and my own.

Tomorrow?

How does anyone know when or where a thing starts happening? When, where does an acorn start happening? In the winter? The spring? In the stem? The branch? The trunk? The roots? The earth? The Milky Way? Who can tell?

Once closed away in my room upstairs, I examined the brass chest carefully. It was a handsome piece of workmanship. In relief on the lid was a cavalier seated before a bowl of fruit and a goblet, holding up to his face a lamb; in front was a Venetian scene with gondola, gondolier, and lovers; and on the ends were pastoral settings showing foliaged hills, flocks, and shepherds holding their crooked staffs. With the small blade of my pocket knife I triggered the tiny lock and had the chest open in an instant. It was padded on the inside with blue velvet and contained a folded note and two slightly wilted wild primroses, the kind that grow in profusion during springtime along roadways and spray up like surf and whitecaps in southern pastures. The note read simply: *I love you forever—Sylvia.*

Before suppertime Sylvia was afoot, calling to me from over our garden fence. She wanted the brass chest back.

Nothing disloyal. Our love chest, she revealed, was what her mother kept her earrings and jewels in, and though her mother never wore earrings and jewels much now, if she ever took a notion to and found them gone, then she was sure to raise the roof and sniff out the culprit and punish him beyond description. Sylvia suggested to me that I was in possession of stolen property. Which was a fact. Would this all have turned out this way, I wondered, if I had not fallen out of the chinaberry tree? if Sylvia hadn't written the note? if Shelly hadn't come into the bathroom? if Clayton hadn't ridden my bicycle? if he had conveniently fallen out of a pecan tree and broken his neck? I could not tell. "Life," Mother had said, "is a marvelous but crooked row of stacked dominoes, stretching out of sight, always getting set off just before you are ready."

"What did you do with your mama's earrings?" I asked, wondering about the magnitude of our crime.

"Put them in a sock," she said.

"A sock?"

"Yes."

"Whose sock?"

"I don't know. Just an old black sock."

Jesus, I thought, earrings and jewels and not even knowing whose sock you put them in!

"I stuck them under my pillow," she said. Good grief.

I drew the brass love chest out of my pocket and handed it to Sylvia.

"You haven't peeked inside, have you?" she asked. How could I have? I didn't have the key.

"No," I said.

"Swear?"

"I swear."

"Cross your heart."

I scratched a guilty X across my chest. All in one graceful motion, Sylvia inserted the key into the chest, clicked the lock, lifted the lid, fingered to me one of the mortally ill primroses, and snapped the chest shut; she then leaned across the fence and pecked me gently on the lips. With a gesture of dramatic fervor, she sighed, "Forever!"

But she had kept the love note. The little streak of green was still on the waistline of her dress. What could "forever" mean now if she had taken back the love note?

"What did you tell your mama when you came down out of the tree?" I asked.

"Like I said—I told her *everything*."

"What *is* everything?" I needed to know.

"That you kissed me," she said, exasperated at my ignorance.

Well, at least—for the moment—I was there when it happened. And, I reasoned afterward, it could not have happened if I had not been there. I was dangling the sad little primrose on the end of my index finger when Sylvia bobbed down the path. But *forever*. Forever *what?*

"What about our ride in the De Havilland?" I called after her.

"I'll have to ask Daddy," she sent back.

III

Tomorrow, tomorrow, tomorrow, and Clayton Slaughter. That night I planned to be sick tomorrow and wished that, on that fated afternoon, I had not won all of Clayton's marbles.

After supper, I asked Father if there was a verse in the Bible that had to do with pretty flowers. He brought out the great family book and opened it to the place where Jesus was talking about lilies: ". . . Why take ye thought . . . Consider the lilies of the field, how they grow . . . even Solomon in all his glory was not arrayed like one of these. . . . Take therefore no thought for the morrow . . ." I found the same place in my Sunday school Bible and pressed Sylvia's expired primrose between the pages. The last part of the verses I liked best, the words about taking no thought for the morrow. What did it mean? My father, who was trying to listen to the scratchy reception of a prizefight on our huge living room radio, said it simply meant that if you had faith in God, you didn't have to worry and everything would turn out all right.

Mother was less encouraging. The lily, she pointed out, did flourish and was indeed beautiful and did not toil and did not spin, but it most assuredly was not long for this world. "Its real beauty," she said, "lies in its not fretting about the inevitable, which is always a brief tomorrow away. And," she added, "it is a blessing that the lily can't see how pretty it is, otherwise it would most surely perish in its own vanity." Her precept of vanity went over my head; but with Clayton heavy on my mind, her death message came across loud and clear.

❖

My second fight with Clayton wasn't really a fight at all; it was a kind of slow, unwitnessed calamity.

To begin with, the next morning Mother would hear nothing of my concocted illness. She put her palm on my brow—no fever—and sent me off promptly to school, pedaling a bruised and reluctant Red Flyer. Once out in the road, I discovered there was no going back. The air seemed sucked out of the world. The simple act of riding down this particular road at this particular moment was like the difference between dreaming I was snakebit and knowing I was snakebit.

I slowed down. I would be late for school. Everything would be started when I got there: the double front doors would be closed; all my classmates would be nailed to their seats; and Miss Gibbons would frown at my tardiness, chalk my name in the corner of the blackboard, and forbid me recess. Excellent! During that time I would write Clayton a declaration giving him exclusive privileges to ride my Red Flyer.

Praise God from whom all blessings flow; praise Him for the powers of reason! I was pedaling so slowly now I had to touch one toe to the ground to keep my balance.

The road was empty. The Reverend Grayson's house looked deserted. The front curtains were drawn. Had they been drawn yesterday? The chinaberry branches I had pulled down with me the evening before were still in disarray by the walkway, and the reverend's automobile was gone out of the garage. Where was everybody? I could see the corner of the schoolhouse and, in the distance, the church steeple pointing up through the oaks. A musty image of Aunt Rebecca arose in my mind like the odor of opening an old church hymnal; and God Himself was sulking on the other side of the world. Where was Sylvia? In her darkened bedroom? In the school cloakroom? The girls' bathroom? Or in the golden light of our classroom, casually stacking her books for our first lesson on the mystery of English verbs?

No thought for tomorrow . . .

It was already tomorrow. A comforting little fantasy popped up in my mind. I imagined for a moment, after my invented covenant with Clayton, that Clayton and I embraced like medieval knights, reconciled our wounds, and walked arm in arm across the schoolyard, to the enthrallment of Sylvia and the student body and to the applause of the teachers. . . .

Once clearing the arc in the road, I could see the whole schoolhouse, all drab two stories of it, from walkway to playground. The bell had rung. The grounds were bare except for a truant breeze teasing along a loose tatter of paper and the naked flagpole with an impartial crow teetering on top. But my worst fears were confirmed: Clayton Slaughter—overalls, sores, warts, and all—was standing straddle-legged, barring the double front door of the schoolhouse.

Sages of old have observed that you can seldom measure the intensity of an experience by the immensity of the occasion. For instance, there was this British coal miner, hopelessly trapped in a fallen mine shaft, who managed superb self-control by licking cool sweat from the black walls of his tomb and calmly playing his harmonica, until he was miraculously rescued a week later. And yet a week afterward, he fell into spasms of fear and depression over the loss of a single toe to a garden spade. And there was a courageous bomber pilot in World War II who had flown through a month of the most furious aerial combat, all the while maintaining near-perfect calm and undisturbed digestion. Yet when this one London broad forsook him, he lost his appetite completely and was a hazard to fly with, even over the friendly fields of England. Who can tell about such things? As for myself, the sight of Clayton that morning, standing in the school doorway like a grinning gnome, brought more wear and tear upon my body than my first mission toward Berlin.

The crow was gone from the flagpole. You would hardly call it a fight, even though, after all the scuffle and tumble, it took the full teaching staff to throttle Clayton and peel him off me. I have read that in the wild, when a pursued animal is finally and fatally seized, it simply acquiesces painlessly in the jaws of its predator. There may be some truth—and wisdom—in this behavior; for though I struggled mightily for a while, I remember feeling not a blow nor uttering a sound. I recall only Clayton's grin and his gray teeth. Then suddenly I was the proverbial tree in the forest—without audience, out of sight and earshot of the world—struck down by silent lightning.

When it was over, the class were craning their goony heads out the windows. All the teachers, except Miss Gibbons, were mercifully holding Clayton in check. I was groggy, as if I had been dredged up out of the deep.

In the classroom, Sylvia sank her head down in her book when I passed by. Shelly, across the room, looked at me with his forlorn eyes. By lunchtime, half my face had swollen. During long division, my left eye closed. Before the last bell, Sylvia read aloud the last lines of "The Passing of Arthur" by Lord Tennyson.

Clayton, it occurred to me as I pedaled home that evening, had been kinder than I was. At least he let me get off the bicycle.

Chapter Three

The circus was a funny disappointment.

Out of nowhere each fall, our annual one-ringer rolled into Deen, Alabama, on trucks and trailers, amid romp and clamor. Two days later in silence it vanished, clowns and calliope, into the early dawn like a dream, leaving behind empty cotton candy cones, dead pop bottles, and snaggled cavities in the south end zone of our football field, where the butt of the big tent had been anchored. During this one particular fall, the circus struck a lasting alteration in Shelly Webster and me and even in the Wild Man of Zanzibar.

If Sylvia was the first to assail my heart, it was Shelly who first aroused my soul. Not in a teary-eyed way, as when one listens to "The Star-Spangled Banner" or beholds God in golden sunsets. Being around Shelly made you feel a little unsure of yourself. There was something sublimely ghoulish about him, as if you were in the presence of the Hunchback of Notre Dame. Rangy and gently lumbering, never in step with those beside him, Shelly glided above the rest of us, handsome and smooth, like a sailboat on open sea.

It was clear to me, even then, that Shelly Webster had been born wondrously and fatally different from our schoolyard pack. A few cowardly souls in our community had whispered of Shelly—a label even I could catch the gist of—an ugly indictment against Shelly's mother: "Gretta's Folly" they dubbed her son. But out of respect, and probably fear, of Shelly's judge father, this unjust curse, to my knowledge, was seldom hung on Shelly even in private and certainly never in public. With one exception. Clayton Slaughter referred to gentle Shelly openly and shamelessly as a shithead bastard.

Any such label on Shelly was, of course, dead wrong. Shelly in his own way was mountains and sky above us all. The ordinary channels of our classroom learning were unnecessary for Shelly. From thin air, it seemed, he absorbed the essence of our textbooks, which I had to chisel out page by page. His rare arrangement of genes carried him along on crystal streams into nooks of insight and flights of fantasy that nature had denied me.

Shelly's most popular talent was with numbers.

Once Shelly recorded a number in his memory—telephone number, license plate, or serial number—it became indelible and ineradicable. All of which was not especially remarkable; but Shelly could add, multiply, or divide these numbers in his head and, within seconds, come up with infallible answers. One of his feats occurred on the Fourth of July when he was twelve years old. Shelly added the five- and six-digit serial numbers of fifty-two boxcars of our local train as it rattled by at thirty-five miles an hour. The day before, with the aid of a railroad conductor and the town clerk, our mayor had prefigured the sum on what he described as "the incomparable McCormick-Johnson calculating machine." The next day he compared his elaborate results with Shelly's six-minute tally. To the small crowd gathered at the depot, including Judge Webster, the mayor announced kindly and condescendingly that our young mathematician had done remarkably well but had missed the mark by a bare 129 points, and that the correct sum rendered by the official city McCormick-Johnson calculator was 371,983. Shelly remained serene and confident, until a second tally showed the mayor, the clerk, and the incomparable calculating machine itself to have been in error. The correct answer was 372,112, which was exactly what Shelly had figured out in his head.

How well did Shelly do in grammar school arithmetic and later on in high school math? Very poorly. Invariably Shelly arrived, almost instantaneously, at the right answer but by the wrong route. He was especially troubled by such cute, realistic narrative problems as: "If Sam walked seven miles down a country road and met Henry, who had walked in the other direction one third as far as Sam, how far would John have to walk if . . . ?" Shelly always had the answer as soon as he read the problem, but he would wonder aloud to the teacher about such words as "country" and whether they were planted in the problem to obscure the answer. And what was the purpose of the one-third-of-the-way meeting of Sam and Henry? And what did John have to do with all this senseless walking about? After which Shelly would fold over, head in arms upon his desktop, his shoulders quivering in worried laughter akin to tears—then abruptly he would sit upright, like Judge Webster in court, and deliver final judgment: Unless John knew *exactly* where Sam started his journey and if, in *fact*, John had seen neither Sam nor Henry in passing, then he, John, would have to walk forever.

But after Shelly defeated the invincible McCormick-Johnson calculating machine, few teachers questioned his method of ciphering, nor did they thereafter trouble to pick his brain.

Shelly's master talent was music. He was a

musical genius, alone and lonesome among us. In this delicate medium he was so far beyond the rest of us that we gladly excused ourselves from any comparison. Not that we despised his music; we were awed by it and were simply left with nothing in ourselves to measure Shelly by. Shelly was born out of a pure sea of sound and number and could swim in both at birth.

In the years following World War I, before her marriage, Shelly's mother sang grand opera in Philadelphia; later she taught piano in Deen, Alabama. Greek Orthodox by birth and temperament, a mighty woman, Gretta Webster sang upon request at all our gatherings and to congregations far and wide, great and small. On special warm Sunday mornings, with all windows open to catch a summer's breeze, her powerful voice, overwhelming our modest church, swelled across the neighborhood and billowed into the pines beyond. One did not need to be present to hear her sing, merely open one's doors and let her voice roll in.

What vocal gifts Shelly failed to inherit from his mother he made up for in ear and hand. While I was puffing out a poor "Turkey in the Straw" or "The Wabash Cannonball" on the harmonica, Shelly was doing Strauss and Chopin on the piano; and while Sylvia and other pretties in his mother's class had barely graduated from "Sneaky Spook," Shelly was playing Beethoven and Mozart with power and comprehension. Shelly had expansive hands, sensuous and strong. "They are," his mother praised, "a glory and a godsend." An unlucky neighbor took that to mean that Gretta Webster was apologizing for her son's unique talents, and the poor man agreed sympathetically that Shelly's wonderful hands were indeed a "godsend," since they provided the unlucky youth "an escape from the *real* world."

"Escape! *Whose* real world?" Gretta roared at the man, and never spoke to him again.

Which was exactly the way I felt. Why should I give a happy damn if Shelly's *real* world transcended mine or if he could soar into a realer world than mine? Who can tell whose real world is realer, or whose world is really whose?

Sometimes, clowning ghoulishly on the school piano, Shelly would hold up his elongated hands like magic wands, wave them in the light, and chant his philosophy of music: *A silver river going nowhere, everywhere, under towers and bridges, upstream, downstream—hands never touching the crystal seam . . .*

"My hands can breathe," Shelly would clown, shifting his bulging eyes from side to side. "See?" And he'd smile, holding his hands above the keys, then run wild on a piece he'd composed about a forsaken shadow trying to catch the sun.

Funny thing how Shelly could wax so eloquent

on things of his own interest, then drop off suddenly into the doldrums.

II

In a way it was Shelly's fault that we got tangled up with the Wild Man of Zanzibar.

It was October's bright blue weather when the Harris Brothers' Circus rolled by the schoolhouse one Friday morning. All classes turned out to watch. For a month the traveling show had been proclaimed over the countryside on billboards and posters. As the caravan passed, roustabouts were already in the process of unwrapping and getting in the swing for the first night's stand.

On a rubber-wheeled platform, a five-piece band in shirtsleeves was blaring away. A couple of clowns were doing cartwheels down the road. There was a leopard pacing in a cage. Painted on one carriage was half a woman in tights, her enormous white thighs in a spread stance, with OF wedged under her crotch and FRANCE between her bare feet. It was followed by a trailer bearing the rest of her, a rhinestone-belted torso cut out of plywood, her face with a red smile as bold as a cut watermelon, and over her whopping breasts, one word for each: FABULOUS FRANCES. At the very end of the procession came a rainbow-colored calliope steaming and oom-pah-pahing "Over the Waves."

It was the calliope that got to Shelly. Shelly and I didn't go back to school that morning. As surely as we would have followed the Pied Piper out of Hamelin, Shelly followed the music machine all the way to the high school football field, and I followed Shelly. Shelly was fascinated by the wheezing old organ. Not because of the quality of its sound or its tune, but because, while the men set up the merry-go-round, the abandoned machine kept playing all by itself.

"We better get back," I said, "or Mr. Winters will be tuning up our own ass," although I knew instinctively that our principal was not going to whip Shelly for his absence. Thus, in fair play, Mr. Winters would spare me too. Shelly was profitable company.

Uncle George explained that the Harris Brothers' Circus was not a bona fide circus at all but a "bastard," meaning it was a crossbreed, half roughneck carnival and half lowbrow circus, which made it a cur compared to the prestigious, high-pedigreed Barnum & Bailey, which hit the big spots like Atlanta, Montgomery, and New Orleans. But our circus produced more enduring memories than the legitimate big tops with their acres of tents, their clean clowns and funny cars. So what if only a single big tent, a scrawny elephant, and a cigarette-smoking Golden Princess didn't make it "legitimate."

Our Harris Brothers' bastard was unique, year by year. Not because it intended to be but because it couldn't help it. With its crew of riffraff and rednecks, it could not help being one of a kind. And this show was eons and blue moons better than the sterilized, institutionalized big tops pretending to permanence and "educational" benefits. Our ragged one-ringer on its two-night stand made no pretense. As Aunt Rebecca had long ago proclaimed for the whole human race, this show was merely "passing through." There was something of the charlatan and vagabond about the Harris Brothers' assault, a gypsy air of mystery, ill repute, deception, and flimflammery, an alluring aroma of sin.

The calliope belched and stopped its song in midair, its damp notes dying away toward the schoolhouse.

Two men, one of them quite slim, with sideburns and oiled black hair, were hinging the plywood top of the voluptuous Frances to her waist. In one hoist they swung her into being. She rose to an arresting ten feet. There she was all together: FABULOUS FRANCES OF FRANCE—*Adults Only*.

A pleasant, straw-hatted farmer with a cane was watching the erection of Frances with mild disbelief. The man with the slicked-down hair threw a bolt that locked Frances into place. He called out to the old-timer. "Hey ho, Daddy-o," he said, motioning an elbow toward the plywood Amazon. "For two bits and a peek tonight, you can throw that cane away."

That night Shelly and I would discover, to Shelly's delight and my mortification, what made Frances so fabulous.

The same two men were now busy arranging the Wild Man of Zanzibar's arena, erecting a tent annex to his trailer cage, which had painted bars on the outside, glass box windows across the top, and a half-glass door at the end. The white canvas flip-up front to the annex tent was covered with illustrations and an inscription: *Wild Man Captured and Trained for Your Pleasure and Amusement—Eats Live Chickens.* To the side was a portrait of a wild man, a nightmarish likeness of a furious brown creature with fangs and flaming red hair and beard, seizing a fleeing rooster by the legs and drawing the stricken bird into his clutches. There was something almost comic about the poor rooster, its red comb raised high in alarm and its eyes cocked back at the pursuing monster, not so much in terror as in bemused vexation. I wondered if the artist intended this effect or lucked upon it.

Not so Shelly. When he saw the depiction of the helpless captured fowl, his heart sank. I was not surprised. Shelly had once shed tears over a homeless, slack-teated bitch. "There was nothing, nothing, nothing she could have done about it," Shelly lamented. He followed the bereaved animal to her den in the woods and retrieved her and her starving pups, every one, to the comfort of Judge Webster's home. Shelly saw beauty in all animals, even the smallest. Like the Hindu zealot Mahavira, he avoided stepping on ants and other insects, explaining that their size in no way diminished the marvel of their creation and construction; it seemed, he said, the smaller these creatures were, the less we regretted treading them into the earth. He scolded me bitterly for my long-standing slingshot wars against jays and catbirds, and once threw me to the ground for my sins and demanded my reform.

When the two roustabouts disappeared, the door of the Wild Man's painted cage opened, and out stepped a tiny, bewhiskered brown man. He was beckoning to me and Shelly.

All of Shelly's natural pity for the helpless and downcast ran right off the glaring canvas flap where the poor rooster was struggling for his life and onto the ridiculous little brown man standing in the doorway.

"Come." The little man gestured impatiently with his stubby bulldog arm. "Quickly—and shhh," he said, sealing his lips with his finger and glancing from side to side like a fugitive.

What did he want? Who could he be? Certainly he was not the Wild Man of Zanzibar. He was too small. He had no fangs.

An English poet has spoken of an artistic technique that releases the mundane mind to enjoy the deeper pleasures of the imagination. Called "the willing suspension of disbelief," it is like going willingly along with Dorothy on her journey through Oz. Well, Shelly didn't have to "suspend" any such thing. Shelly was born in Oz. If Shelly had had to believe in our reality, he would have had to suspend his perfectly normal Land of Oz so he could enter the absolutely incredible world the rest of us inhabit. So there was nothing especially unnatural or unnerving to Shelly about the little deformity that stood before us.

"I'm Zulu from Zanzibar," the little man said, his voice miniature and hollow, as if it came from a small wooden box buried within his chest. His eyes were flint black, his beard and hair a wiry coconut brown, and his little fists like overbaked biscuits.

"I know," Shelly said, not seeming the least surprised.

"Have no fear," Zulu said urgently in his small voice. He held the door open. "Hurry. Inside." He motioned. "Not an eye is to fall upon me until I perform my horrid act." Shelly had already entered Zulu's painted cage, and the little fellow was assisting me from behind, pressing his knuckles into my spine.

It was not a cage at all. It was a home, comfortable and complete with sofa, table and chairs, closet, icebox, kerosene stove, and bunk bed. One entire inside wall—the one with the painted bars on the outside—was a mural composed in foliage green, a jungle scene, the sun a blazing orange on one side and a cool night moon on the other. In the middle of the painted forest was a little brown man riding a tiger.

"I am a great artist," Zulu said, nodding at the painting. "This is my native land of Zanzibar, to which, with God's aid, I may soon return. I presume, in my heart," he said, pointing a stubby finger to his chest, "that you are both *Christian* lads."

"Yes," we answered together. How could anyone be week after week in Aunt Rebecca's Sunday school class and not be a Christian?

"Have no fear," Zulu said. "I have only to thank God that at this unlucky span in my sad life I have been granted such good fortune."

"That you won't have to eat any more live chickens?" Shelly prompted.

"Alas, never again, God help me." Zulu sighed. "I weep to think of what a disgrace and abomination I have been driven to, and what a rogue I have become to God and man."

I was astonished at the little man's humanity. Mother would have been impressed with his command of language. I had expected him to let out a few weird whoops, do a flip or two, and scamper about.

"You don't act very wild," I said.

With that, Zulu sprang and, in one bound, landed in the middle of his large table, crouching there, drilling us with his black eyes. We were startled.

"Of course I'm not wild," he declared in his compressed voice. "But they have tried to make me so! They have taken me from my gentle land of milk and honey, my country of sunshine and moonlight, and made me into the bloodsucking monster you see before you."

Shelly was looking at the huge jungle picture, with the kindly little brown man in the middle, riding his tiger. I wondered if the tiger man was Zulu.

"Why don't you just stop eating chickens and go back to painting pictures?" Shelly said.

"That's just it," Zulu said. "They won't let me. I am a captive here, their prisoner, held in bondage against my wishes and beyond my feeble powers to escape. Look," he pled, leaping from the table and waddling like a duck to his bunk bed. "Do you know what these are?" he said, picking up a steel cuff on a chain. There were four chains, two at the head of his bunk and two at the foot.

"Shackles," I said.

"Yes," Zulu confirmed. "Every night they come—these unholy giants—to cuff and chain me like a galley slave, restricting me forever so that I may never return to my gentle people and to my wailing wife and children."

"You've got a wife and little babies?" Shelly asked darkly. He was touched.

"Yes—God granting me in His infinite mercy that they might still be alive."

"Why don't you just walk out of this circus and never come back?" I said, beginning to feel sorry for him.

"My God, dear child!" Zulu was incensed. "Can you imagine a tiny man, as I myself am, simply walking out unprotected into this world of hungry giants and expecting to avoid their eagle eyes or their clutches? They would swoop down upon me in an instant, snap me up like a struggling beetle, and swallow me down into a gluttonous hell more dark and miserable than the one I now endure.

"Look," said Zulu pitifully, pulling up one sleeve, then the other. There was a vague pink ring around each wrist. "And this." He pulled up his trousers legs. Around each ankle was the same pink circle of his bondage.

Shelly was on the verge of tears.

"In my country I was king," the Wild Man continued, turning his shrunken form around daintily, like a girl. "Behold me now in my helpless misery. We dwarfs are God's unique creation—never call us midgets!" he wailed. "We are a special race of men conceived before the origin of the world and created during the flood because of Adam's sin, so that, in the event of Noah's failure, we should inherit the earth. But alas and be damned, the success of wicked Noah has subjugated us to his tyrannical race of giant monsters, who count themselves as gods and make us the pets and play-pretties of their vulgar conceits. We are not children!" Zulu cried, even more intensely. "I am thirty-three inches high and one hundred years old!"

Shelly and I were hypnotized.

Zulu gave a little backward rump jump and landed in a chair, then burrowed his forehead into his biscuit paws.

"Christian lads," Zulu sobbed through his whiskers, "I pray God—will you help *save* me?"

"Ye-e-es," Shelly whispered.

"Excellent well," Zulu said, recovering immediately. He bounced from the chair and, to my surprise, skipped—swaying like a little girl—to his curtained closet, returning in a moment with a cigar box. Before opening it, he hopped up on a stool by the half-glass door, looked north and south, then closed the blinds. The house cage grew dark.

On one end of the large table were a kerosene lamp, a hand bell, a Bible, a fruit jar, and a huge Texas ten-gallon hat. Zulu lit the lamp, which threw a canopy of copper light around the three of us.

The cigar box held fifty one-dollar bills. Zulu slowly counted them out before us into a stack beside the Bible. It was an awesome pile.

"Handkerchief," Zulu instructed, extending a paw.

Shelly and I struggled into our hip pockets and drew out our handkerchiefs. Zulu surveyed them both and chose mine, a large silk Sunday kerchief that Aunt Rebecca had given me for Christmas and in the corner of which Mother had stitched my initials, SOS.

"Excellent well," Zulu said. "Have no fear. God has sent you Christian lads to seal my salvation."

I wasn't so sure God had done anything of the sort. It was the calliope that had beckoned Shelly to the circus. I had followed Shelly. And, in a way that nobody understood but me, it was that silly, doomed rooster painted on Zulu's tent that had got us both exactly where we were. But where exactly were we now, standing before this little hobgoblin in a hood of copper light?

Zulu opened the Bible, laid my handkerchief upon it, arranged the money in the middle, and—as if this had been a practiced chore—rolled the bills into a perfect cylinder. When he tied off the handkerchief ends, the rolled money looked like a fat sausage. Zulu handed me the money.

"It is all I possess save what rags you see hanging upon these poor bones," Zulu said, "and it is yours alone, every cent of it. I vow I want none of it ever again while I live and breathe on this wretched earth." With both his paws, Zulu pressed the money into my hand and said, "I pray by our blessed Savior's saving grace, and with such help as I may beg from you two Christian souls, that I, by Sunday morn, shall be set free from this caravan of sin and shame."

Zulu's oration sounded remote and mechanical, like a wind-up gramophone. Was it rehearsed? Or was Zulu's voice merely a sad manifestation of his fate, or another mutation of his already shrunken body?

Zulu didn't request—he demanded—that the money be ours, totally and absolutely! No strings. Except for secrecy.

"Here," he said, and plucked the rolled bills from my fingers. Standing tiptoe, he stuffed the money into the bosom of my shirt. I was glad he had given *me* the money, not because I wanted to take advantage of an unfortunate midget but because Shelly, without batting an eye, would have given the money straight back to Zulu. The little man pushed the Bible toward us.

"I pray you, swear with your hand on God's holy word not to breathe of this to a living soul until you have released me to your sheriff on Sunday morn."

Shelly was hooked. All creatures small and forlorn Shelly cherished, and Zulu was certainly the smallest and most woebegone man we had ever beheld. But questions kept popping into my mind.

"How can we—" I began.

"Swear," Zulu repeated in his pitiful Victrola voice.

Shelly swore by God on the Bible at once. I held my hand a safe distance over the book and mumbled something.

"You want to just give yourself up to Sheriff Holdster for doing *nothing?*" I asked.

"Yes. Not alone for my protection but for you two Christian lads, who so kindly will render to me your services." Zulu pulled on his beard philosophically. "Have no fear. I will suffer no hurt to befall you."

What could possibly befall us?

"But you haven't *done* anything," I said. "Just ate up on a few dumb chickens."

"Ah, but—"

Zulu, chest-high to the tabletop, settled himself into a special high chair and pulled a large white fountain pen and a sheet of paper from the drawer. Then he began writing. "Don't you see?" he said. "I will, with your Christian fortitude, escape not *from* the law but *to* the law—after which you will *own* me."

I shrugged my disbelief to Shelly and looked again at the jungle scene from Zanzibar, with the little brown man riding the tiger. The kerosene light made the tiger man's eyes sparkle like black diamonds. Zulu was drawing up a contract, and while he was flourishing away with the ivory pen, his last words began soaking into me, slowly, like beads of water on a dry plank. Zulu not only wasn't wild; he wasn't stupid either. So far he had been one step ahead of us all the way.

"Own you!" I croaked.

"But of course," Zulu said, still scribbling along with the great white pen. "What better reason could you have to return for me Sunday morn than to own me legally—beard and body?"

"But suppose—" I began.

"Silence!" Zulu commanded. "Your name?" he asked, looking first at Shelly. Zulu poised the big pen over the document ready to write.

"Shelly Leopold Webster."

"Middle names are entirely superfluous," Zulu complained. "They are an outrageous conceit and a sign of Noah," he said, raising his voice but writing carefully all the while. "True dwarfs *never* have middle names of their own. Never!" When he finished recording Shelly's name, he looked at me.

"Silas Simeon," I said, carefully omitting the O'Riley.

Zulu's outburst about middle names had made me uneasy. With the kerosene lamp flickering, with this little troll scribbling and wheezing in the copper light, with Shelly happily humming "Over the Waves," and with my heart thumping against Zulu's wad of money, I stepped on my toe to see if I was dreaming.

Shelly, humming and now swaying, was perfectly at ease.

"How much money do you have?" Zulu asked, looking at both of us.

Oh, Jesus, I thought, Zulu wants his money back.

"Not that," Zulu said, reading my eyes. He pointed at the roll of money inside my shirt. "Those worthless sheets of green, each and all, are yours so long as you both may harbor them. Grapple them unto thy soul with hoops of steel." This last sentence hit me like lightning. I remembered, from Mother's reading Shakespeare to Blue and me, that these words came from the garrulous Polonius.

"There." Zulu pointed at our pockets. He was talking about *our* money.

We dug into our pants. Shelly fished out a dime, two nickels, and four coppers. I had eight cents. We flopped it all on the table by Zulu's Bible. Before the coins stopped spinning, Shelly summed them:

"Thirty-two cents."

"Excellent well," Zulu said, writing down the amount. "You have purchased Zulu of Zanzibar for thirty-two cents."

Shelly was delighted. I was thunderstruck.

Zulu lifted the ivory pen ceremoniously and turned the document around for our inspection. Zulu's penmanship was exquisite to the point of being illegible. It reminded me of my great-grandfather's letters penned during the Civil War, with every *A* and *I* and *T* swirling in sensuous convolutions around the words they embraced. Zulu's document read:

> I, Zulu of Zanzibar, on this day of October 8th, 1937, in keeping with the laws of my country, and to secure my freedom from bondage, do sell my wretched self, body and soul, to Shelly Webster and Silas Simeon for the sum of thirty-two (32) cents.
>
> (Signed) *Zulu of Zanzibar*
>
> ____________________
>
> ____________________

Zulu had drawn two lines for our signatures. Shelly took the pen and signed enthusiastically—but not before inking a line through the word "soul." He held out the pen to me. Sweet Jesus. What was going on? What was Shelly getting us into?

"Thirty-two cents!" I said. "That's not enough to—"

"Suffer no thought upon it," Zulu said. "Money is of absolutely no consequence *when honor is at stake.*" Yes, our wild man had indeed read into at least one of the old bard's famous tragedies. But at the time, however legal all this seemed, thirty-two cents struck me as a pitiful little bit to pay, even for a dwarf.

"Suppose—" I started.

"Nonsense," Zulu cried. "I am a bargain at any price. My jungle painting alone is worth a million dollars, and if you wish, I bequeath it and this carriage that graces it to you both this very instant."

"Silas." Shelly was tugging at my sleeve. "Let's not make Zulu eat any more live chickens," he said.

What had I to do with this little goblin and his eating chickens?

"This is committing slavery," I said.

"It is of no consequence," Zulu assured me. "Pay it absolutely no attention. I am bound by no laws save those of my own dear green paradise of Zanzibar, where my sobbing wife and babies await my return." Zulu studied our eyes and added quickly, "If you wish, I will buy me back on Sunday morn with this very thirty-two cents." He held up the coins in his fist. "And then I will be free, and if you wish, you will be free of me forever."

It must have been at this moment that Zulu entered my Jar of Marbles. I was soothed by the knowledge that Shelly's father was a judge of great repute and would allow no calamity so insignificant as Zulu to befall me. I took the pen from Shelly and scratched down my name.

"Excellent well," Zulu said, recovering his giant pen. He hopped down, folded the contract, sealed it in an envelope, and slipped it into my hip pocket.

Shelly beamed. I have to confess to a tiny flush

of pride such as my grandfather must have felt a century ago upon bringing home from auction a strapping slave.

There were other questions. How were we to spring Zulu from his four shackles Sunday morning?

"Do you think me a complete fool?" Zulu said. "I am a great locksmith. I have fashioned skeleton keys for all locks within my ken. Have I not better eyes and more nimble hands than these crude giants who play God and go roaring their ignorance throughout our world?" He pulled open the table drawer and produced a key for each of us.

But how were we to sneak Zulu off the circus grounds Sunday morning undetected?

"A problem of no consequence," Zulu declared. "There is absolutely no hindrance to it." We were to bring my bicycle, seat him on it astride a pillow for elevation, and simply roll him off to freedom between us. To demonstrate a greater height, Zulu slipped out of his high chair and plopped on his huge Texas hat, which made him look even shorter and more ridiculous. I couldn't help but laugh at this little imp squashed down under his great bonnet.

Then, to my surprise, Zulu whipped out two imaginary six-shooters from imaginary holsters and fired imaginary bullets into the kerosene lamp. Spontaneously, Shelly made his large hands into pistols and, likewise, pumped two imaginary shots into the flickering light that Zulu had already blasted into imaginary darkness.

"Blam! Blam!" Shelly repeated.

"Excellent well," Zulu exclaimed, applauding Shelly's marksmanship. "Who would not mistake us for Tom Mix and Hopalong Cassidy? Am I not a great actor?" He pranced about like a bantam rooster.

Now Zulu grew deadly serious again. We were to promise to see with our very eyes the Fabulous Frances of France in action and then his own "abominable" act that followed. Why on earth this?

Otherwise, Zulu explained, "You would never know the caravan of horrors that devours me, digesting my poor body and soul ounce by suffering ounce as in the belly of a snake."

"But the Frances show is for adults only," I reminded him.

"It is of no consequence whatsoever," Zulu said, waving my question out of the air with his little arms. "I will admit you into a secret entrance I have prepared. Have I not told you that I am a great magician second only to Harry Houdini? You must see all. I have thought of everything."

"Where do all the roosters you eat come from?" Shelly asked.

Zulu was stumped. He thoughtfully removed his ten-gallon lid, took aim, and sailed it toward an invisible target at the rear of his quarters. It landed securely on a peg and hung in the shadows like a gigantic bat.

"That is of no matter to children," Zulu said. "These hellish sins have all been decided and devised by the very Goliaths I despise and whose hot blood I could drink off in one quaff."

Zulu could be downright scary.

Zulu's final ploy didn't faze Shelly but took me by complete surprise. Shelly not only took Zulu's offer in stride but later added to it his own unique brand of genius and showmanship.

What Zulu wanted—so that we would be bound in trust to each other—was wonderfully generous and simple. He explained that so long as we had taken *his* money, we shouldn't mind, as a matter of common trust, matching it with fifty dollars of our own. "Trust money," Zulu called it, to ensure our return for him on Sunday morning.

Shelly and I were to freely take his fifty dollars home with us; match it with our own trust money; return tomorrow night to witness the unmentionables of Fabulous Frances and Zulu himself; secure all the money in the fruit jar on his table; bury it anywhere on the football field we wished; return Zulu's spade; then dig up all our money Sunday morning for our very own—but only after releasing yours truly, Zulu, to Sheriff Holdster. It was foolproof.

I couldn't believe it. But it was easy to spot the poor midget's weakness. Who, unless he was a scatterbrain, would just haul off and give kids fifty bucks to run off with? Like Shelly, I felt sorry for Zulu. But for different reasons. Shelly felt sorry for Zulu's sad, squelched body. I felt sorry for Zulu's sad, weak head.

Then Zulu started to cry. "But hold," he sobbed. "Shall I entrust to you my freedom, my life and all, only to see you two Christian lads betray me in my hour of need, leaving me naked and enslaved by these monsters whom I loathe?"

Then that marvelous wheel inside Shelly's brain began to turn. "Have no fear," he cried, going into a squat and doing a little duck walk around Zulu. "It is of absolutely no consequence." Rolling his pop eyes from side to side like Groucho Marx, Shelly said, "It shall all come to pass. Pay it absolutely no attention."

Shelly was putting on a Zulu act! His mind, unmatched for memory and sound, was set in motion. Shelly sprang erect, towering over Zulu, and lifted the astonished dwarf to the ceiling and set him down on the tabletop.

Shelly rambled on poetically: "No harm shall befall thee whilst thou art in our care. Absolutely none whatsoever, even though the flames of hell engulf us all without mercy. For I am thy shepherd. Yea, though you walk through the valley of the shadow of death, fear no evil . . ." Shelly spelled out the word, adding volume to each letter: "e-v-i-l!"

How, I don't know, but after a while Shelly moved backward out of Psalms and into the Book of Job:

"To the hideous monsters that sadden you," Shelly continued, "have *no fear*. Who are they that darkeneth counsel by words without knowledge? Gird up now thy loins like a man, for I will demand of thee and answer thou *me!* Where were these God-mocking Philistines when the foundations of the earth were laid, when the morning stars sang together and all our little men of paradise shouted for joy. . . ."

How far back and forth into the Scriptures Shelly skipped about, improvising, I can't remember; but when he finished, Zulu was standing transfixed on the tabletop, as rigid as a railroad spike driven into a stump.

Shelly wasn't finished. He swept up the fruit jar and walked to the door on stiff shanks like a Frankenstein creature and stepped outside. Almost before his shadow had left the doorway he returned, the jar half filled with sand; he set it solemnly on the table. What could I say? What was going on in Shelly's mind? Was he taking over Zulu's act? Was Shelly his real self? Had Zulu been acting? Or was this Zulu's real self, all thirty-three strutting inches and one hundred years of him?

Shelly picked up Zulu and stuck him on the floor

as if he had been a doorstop. Next Shelly poured the sand on the table and, after smoothing it out, wrote in it with his finger:

I OWN 3/4 OF ZULU
SW

Shelly then lifted the petrified midget and set him down in his high chair, squarely before the inscribed sand. I wondered how Shelly figured he owned more of Zulu than I did. Then I remembered that my contribution to the Zulu purchase had been only eight cents out of the thirty-two.

"Sign it," Shelly whispered confidentially into the dwarf's ear.

"But, dear Christian lads—" Zulu began.

"It is of absolutely no consequence," Shelly said. "Initial it." He rolled his eyes fiendishly, as if he were one of the monsters whose hot blood Zulu would gladly have drunk off in a gulp.

Zulu stuck his forefinger in the sand and inscribed "Z OF Z."

"Excellent well." Shelly swept the grains into a pile. He then scooped the sand up with the back cover of the Bible and, making a trough, poured it all into his spread handkerchief. After tying the four corners into a knot, he put the sand contract in his shirt pocket and stood the elf, still transfixed, back on the table. I could tell that Shelly's performance was over now, as surely as if one had pulled the curtains on a stage play.

❖

When we returned to the schoolhouse, it was lunchtime, and Shelly had withdrawn again into his sanctuary of indifference.

Mrs. Roberts had seen us coming. She had a way of eroding you from a small hill into a gully with one glance. When we opened the door, Mrs. Roberts met us face-on.

"I brought Shelly back," I announced, like a crusader arriving from the Holy Land.

In the cloakroom, I put Zulu's fifty-dollar money roll in my jacket pocket. Shelly put his sand contract in his lunch box.

"Nobody can read that sand now," I said.

"I can," Shelly said.

Chapter Four

After a quick supper, Shelly and I were standing that night under the big mushroom-shaped oak in the Websters' front yard.

Greater than the mystery of Shelly's Zulu act was where Shelly had gotten the fifty dollars. He had ten crisp five-dollar bills in a white envelope as if they had been handed to him by God. Had he lifted the bills from the Judge's wallet? His mother's purse? Where? What was Shelly getting us into? Judge Webster and his magnificent wife, Miss Gretta, had always trusted me to steer Shelly out of harm's way, or at least, with simple Sunday school discretion, to keep us both within safe walking distance of the straight and narrow. Nor could they have missed noticing my devotion to their large maestro and genius. But good Lord, I thought, if Shelly and I were guilty of committing slavery, were we not now guilty of stealing too?

"The money. Jesus!" I whispered.

"Shhh," Shelly teased, holding a long finger to his lips. "How much you got?" he asked me.

I had, after serious agonizing, taken half my coffee-can savings toward a bolt-action Sears Roebuck .22 rifle—a painful withdrawal of seven dollars and twenty-five cents. My father had given me a dollar and a half for the circus. I started counting it out.

"Eight dollars and seventy-five cents," Shelly said. "Excellent well." He plucked five one-dollar bills from my hand and put them in his pocket.

"Don't go getting started up on that Zulu act again," I said. "Where'd you get all the—"

"It is of absolutely no consequence." Shelly grinned and patted me on the head.

"Consequence! Hell's bells, you're going to get our ass in trouble."

Shelly was figuring. "That leaves you three dollars and seventy-five cents for the circus and five dollars and eight cents ownership in Zulu to my forty-five dollars and twenty-four cents, minus thirty-two cents equals fifty times point one zero equals five times two for one hundred equals ten." Shelly considered his calculations. "When we dig up all the money Sunday morning, you get ten dollars and I get ninety," he said.

My heart sank. First I had thought Zulu wanted

all his money back, and now, by grammar school logic, Shelly was going to get the lion's share.

We stopped in front of Reverend Grayson's house and rolled all the bills together in one bundle, then tied them up in my handkerchief. To my surprise, Shelly kept the roll this time and stuck it inside his shirt. A whopping hundred bucks. What could I do?

The Graysons were eating supper. I stood under the chinaberry tree. Through their front window I could see Sylvia, smiling, her face flooded in golden hair, putting food to her mouth. How is it, I wondered, that lips that I—oh, God—so sweetly kissed could have anything to do with food!

Could Sylvia see me now? No. Had she forgotten her promise to fly with me in the De Havilland? The fork of this fading chinaberry tree was as high as I had soared with Sylvia. There was something nicely dishonest about spying on Sylvia trapped inside in light while I was outside, secure in the dark.

We were on our way again to the circus, and I could hear the calliope piping away on the far side of the football field.

"Or," Shelly said, coming out of silent contemplation, "you can have *all* the money and I get *all* of Zulu."

I hadn't thought of this. Was Shelly crazy?

"What would you do with *all* of Zulu *all* the time? I asked.

"Keep him from eating live roosters," Shelly said.

Sweet Jesus.

"Suppose Zulu won't stop?" I said. "Suppose he's like Mr. Willie Harper is about liquor and just keeps on hogging down chickens until somebody shoots him like a dog?"

"It is of no consequence," Shelly said. He reached inside his shirt and came out with the wad of money. "*All* the money for *all* of Zulu?" He pointed the money at me.

It was then that I realized Zulu was more interesting than money. Or was I getting as crazy as Shelly? Suppose I did let Shelly have all of Zulu for a hundred dollars? What would Judge Webster and Miss Gretta say if *I* brought Zulu home—all Shelly's—to Shelly's house on *my* bicycle? And me with all that money! And all for selling Shelly a wild, chicken-eating midget! This would be slavery times two. Judge Webster would knit his brow and swell with speculation. Mother would wonder at my sanity, and Father would burn my ass up.

"Fifty–fifty or nothing," I said.

Shelly thought.

"Fifty–fifty," Shelly agreed, holding out the roll of money. He then reached into his shirt again and came out with the handkerchief of sand. "But three-fourths of Zulu for me," he said. Shelly had me beat on numbers, and I knew it, but I still had Zulu's elaborate contract in my pocket, the one written in ink.

"Excellent well," I said.

Now they had me doing it.

"Excellent well," Shelly repeated. Before he could stick the money back inside his shirt, I picked it from his hand.

"Better let me hang on to this for a while now," I said.

II

If our circus was a bastard by day, she was a wench by night. Perfumed by popcorn and fresh pine sawdust, festooned in colored lights and tasseled tents, she took on all comers.

Shelly and I made a beeline for Zulu's house cage, passing on the way a black boy hosing down the lone, slack-skinned elephant; the twinkly-eyed fat woman, sitting alone inside her white mound of dimpled flesh; children fishing colored celluloid ducks from an artificial stream; men shooting corks from air rifles at packs of cigarettes; high school kids throwing warped cottonseed baseballs at pyramids of iron milk bottles; the strong man, standing over his dumbbells, drinking a Coke; and, in a divine moment, the Golden Princess of the High Wire—the very image of Sylvia—flashing across her open doorway like a fleeing Cinderella.

Shelly tapped on Zulu's door. Inside, some spirited conversation was going on. We could hear Zulu's tin-can voice rising in contention and falling in secrecy. I was about to push on in, when Shelly stuck out his arm.

"He's ours," I reminded Shelly.

"Shhh," Shelly cautioned. "Not his voice. Not his breath."

The door opened. There stood the slim roustabout with sideburns and black oiled-down hair, who had helped erect Zulu's tent and the Fabulous plywood Frances. He had gray, cavernous eyes and dirt-colored skin. Dangling from his lips was a smoldering cigarette with an inch-long ash. My eyes distrusted him before I did.

"Ah, it is you."

It was Zulu. Like a house animal, he strutted toward us from under a layer of cigarette smoke. Except for a pair of dark trunks, he was naked and, in an odd way, handsome. I was amazed at his stubby compaction. If his thigh had been slit open, I was sure his pent-up sinews would have burst out like rubber bands from a sliced golf ball. It was not hard to believe he was a hundred years old. I imagined that, with his body compressed into a space one third our own, Zulu could easily live for centuries.

When we entered Zulu's cell, the little man quickly read my eyes. "Pay him no attention whatsoever," Zulu said, shooing the slim man outside and slamming the door. "He is an ignoramus, whose brain is made of monkey dung." Zulu walked to his bunk bed and picked up two of the shackles. "His sole task is to restrain me, cuff me at night with these so that I may do no violence to his masters, who lord it over me eternally and whose very shadows I avoid and spit upon." He waddled up beside Shelly and, in buddy-buddy fashion, cast his little arm up and across Shelly's rump and patted him on the thigh. "Have no fear," he reassured.

No fear of what? I wondered. And why had Zulu chosen Shelly for this special affection?

"We got the money," I said.

"New bills," Shelly said.

"A hundred dollars," I said.

To impress Zulu, I produced the roll, undid the money from my handkerchief, and laid open the raw cash on the table as proof positive.

Zulu barely glanced at the bills. "The money is of utterly no consequence whatsoever," he said, "save to prove our mutual trust and loyalty. May God grant long life and salvation to you Christian lads, who know that the love of money is the root of all evil."

"I'll count it out," I said.

"God forbid!" Zulu protested. "Freedom is what

I crave. I'll not have the stench of avarice upon it."
Avarice. I had heard the word, but now came the first inkling of its meaning.

Either from pity for poor Zulu or in fear of pecuniary contamination, Shelly was about to cram our money into Zulu's jar forthwith, then and there—forsake it and, as far as I knew, dismiss it altogether from our sight and possession. I made a grab for the roll. Shelly was too quick. He held the money aloft, pressing it against the ceiling, and, swaying his hips like a hula girl, started humming "Over the Waves."

Zulu went into a little nervous spasm, spinning on one heel like a top, then stopped short and burst out, "By God in Heaven, *no!* You both must hold fast to the whole abominable lot of it until it is buried secretly in God's good earth, beyond the reach of anyone but yourselves." Which suited me, even though Shelly was now dangerously flaunting our good fortune. He stuck the roll of naked bills into the bosom of his shirt and left my empty handkerchief on the table.

Afterward Zulu gave us free tickets to his chicken-eating act. With a finger he beckoned Shelly to lean down out of the altitudes and, on tiptoe, whispered something in Shelly's ear. Then he led us through a hidden door in the back of his closet and out into the tangy circus air.

III

True to his word, Zulu had indeed prepared ways and means for our viewing of the Fabulous Frances. It was a body-sized, musty canvas envelope, including a stand-on box, that perfectly concealed Shelly and me against the outside belly of the famous lady's tent. In the center of the tent wall was a private set of see-through, see-all slots for our eyes. I could tell by the frayed edges of the slit entrance and the sagging peepholes that, however innocent our viewing was to be, this was no recent invention.

Townsmen were streaming steadily now into Frances's canvas domain. The stage—about the size of a big barn door—was draped in red carpet, with a solitary stool in the middle; to the adjoining right was the lady's chamber. The stage background was a thin, wavering, translucent curtain with moonlit, misty impressions of naked girls shimmering and undulating on a seashore. On the ground to the left was a man in an open vest and a derby hat, sitting behind a set of drums.

Judging from the fare printed on my free ticket to Zulu's act, I guessed that this, too, was a twenty-five-cent show. Shelly's disregard for our trust money was bothering me. I pulled out my clean handkerchief.

"Better let me wrap up those bills again," I said.

Shelly didn't hear. He was glued to his peephole. The man at the drums hit a few licks.

The place was filling up. I was not surprised to discover Uncle George and Sheriff Holdster in the audience, but when our principal, Mr. Winters, and the kindly old farmer with the cane showed up, I was shocked. I don't know why. I had no idea what Miss Frances might do. Maybe stride bare-ass across the stage and fling an acrobat over her shoulders—nothing I'd dare breathe to Aunt Rebecca or mention to Mother; but on the other hand, it could be nothing to permanently alter my Christian bearing.

With a flurry from the drummer, out hopped a feisty, stiff-legged barker in a short-brim cannonball hat, wielding a megaphone. I could tell he'd been drinking. He began mouthing off about the feats of Fabulous Frances and her incredible passions for the bizarre.

I was burning to know what it was that Zulu had whispered in Shelly's ear.

It was "the light," Shelly told me.

"What light?"

"I don't know," Shelly said. "Zulu just said, 'Keep your eye on the light.' "

I was as much in the dark as ever. I had to wonder sometimes if Shelly was worth all my trouble.

The drums stopped. The barker stopped. Then she appeared—Fabulous Frances in the flesh. The whole stage trembled when she alighted. And Jesus, hide your eyes—was she evermore *in the flesh,* every jiggling white pound of her, with two silver dollars harnessed in tandem to her enormous breasts. She was clad in pink tights too tight and scant for any hide or hair of modesty. Her plywood likeness belied her not: streaming black hair, buckshot eyes, a bold face, and a lipstick smile as broad as a slice of raw beef, and across her shoulders a bullwhip. The audience drew its breath. She was an arresting blend of Mae West, the Wife of Bath, and Luis Firpo, the Wild Bull of the Pampas, whom only Jack Dempsey could subdue.

Clayton Slaughter's daddy was in the crowd, standing behind Mayor Prowler. Sideways, Mr. Slaughter's face stood out like a rusty ax head. He was wearing a gray felt hat with the brim pulled down as if it was raining.

Suddenly a chimp leapt from Frances's trailer door, dragging a rope, and scampered across the stage. Frances unslung her whip and, to the drummer's cue, cracked the air above the crowd. At which the chimp turned, bounded back with great acceleration, and sprang into the air toward the monumental woman. Frances caught the chimp on one hand and lifted him skyward like the Statue of Liberty.

Applause.

Down bobbed the chimp and loped over to the

chained-off spectators. It was not a rope the monkey was dragging; it was an electric cord with socket and light bulb at the end that he held in his hand.

"It's the *light*," I said. "It's the light Zulu was talking about."

"Not yet," Shelly said. "It's not *on*."

"Watch it," I said.

"I am," Shelly said.

The chimp jumped over to Sheriff Holdster, clicked the light on, and waved it under his nose, then wabbled over to our side of the tent and pointed the bulb in our direction, flicking it on and off.

"Now that's it. *That's* the light," I said.

"Yes," Shelly said.

The chimp loped over our way, closer. Could he see us through the eye slots? Shelly was getting excited.

"Better button up your shirt so the money don't all fall out," I said.

"It's not a monkey," Shelly said. "It's Zulu."

So it was. It was Zulu in a monkey suit. No doubt about it. *Zulu the great actor*, I thought. Ha! The crazy little runt has fooled them all but Shelly and me—even Mr. Winters.

Although Shelly was in my Jar of Marbles since I couldn't remember when, he had always been a mystery to me. If fate had been kinder to him, I'm sure he would still be so today. Shelly cringed if he saw a mouse caught in a trap. So how he managed to watch the rest of the Frances show that night with such pure delight, without chucking up, I have been able only to guess. *Disappointed* in Zulu is not the word. I was mortified. I was in too deep by then not to believe that, somehow, all Zulu's shenanigans were forced upon him, that he was not the sinner but the sinned against. But when Frances dropped her panties and sat down naked on the stool and spread her legs, and Zulu pranced around her flanks, making lewd and vulgar gestures toward her privates with the glowing bulb, I couldn't help but wonder if he wasn't enjoying it all.

The rest of the act was too disgusting to watch with both eyes. I started to put my hand over Shelly's peepholes. But no. Shelly was as pleased as a biologist over his microscope. Then all lights went out, except the one Zulu was wielding.

Where Zulu finally inserted the glowing bulb, I don't have the courage to say. But when the bold lady's groin lit up like a pink grapefruit, Shelly was delighted.

What did Shelly think of this humiliating performance?

"Excellent well!" Shelly exclaimed.

After that, Zulu cut off his vulgar light, Frances vanished, the top lights came back on, and that was your two bits' worth.

IV

The thing that hit me the strangest about the whole Frances episode was that Shelly seemed more concerned about the light bulb than he did about Frances or Zulu. He explained later that any sudden change in temperature or pressure might have caused the bulb to implode, shattering itself completely and causing great discomfort to Frances. I ran across the word "implode" again a decade and a world war later. It means, prophetically for Shelly, that under outward pressure, surrounding walls *crush in* upon you.

It was weeks after the light bulb stunt when I realized that Shelly hadn't been in the least concerned about the morality or immorality of the act. Once his attention had been drawn into fine focus and he was alone on his own inner stage, he soared like an asteroid above and beyond the gravitative audience around him. It was at such times as these, for brief periods, that weightlessness lifted Shelly above the heavy world surrounding him.

Maybe Shelly's amoral philosophy was right. After all, Zulu had done no harm to the ample Miss Frances; and he had performed his duties not only with her consent and cooperation but, apparently, also to her profit and pleasure. To Shelly, Frances was—unlike the enslaved Zulu or the doomed rooster—too big and self-sufficient to feel sorry for. As for Zulu, Shelly said, with good sense, "Doing that to the light bulb is better than eating live chickens."

❖

Zulu's own show was a masterpiece of madness and deception. It was also the near undoing of gentle Shelly. The enactment so completely drained him that, for a moment, he fainted away, and it was not until some time after the ordeal, and Zulu's visible return to sanity, that Shelly truly revived.

Zulu's arena was packed. The same barker, with the prancy, fox-terrier legs, was mouthing off to the crowd through the megaphone. Shelly and I were standing as close as we could get to the action. With the pulling of a cord, the painted canvas of the fleeing rooster and the Wild Man of Zanzibar rose, and there was revealed a real half-trailer cage with real steel bars and a closed-off compartment adjoining the end door to Zulu's private quarters.

There was no subtle theatrical suspense, no building up toward the main action. Zulu was all climax from first to finish—a Zanzibar midget with a King Kong performance. The curious thing was that Zulu's shrunken form made him more awesome than if he'd been a giant. Above all, Zulu was the unexpected. His jack-out-of-the-box shock strategy sent children scurrying through a forest of legs and to the rear of the crowd. Out of nowhere Zulu flew, screaming, from his enclosure, and landed, hands and bare feet, on the center of the cage bars like a colossal frog, screaking a primeval cry that would have made Tarzan sound like Prince Charming. He wore a tiny leopardskin, hung over one shoulder and draped loosely over his groin. Glued thus to the bars, he increased his maniacal wailing and shook himself so violently that the whole cage clattered from end to end. Then he sprang clockwise from bar to bar, pumping monkey-like back and forth with all his might and glowering at the stunned spectators with his hot charcoal eyes and, yes, foaming at the mouth!

Had Zulu fallen so deeply into his own feigned frenzy that he had really gone stark, raving mad? Was it possible to act yourself into insanity? Then back out again?

The chicken that was released from the enclosure into Zulu's cage was not the noble game cock depicted outside on the canvas. This bird was a perturbed Rhode Island Red hen, a plump, egg-laying pullet that fluttered into the cage, gaining her feet uncertainly but with a kind of barnyard dignity, then clucking about in her moment of displacement, when—like a thunderbolt—Zulu fell from the bars upon her. It was an amazing and thrilling display of showmanship. Shelly fainted promptly away, clinging limply to the corner tent pole. Without missing a lick, Zulu seized the squawking bird by its neck, cranked her into a whirl that wrung her body free and flopping across the cage, then flung the head, eyeballs bulging and beak still dripping and gasping, into the audience. Finally, screaming like a gargoyle out of Hades, Zulu pounced upon the shuddering brown body, burying his muzzle in the red cavity and flinging feathers to the winds. . . .

It was a shame Shelly didn't endure to see Zulu's act through, even though, I had to admit, it was pretty gory.

Whether it was the fate of the poor hen or Zulu's plight that blasted Shelly the hardest, I could not tell. I led my friend like a drunken man to the football bathhouse, where I wiped off his face with a wet sock. I could see the naked money lying abandoned inside his open shirt. To secure our investment, I transferred the roll to my own breast and buttoned up tight.

It was some minutes before I got Shelly stabilized enough to approach Zulu's trailer. With my rubbery buddy still too woozy to intervene, I opened Zulu's door and barged straight in, just in time to glimpse the black-haired man enter the closet and vanish. Zulu emerged from the same enclosure.

Surprisingly—so soon after all the blood and feathers—there was Zulu washed beamingly clean, completely transformed. He was decked out in a kid's cowboy getup, with green silk shirt, red bandanna neckerchief, boots, holsters, cap pistols—all that under his whopping ten-gallon hat.

With Zulu's transformation, Shelly quickly revived. He picked up Zulu fondly and stood him on the table.

"Was I not magnificently revolting," Zulu announced.

It was true. I never would have dreamed that so much violence could be generated in one pint-sized midget and released with such sustained fury. I wondered that he still had breath to carry on.

"You scared the living hell out of Shelly," I said.

"It was not in you lads that I wished to strike fear," Zulu said, prancing across the tabletop, "but in those mulish goons that come to gawk at me. I hate the very pupils of their milky eyes. They can see nothing in me. It is I who see *them*."

"Then . . . you didn't . . . eat the chicken?" Shelly said haltingly, almost begging.

"By God's beard and breath, no!" Zulu cried. "Do you think me a cannibal? Do you think I claim kin to those carnivorous wolves who for a quarter of a dollar suck me into the hollows of their eyes? It is they who are bloodthirsty, not I. I am a vegetarian and never allow the unclean flesh of animals to corrupt my belly."

"You sure got plenty bloodied up out there," I reminded him.

Now what was Zulu up to? Was he going to do it again? Yes. He hopped off the table, ambled around to Shelly in a mannish and fatherly way, put his arm around Shelly's hips, and patted him on the thigh. What could this mean?

"It was an *act,*" Zulu said, admonishing me about his chicken spectacle. "It was an outrageous deception. The world is a stage. Out there, there are stages upon stages upon stages. But the empty-eyed don't know," he cried, pointing to an imaginary audience. "I am a great actor. It is they who crave blood, not I." Zulu was getting carried away. Shelly started searching into his shirt for our "trust" money.

Before anything else went cockeyed, I stepped forward to seal our covenant with Zulu. I unbuttoned my shirt, dropped the money roll into the fruit jar, and screwed the lid on—our earnest money to bury tonight. Then on Sunday morning we would engineer Zulu's deliverance from his caravan of woe and his restoration to the paradise of Zanzibar.

V

We were lucky. Zulu had a spade—a small one—laid out on the table for us to bury our "trust." But this—our whole trembling hundred bucks—Shelly was totally oblivious of. He would just as soon it had flown to the winds with the poor pullet's feathers or vanished into the dreamy land of Zanzibar.

The only unrestful thing about the burial happened as we were passing the big tent. I saw, lurking in the foreground, the slim, black-haired man, with a flashlight. He crossed in front of our path like a black cat; and almost at the same moment, a bell rang out.

"B flat," Shelly sounded off before the ringing faded out of earshot. To Shelly's wonder, when we got to the trail the slim man had taken, I stopped to examine his tracks in the damp grass; then, just in case this man meant bad luck, I stepped over them. I would have warned Shelly to do the same, but I feared his disgust at such childish superstition.

In the few wandering shafts of circus light, we committed our jar money securely to earth under a dogwood tree at the dark end of the football field. I dug the hole with Zulu's spade. To ascertain if anyone aborted our secret, I pulled from our money roll a dollar bill, tore off one corner, and placed our "security" dollar on top of the jar. Then I buried all and placed a rock as a marker. The circus lights were going out. The whole interment had been as easy as pie.

❖

Returning the back way through the labyrinth of staked-down and roped-off show tents, I had to wrestle Shelly away from trying to release the hissing, hollow-gutted leopard pacing his bars and searching our faces with his yellow eyes.

When we entered Zulu's quarters, the only light

was the nervous kerosene lamp, bouncing shadows and spokes of orange along the walls and into the green jungle mural where the little brown man rode the tiger. A charred match was smoldering in a saucer beside the lamp. Zulu, naked again except for his brown trunks, was lying spread-eagled on his bunk, with the steel shackles placed in careful proximity to his hands and feet. I was about to announce our return with the spade when, like a ghost, the slim man reappeared. This time he emerged from the curtained enclosure, puffing as if out of breath and making urgent strides toward Zulu's bed.

"Halt," Shelly commanded, cocked forward like a halfback set for action. Except for Zulu's intervention, Shelly would have nailed the thin man to the floor.

"Bear the poor wretch no malice," Zulu sighed. "He is but a carnival clod, an ignorant engine of clay driven here to confine me for his master's dark designs." When Shelly's eyes released him, the melancholy man set to work, hurriedly clamping the manacles to Zulu's wrists and ankles; then, following the same route by which he had entered, he slunk away, snapping the hidden door shut behind him.

It was past time to be home. Sweet Jesus, was I ever glad our trust money was safely sunk in God's blind earth. I laid Zulu's spade on the table, between the Holy Bible and the hand bell.

Shelly made sure our lugubrious little burden was made comfortable, pulling up the covers over his bowed legs, tucking him in, ankle chains, chin, and all, and patting him gently on the forehead. After which Zulu numbered once more on his stubby span of fingers the stages for his liberation: one, our continued secrecy and presence at seven o'clock sharp Sunday morning; two, my bicycle to roll him away on; three, the pillow to set him upon; four, the ten-gallon hat to give him the illusion of greater height; and five, our recovered jar money, the tangible bond of our trust until we turned him over to Sheriff Holdster. We shook hands in alliance, and Zulu crossed his chest like the Pope.

Before we left, Shelly remembered the lamp. While he blew out the light, I—for the hell of it—seized the hand bell and rang out a tumultuous clanging that charged the room. When we were outside in the dark, the bell still resounded in my ears.

"B flat," Shelly said.

VI

The ten new five-dollar bills had indeed come from Judge Webster. He had lost them one by one and week by week playing chess with his ingenious son. Shelly said he and his father played each Sunday night, for a brand-new five-dollar bill a game. Shelly never lost.

"I've got a whole stack of them," Shelly said after we left the circus. A *stack?* I wondered. Had Shelly, the mastermind of number, not even counted his money?

It was only before I went overseas that Judge Webster spoke to me of the chess games. "I never *let* Shelly win," Judge Webster said. "He just always *did.*"

The next morning before daylight, the day before Zulu's liberation, Blue and I went to see if the jar money still lay well buried under the dogwood tree. The circus was asleep. I pushed the marker stone away. Under the leaves and the thin layer of soil, there was my three-cornered dollar bill. All was well. I dug no farther and fixed the security dollar, the dirt, the leaves, and the rock back as they were. Blue wanted to dig up the jar money. He wanted to *see* it and then bury it on the riverbank.

"How you know the wild man ain't dug up the money already and put the dollar back to fool you?"

I didn't. "Because he's chained up. Why d'you reckon he'd give us all that money to bury anywhere if he didn't trust us?"

"How come he stays all chained up if he got all them skeleton keys?"

I didn't want to think about it. I was thinking

about the sneaky thin man. It never occurred to me at the time, or to Blue, that Blue might have gone all on his own that night to see Zulu and the Fabulous Frances if Blue had been white. But it did occur to me, after I told Blue about the lewd Frances and the light bulb, that I had contaminated Blue, that *Blue* had seen, with *my* eyes, white, naked thighs that were for him absolutely and unforgivably forbidden.

"Don't even *dream* about what I told you, or you can drop dead," I said. Even so, the next day, with his very own eyes, Blue did see Zulu.

Saturday night, from my upper room, I could hear the rainbow-colored calliope thumping out "Over the Waves," and I envisioned our mad Zulu wielding his wicked light bulb and falling from his cage bars upon the headless pullet.

❖

Sunday, the day of Zulu's liberation, had arrived.

As I rolled my bicycle past the Graysons' early that morning, I imagined Sylvia asleep on a cotton cloud. When I arrived at the antebellum Webster mansion, Shelly, chin in hands and as solemn as Buddha, was sitting on the front steps.

Shelly figured the pillowed seat I had fixed for Zulu was too short. The normal elevation of the bicycle seat, added to Zulu's sitting height—allowing for Zulu's extra-short legs but near-normal trunk plus his rump—would be approximately two thirds of our own thirty-six sitting inches, which would reduce to twenty-four inches of Zulu, or roughly twelve inches short of normal height, which thus, allowing the four-inch illusion of Zulu's ten-gallon hat plus four more inches for my thin doubled pillow, left four inches of Zulu's elevation still to be desired.

Shelly went back into the house and got another pillow. We strapped both pillows on the bicycle seat with an old army belt. My bike looked like a sick one-hump camel.

Remembering that we had given our *word* on secrecy to Zulu, I asked, "Did you tell anybody?"

"No," Shelly said. "You?"

"No," I said. "Nobody. Not a soul. Just Blue."

"You got Zulu's contract?" Shelly asked. "The one he inked down?"

I felt in my back pocket for the sealed envelope.

"Yes. You got the one you wrote down in sand?" I couldn't help but smile.

"Yes," Shelly said.

"Got your handcuff key?" I asked.

"Yes."

From the church corner I could see the courthouse clock. It was six forty-five—fifteen minutes to dig up our money, uncuff Zulu, and roll him away to Sheriff Holdster and freedom. In the distance at the end of the football field, I could see the autumn dogwood tree ablaze in blood-red leaves and berries where in spring white-cross blossoms would be.

Having few illusions that our possession of Zulu would stick, I wondered if we might not persuade the loquacious dwarf to remain in Deen and, as our investment, perform for us—without decapitating chickens, of course.

It is known that there occur two dreams common among us all, each dream leaving us in a state of humiliating futility: one is the startling vision of being caught naked in a crowd of busybodies who scarcely, if at all, acknowledge our predicament and who, to our greater shame, do nothing to relieve our nakedness; the other dream, mainly from childhood, is the terrifying fall from great height—the rapid acceleration, the electrifying descent, and the shocking burst into consciousness before the fatal collision with earth. On this Sunday morning, Shelly and I got the equivalent of each dream or, better, a double-barrel blast of both:

The circus was gone.

Zulu was gone.

Our trust money, jar and all, was gone.

Shelly stood silently, rolling his banjo eyes and smiling abstractedly at the vacant football field. I was leaning faintly over our moneyless hole and hanging on to my ridiculous bicycle.

VII

Blue rode with my father and me to the jailhouse minutes after the money-jar catastrophe. Shelly, Judge Webster, my father, and I had been summoned by Sheriff Holdster. It was then that Shelly and I learned of the origins and ways of the Wild Man of Zanzibar. Sheriff Holdster knew all about the flamboyant dwarf and revealed it to Shelly and me in succulent but painful detail.

Zulu, as I now well knew, was not wild, at least not in a clinical sense; and he most definitely was not from Zanzibar. A flimflamming, liquor-guzzling mulatto preacher raised by a defrocked missionary from Brazil and educated in part at Loyola University, he had achieved renown as a seagoing cabin "boy" out of the port of Mobile. His bestowed alias from Savannah to New Orleans was "the Bishop." Of late, his accomplice had been a slim Mexican by the name of Demetrius Gonzales.

Shelly was unperturbed. He acted as if the sheriff's withering revelations had somehow exposed wonders yet to be explored.

"Excellent well!" Shelly said happily.

The sheriff's disclosures took the form of an inquisition:

Did we not suspect that the Mexican *saw* us bury the money?—Yes.

And did we not remember the flashlight and the signal bell?—Yes.

And did not Zulu have his spade ready for us?—Yes.

And didn't we have to bring the spade back to Zulu's quarters?—Yes. (I remembered Shelly's labeling the bell ring "B flat." Why hadn't Shelly put two and two together?)

And didn't Zulu show us the red, chafed shackle marks on his wrists and ankles?—Yes.

"Mercurochrome!" Holdster exclaimed. "You kids got sucked in by an expert!" The sheriff slapped his britches in glee.

Did we not *see* how gullible we were? The cuffs, the keys, the spade, the bicycle, the Bible, the money, the Mexican, the lamp, the bell, the bloody chicken—all ingredients in Zulu's larger act!—Yes, yes. As Zulu had said, there were stages upon stages out there. . . .

Holdster could not have known that I had watched his eyes beholding the Fabulous Frances as the bulb had lighted up her groin—the same bulb that Zulu had twitched under our sheriff's nose.

"So now then," Sheriff Holdster inquired sweetly, "the Bishop did remind you that you are both *Christian* lads?" With deepening knowledge, Shelly and I looked at each other. "You *are* Christian lads, ain't you?"

So yes, yes, Zulu was the greatest inland pirate on the Gulf Coast. He had worked this gimmick, with slight modifications, dozens of times. It had never failed him. "Why us?" I asked.

"Because you are as green as grass and as innocent as one of your mama's mockingbirds!" Holdster beamed. He enjoyed a smile with my father and the Judge. "The Bishop learned long ago never to trust grownups."

What could this mean?

The most arresting news of all from Sheriff Holdster was that Zulu had not escaped with the circus but was right here and was resolved to live in Deen, Alabama, forever.

"Here? Where is Zulu?" I cried, thinking of our jar money.

"In jail," the sheriff said.

Holdster explained that after the circus shut down Saturday night, the Bishop went on a moonshine spree at a local beer joint with some black brethren, who picked him penniless. After which Zulu had climbed up into the woodwork among the merchandise and bombarded his hosts with missiles of Tabasco sauce, pickled pigs' feet, canned sardines, and Vienna sausage.

"Including *me!*" Holdster said, pointing to a lump on his head.

I looked to Shelly for help.

"But he's *your* property!" the sheriff pressed. "You do *own* him?" he asked, looking first at me, then at Shelly. "You *do* have the bill of sale, the *contract,* don't you?"

"In ink, in ink," Shelly sang. "In blue-black ink." Shelly was alluding to Zulu's soaring script in our original contract, which I had in my pocket.

"You bought the midget for how much?" Father asked.

"Thirty-two cents," I said.

"Sweet Jesus," Father muttered.

"The evidence. Let's have the evidence," Judge Webster suggested, pointing to my hip pocket.

"That?" I nodded backward toward my rump.

"Yes, Silas, *that,*" Judge Webster said.

I came out with Zulu's sealed envelope and opened it.

"Read it," the sheriff said.

"Aloud," said Shelly.

"Aloud," said Blue, who was becoming more interested and moved in closer to me.

I unfolded the document and looked at it.

"What do you see?" Holdster asked.

"Nothing." It was true. There was not a scratch upon it.

"Magician's ink!" Holdster declared, like Sherlock Holmes. The sheriff was proud of himself. "I knew it!" he said. "You don't own him after all!"

A silence. Then. . .

"Yes we do," Shelly said.

With Shelly all things were possible. I remembered . . .

"Show them *your* contract," I said to Shelly. "The one *you* wrote down." I could hardly wait.

We followed Shelly to the sheriff's desk, where Shelly pulled out his handkerchief of documented sand. Blue moved in closer so he could see. Shelly, who stood a head taller than the sheriff, unknotted his handkerchief and poured the sand in a pile on the desk, then smoothed the grains gently into a plane. We watched.

The sheriff smiled. "Nobody can read that," he said.

"I can," a small voice said. It came from the doorway behind us.

It was Zulu. He was completely outfitted in his cowboy gear—chaps, cap pistols, ten-gallon hat, and all—and waddled forward like a dehydrated Hopalong Cassidy. "Have I not told you that I am a great actor and locksmith? The jail here is but a sham, a guise, a playpen for children," Zulu huffed. He clambered up into the captain's chair by the sheriff's desk and turned to scrutinize his audience. Then he fixed his attention on the little patch of sand. Bending stiffly from the waist, he very deliberately wrote in it with his finger:

I OWN 3/4 OF ZULU
SW
(Signed) Z OF Z

What had become of my one fourth of Zulu?

With a theatrical twist, standing tiptoe with arms and hands heavenward, Zulu produced, out of the barren air, ten brand-new five-dollar bills. He faced Sheriff Holdster, holding him steadfastly eye to eye, wagging his tiny fistful of money under the sheriff's nose as he had the light bulb the night of the Frances act, and cried, "Who here among us is without sin, and who here has shed a quarter to see the blasphemous Frances?"

Then Zulu bounced down from the chair and folded the new bills into Shelly's palm. After a chubby embrace and a pat on Shelly's hip, Zulu wheeled about on one heel, stopped short, and handed me one dollar and thirty-two cents, a dollar more than he owed us from our original contract.

Then Zulu crooned out in his cigar-box soprano:

"Am I not a great magician and a genius? If it were not so, I would have told you. Entreat me not to leave you, for thy people shall be my people."

Shelly lifted up the little preacher affectionately and set him down squarely in the field of inscribed sand. Then, from his surprising memory, Shelly appended:

"And our people shall be thy people."

"Excellent well," Zulu concluded.

❖

Before we left the jail, Shelly gave me five of the new five-dollar bills; and on the way home, out of the goodness in my heart, I gave Blue one of them.

As we passed the schoolhouse, I noticed the splay of blood-red leaves and berries of the dogwood tree at the end of the football field. I looked at the dollar bill Zulu had given me. The right corner was torn off. It was the "security" dollar I had buried with our jar money.

Chapter Five

How could I have known that my zany flight with Blue would have anything to do with Shelly's misfortune or that a world war already brewing would cast its shadow on Shelly in his own backyard?

My jaunt with Blue was in June 1938. But it had its origins, like invisible beads on a string, when Uncle George Simeon was a flier with the American Expeditionary Forces in France some twenty years before.

My literature on the marvels of flight was concrete: Cottier's pictorial account of World War I, *The Wings of War; The Spirit of St. Louis* by Lindbergh; *Tom Swift and His Flying Machine;* Rex Ralfe's practical text on *How to Fly;* and anything I could lay my hands on about World War I aces Eddie Rickenbacker and Baron von Richthofen. *How to Fly,* a worn manual from a slot long pressed closed on Uncle

George's bookshelf, had gradually become my own from extended borrowing.

Though Shelly's prolific dreams produced thrilling night flights, which he often set to music, his knowledge of flying was mainly abstract and surrealistic. He enjoyed the fantastic grotesquerie of the medieval painter Bosch and the prophetic flying creations of Leonardo da Vinci. Shelly's most extravagant flight literature was Felix Vaughn Knox's *The Art of Levitation and Corporeal Projection*. This was a conglomerate of wild ponderings on the powers of mind over gravity and the projection of the human body into space by "introcognitive realization." Shelly's more sober such readings were in Carl Jung's renderings on dreams, *Symbols of Transformation*, and P. D. Ouspensky's *Tertium-Organum—A Key to the Enigmas of the World*. All these metaphysical gems, and more, Shelly had gleaned from his father's library.

Blue's literature on flight was zero, unless it came from his mother's library: the Bible. But even from that dauntless source I recall scant reference to mere mortals becoming airborne, unless it was the time Elijah, following a chariot of fire, got sucked up into Heaven by a whirlwind, or, maybe, the bodily resurrection of Jesus.

Despite my pleas and planning, despite my instilling in Sylvia all the glories of flight, and despite proclaiming Uncle George to be the best pilot in the world, I had failed to get Sylvia aloft. Secure in the cockpit behind Uncle George, Sylvia would have flown with me. She was not afraid. We could have flown together in bliss more thrilling than kisses. "You promised!" I pled. But Reverend Grayson said no.

Uncle George was a real World War I ace, who shot down three German fighter planes. He once shook the hand of our own Rickenbacker and faced the great Von Richthofen in aerial combat over Normandy. I kept a large picture of Uncle George in my bedroom—Uncle George in his cocky flying cap and goggles, his leather jacket, his white scarf. He had flown a two-hundred-horsepower French single-cockpit fighting SPAD (Société Anonyme Pour Aviation et Ses Dérives) biplane. It had a thirty-caliber machine gun that fired past the synchronous prop without shooting the blades off. After the war, Uncle George never married. He said there were three mysteries in the world to be wary of: dreams, warts, and women. But Uncle George was never without women. Later I became the apple of his eye. He taught me to fly.

As far as I knew, Uncle George was the only flying cattle farmer in Alabama and the only living soul in Deen who owned an airplane. In 1934 he sold a fancy registered bull and bought a 1928 De Havilland DH-60 biplane, which he called the Gray Lady. An angel of awe and temptation to me, she rested in a special annex at the rear of Uncle George's hay barn. More times than I could count, I had flown the Gray Lady from between Uncle George's knees; yet now that my voice was changing and my own knees beginning to crowd the cockpit, I had still not flown the De Havilland strictly on my own.

So it happened that while in the presence of the Gray Lady one summer afternoon, Blue said:

"Si, let's fly to Texas and be cowboys."

II

Why *Blue?*

Bama, Blue's mama, said that when Blue was born, his daddy held him up to the light and said, "He ain't black, he blue." And so he became Blue Booker T. Bobiden (Bō bī' den). His was more than a name. It was a poem. And a poem he became to me. He was my black poem, and I was the white paper he scribbled on. In our sharply segregated cotton belt world of the Great Depression, we were perfectly at one and free with each other and never questioned our absolute uniqueness and equality. Blue's daddy had got his leg ground off in a seed conveyor by a big worm auger in our cotton gin and bled to death. After which my father adopted Bama and Blue to come live on our premises as cook and yardboy.

In our barefoot days, Blue and I romped and wrestled, fished and swam the river, talked and dreamed together, and, in our pensive hours, labored over the nature and location of the human soul.

As best I can figure now, Blue was the Platonist; I the pantheist. Blue had seen hogs slaughtered and figured hogs and folks weren't much different inside and allowed that your soul "got no business being hemmed up with all them stinking guts." As evidence, you could actually see your soul following along outside you by looking down at your shadow. This was your *little* soul, the *little* shadow. The big shadow was night, God's soul. To prevent his little shadow from getting lost in the great night, Blue kept his little soul stuffed in a snuff can on a mantel over the fireplace. Blue's belief required eternal diligence: In a crisis, and especially at the moment of death, you must always know *exactly* where your soul is so you can find it and get it to lead you unerringly onto the proper path and thence to Heaven.

My theory of immortality was more in-the-flesh. I figured that my private soul was a little blob of liquid light that got inside me through my eyeballs and circulated around (you could never know exactly where it was) in my body like a little egg bubble. If I died, it was supposed to float up to Heaven with a tiny *me* inside. When God's eye fell upon my egg bubble, it would hatch open, and lo, there I'd be, born anew.

One thing our theories had in common (although Aunt Rebecca would have disapproved): We eliminated Hell altogether.

On a hill overlooking Deen, Blue went to a segregated black school painted white, and in town I went to a segregated white school painted brown. During the '30s, it was a source of confused pleasure for me to discover that Blue and I carried home some of the same textbooks. Was it true, I wondered, that the same Christopher Columbus and Benjamin Franklin and Henry W. Longfellow who showed up in my books would show in Blue's too? One night I borrowed Blue's schoolbooks and searched them through in vain for telltale marks in paper, picture, or print that would rightly set Blue's books apart from **mine**. With not the slightest sense of vanity or racial pride, I was sure the discrepancy of perfect duplication had been either a coincidence or a printer's mistake.

Twin wellsprings to our imaginations were Bama's home-concocted characters and Mother's readings from her favorite books. In her fussy way, Bama was the best story instigator ever. She started a tale in grand fashion but never finished it. Blue and I had to do that.

Bama's stories were always variations of two: There was Old Black Crow, a king-sized raven of ill omen who flew about the country stirring up all manner of trouble with anybody, anywhere, over anything; then Bama would have the wicked old bird fly away, leaving Blue and me to settle the turmoil.

And there was the relentless Mr. Glumbergrumble, of no known race or origin, who was eternally grumbling about something—the weather, his food, his health, his clothes, his kin, and on and on. Bama would build up the grumbler's discontent to outlandish proportions, then leave off to let Blue and me figure out how best to punish the old killjoy. We solved, or shattered, many a dispute brewed up by Bama's Old Black Crow, though seldom by the most judicious means. But it was the insatiable Mr. Glumbergrumble who allowed us our sweetest freedom for inflicting justice.

If Mr. Glumbergrumble had complained about too much or too little rain, we were sure to have him swept away in a flood or bleached bone dry in a blazing desert. If his complaint was about food, its scarcity or poor preparation, we would starve him until he begged to eat our vittles of rotting rats crawling with maggots mixed with buzzard vomit. Or about clothes—Blue and I would never create any punishment so dull as merely having the old curmudgeon make his own garments out of dirty fertilizer sacks. Nothing like that. We'd have him dipped naked in a barrel of mushy cow shit, sun-dried to a crisp, and then stood up as a shameful statue in the courthouse square (where dogs peed on him), until the Lord blessed his release with rain.

There was one memorable indictment we pressed to the ultimate upon the old grumbler. It had to do with hot weather. For Bama it was an article of faith that weather, all of it, was God's blessing to mankind and that bad weather, never to be frowned on, was better than no weather at all. On a steamy day in mid-July, as Bama hustled over our hot cook-stove, she set Mr. Glumbergrumble into a blasphemous tirade against the summer heat, then stopped. . . . Blue and I knew what to do.

During Dante's journey through the inferno of Hell, we could have given the great Italian poet a few pointers in his punishment of Old World sinners.

It is impossible to remember all the stages of purification we put the grumbler through. But the first was to strip him naked, pack him in a tub of ice, and haul him off in a wagon to the North Pole. Blue and I, of course, were sufficiently bundled up to withstand the hundred-degree-below-zero temperature. Never mind the poor horse. As a final measure, we engineered the diminishing Mr. Glumbergrumble into a mound of clear ice, chipped him out of bondage, and brought him back home in a solid block, then set him on the back porch in the sunshine to melt out. By this time our captive had been reduced to little more than a giant beetle suspended in an ice cube.

Enough, I thought. Let the old malcontent thaw out and walk away to consider his transgressions. Not yet. Blue waited until all the ice dripped away, then let Caesar, Mother's cat, eat him.

Mother was more than a link between Blue and me; she forged in us a common bond stronger than either of us. Her private Rose Room, wallpapered with myriad rosebuds and blooms, was the sanctuary where she wrote her secret poems and where lounged her precious cats, the regal Caesar and Miss Gingersnap. Caesar, an indomitable half-wildcat, was an honest-to-God ball-bearing warrior that no dog, once wise, ever challenged; and Miss Gingersnap was a sweet-purring gingerbread mammy, who never failed to chase a string. Also in the room, to illustrate Emily Dickinson's famous poem that begins "Because I could not stop for Death / He kindly stopped for me," was Mother's favorite picture, of a kindly coachman in a frock coat, urging his horses on and, in his carriage, conveying a lady outward and upward. I instinctively took the lady to be Mother. I had no idea who the coachman was. It was in this room that Mother read her Shakespeare and sipped her sherry and read to Blue and me.

I suspect that mothers are usually more successful

storybook readers than fathers. Mothers know instinctively how to read a fairy tale. Listening to a father read a fairy tale, children, to accentuate the masculine, often stiffen their imaginations into adult shape and shut out that delicate tone and pathos that mothers inject for the proper perception of witches and monsters. Mother, a poet and a lady of literary astuteness, read with passion and understanding. If Little Red Riding Hood's wolf deserved to be slain, he was nonetheless the stealthy, flesh-hungry wolf that he was. Even though Bluebeard was a diabolical murderer beyond reprieve, he was not to be stricken out of our pity or curiosity altogether. And any reading of "Beauty and the Beast" that failed to create genuine sympathy for Beast would to Mother have been disastrous. The surging, probing soliloquies of Lear and Hamlet left Blue and me chilled and wrapped in sound. *Grimm's Fairy Tales, Robinson Crusoe,* and the original *Uncle Remus* were our favorites. On rainy or stormy nights in her Rose Room, Mother read to us long and devotedly until her voice failed or until we, sunk down in Mother's great sofa, tumbled over asleep.

Regarding the Tar Baby story, Blue and I agreed on one thing: Brer Fox was the culprit. It was also absolutely clear to me that Brer Rabbit was the hero. He was the harebrain that finally outfoxed Brer Fox. Blue gave the cottontail credit for getting himself unstuck and getting the fox to throw him back into the brier patch. But Brer Rabbit the hero? Not to Blue. The hero, first and last, was the Tar Baby. And in the Robinson Crusoe tale, Blue always reminded me that "Friday was there first."

Besides Mother and Bama, there was another common denominator for Blue and me: Gullet's picture show. The movie house was an old tin-roof clapboard barn, the loft for blacks who had a dime, the hard dirt floor for whites, with straight pine-backed benches for both. Behind and above it all was the magic cubicle that clicked and flickered out the celluloid giants of the day: Laurel and Hardy, Charles Chaplin, the Marx Brothers, Nelson Eddy and Jeanette MacDonald; but mainly heroes of the old West—Tom Mix, Buck Jones, Tim McCoy, Ken Maynard, and Hopalong Cassidy—*never* to be confused with such singing sissies as Gene Autry and Roy Rogers. When a good western came to town, I always made sure Blue had a dime.

One other thing that held Blue and me together was a fragile Confederate one-hundred-dollar bill that we had found in an old trunk in Aunt Rebecca's barn. Whether the Old South ever rose again or not, we vowed to keep the bill in our collective possession until death did us part. Blue loved ceremony and wished to seal our union with nothing less than our signatures inscribed in blood on the old bill at night.

Which, to begin with, was simple enough. From Bama's chicken coop Blue snatched a wing feather from a frying-sized hen, and to make the writing quill I trimmed the shank and split the point that would hold and dispense our sacred ink. That night we took a lantern, the Confederate bill, and the feather pen out to the barn. In an old stall, we laid out our frail bill on a brick and got down to business.

In the lamplight, my pocket knife, whose last serious operation was on a catfish, looked something less than a surgeon's wonder. Blue rejected my suggestion that we borrow some blood from one of Bama's coop chickens and said of the impending surgery that I ought to go first, because I was white. Blue decided his bloodletting would come from his left hand and kissed the palm. I would go for mine on my left thumb. I sought my vital juice with a sharp X right under the nail, and up rose the red. Blue went for his with the blade point into the meat of his palm heel, and out came his red too. The rest of the operation was neither simple nor entirely satisfactory. In the first place, our limp pen was not exactly designed for a grandeur such as the Declaration of Independence manifested, and in the second place, to have written our full names would have required both of us to bleed ourselves to death. Finally, with what little holy ink we had produced, coagulation set in too quickly for any sustained composition.

"I done run out of blood," Blue said.

After scratching around on the little X in my thumb, I added, "Me too."

Even so, with a lot of squeezing, mashing, and groaning, we got up enough blood between us for me to make a small *S* on one end of the bill and for Blue to make a *B* on the other end. After which we secured our authorized bill in Bama's Bible, midway between the Old Testament and the New.

So Blue and I were lucky. Together we fell heir to a common heritage that permitted us to survive not only those hot summers of segregation but also, I trust, these cold winters of integration that followed.

III

"Fly to Texas and be cowboys!?" I said. "Uncle George'd skin us alive and nail our hides to the shithouse."

How perfectly things fall together out of chaos when we can backtrack them step by step.

But how could Blue, while he was sitting there mouthing these words, have known; or how could Uncle George, years before, when he joined the Baron in deadly combat over Normandy, have known; or how could I have known that all of this would have anything to do with Shelly.

"You can fly in the front hole and guide it, and I'll fly in the hind hole," Blue said.

"Cockpit," I corrected. "They're cockpits!"

I had educated Blue in all the vitals of flight from propeller to rudder. Mother often flew with Uncle George on Sundays; I flew mainly on Saturdays. Behind the stick with Uncle George, I executed all maneuvers and worked the controls with perfect coordination. It was impossible to tell exactly when I learned to fly, because, like Mother's presence in my Jar of Marbles, it seemed like something I had always known. Flying an airplane, I revealed to Blue, was as natural to me as breathing, and furthermore, on occasion, because of my youth and greater agility, I outperformed even Uncle George.

To Shelly's sorrow, I was the only flying kid in Deen. Shelly was sad rather than envious of my good fortune because his sacred zeal to fly, to be lifted up like music and borne above the earth, transcended all adolescent jealousy. Gretta Webster, for all the freedom of adventure she had allowed her son on the ground, forbade Shelly to fly, even with Uncle George, who was the best pilot in the world.

"Yummmm," Blue hummed, poking his head forward and spreading out his arms and palms like wings. "Zzzzzzz," he went, coming out of a right bank and leveling off. "Out in Texas," he said, "we'll be like Tim McCoy and Buck Jones and ride hosses. You ride a white hoss and I ride a black hoss."

"I never saw a nigger cowboy," I said.

"I never saw no cowboy atall," Blue said.

"Then you'd be the first black cowboy," I said.

"And you'd be the first white cowboy to see the first black cowboy," Blue said.

Blue knew as well as I did where Texas was. He had the same map in his geography book and in his head that I had. He could see the lines as well as I could. But with Uncle George, in the De Havilland, I had *been* to Texas. Blue's greatest odyssey had been on a slow mule all day down the road from Deen to Caledonia to see his grandmama. I *knew* that Texas was days and horizons away from Alabama, miles of pines away to the Mississippi River, then across it into the flat sands of cactus country and tumble-weeds. And once you're deep in Texas, Texas is everywhere. To Blue, Texas was a crooked five square inches on page eight in our geography book, then across the creek and down the road a piece.

After all, it was Blue's idea to fly to Texas. And hadn't I learned the art of flying from Uncle George himself, the man who had clasped the hand of Rick-enbacker and touched, if only with his eyes, the in-comparable German baron with his white scarf trailing dangerously in the wind?

And out of my own flying manual, hadn't I memorized every rule and risk, every maneuver and contingency of flight, until I had wearied the old fly-book into a flop-eared rag?

And wasn't it true that the first, second, and third Saturday of every month—as sure as the Lord sent them—Uncle George and I flew in great swaths over the countryside, for those below to gape and point up at?

And every fourth Saturday, didn't Uncle George spend the whole day driving to Montgomery to buy his month's supply of bourbon? Old Raven, it was labeled. "Golden Light," Uncle George called it.

And wasn't this very day, Friday, the day before Uncle George's Old Raven day?

And tomorrow, who but Blue and I would ever know that it was not Uncle George and me buzzing over Deen in the De Havilland?

And then, after a few runs over the Walker Hills, with Blue sitting owl-eyed in the back "hole" . . .

I'd take Blue on a long haul down the Old Selma Road and back over Jackson's Ferry, then across the Alabama River, with a turn over Olahatchee Swamp; then I'd head straight toward Uncle George's landing strip at Arrowhead and set her down, not more than a whoop and a holler from home.

"Texas!" I'd proclaim. *"Texas* and *cowboys!"*

Sweet smiling Jesus. I'd make Blue's eyeballs bug out like a crawdad's.

IV

If Shelly had taken the funny flight with me, he never would have feared for himself. He would have feared for the De Havilland. Shelly revered all vehicles of flight, whether bird, bug, airplane, or, yes, piano, which he could make soar as surely as could Stravinsky. He also feared for Blue. Not that Blue might have been killed had I crashed but that Blue would have been embarrassed, heartbroken, and disenchanted to find himself tricked and not in Texas.

"Leave Blue. I'll go with you," Shelly pled.

"Hell, no," I said.

"Can you bring the Gray Lady back home without hurting her?"

"Yes. I can set her down on a napkin, anywhere."

"I'm going too," Shelly said emphatically.

"*No.*"

Worse than a frown from Mother or scorn from Aunt Rebecca, I feared the wrath of Gretta Webster.

Saturday afternoon, Blue and I slipped the Gray Lady out into the pasture sunshine. I could see Shelly in the back of the Webster mansion. He was up in his father's observatory, with the telescopes, waving a handkerchief at me: *I know what you're up to.* One of the scopes was for viewing the countryside within our horizon; the other, a more elaborate instrument, was for the stars.

Greater faith had no mortal than Blue Bobiden. He arrived for our Texas campaign armed only with his "little soul" in the snuff can, and a chunk of corn bread, both wrapped in a colorful Sunday funny paper. I flipped them into the back cockpit. My provisions were a pair of goggles and a long silk aviator's scarf Uncle George had given me.

"We'll write yo mama and my mama when we get to Texas," Blue said.

"Right," I said.

I was truly sorry Shelly couldn't go. Even before takeoff, Shelly would have composed music and lyrics about the adventure, and Mrs. Webster would have burrowed into our business for sure. Nor would Shelly have intended to expose me. But Shelly, himself an enigma, would have had so little grip on our secret that it would have slipped from him as easily as an eel through boiled okra.

I looped the white scarf around my neck and lowered my goggles. "Contact," I cried.

Blue knew what to do. He flipped the propeller for action. I pumped the choke. On the third flip, the motor caught up into a crisp whir. With a little throttle, the Lady stirred into a fragrant, biting purr that rushed back upon me, lifted my hair, and made the skin of the De Havilland tremble into life. I felt as if I were on the inside of a great fish.

Blue scampered around barefoot into the prop wind, fluttered up upon the lower wing, and, with his toes in the foot hole, swung up and around and plopped down in the back cockpit. His head stuck up like a gopher's.

Uncle George had fixed up a two-way hose contraption—we called it the "tube"—for talking between cockpits. "All abooooooaaaarrrrt," Blue clowned through the tube, making like a railroad conductor. Sometimes Blue's humor could catch you off base.

By now Uncle George would be pulling up to the whiskey store in Montgomery.

I braked the Gray Lady and held her at half throttle for thirty counts. This was the first time I had been up without Uncle George. Without him, the cockpit seemed larger. The little gauges on the panel were farther away, and my legs felt shorter. But the warm, crackling pistons smelled the same—like popcorn. As Uncle George had said a thousand times, "If you can't fly by the seat of your pants, better keep your ass on the ground." But flying, after all, was as natural to me as breathing. I released the brakes and gave the Gray Lady full throttle. Then through the tube to Blue:

"Watch out, Texas!"

We were under way. The acceleration sucked me backward. I pushed forward slightly on the stick to get our tail off the ground. I could see a patch of drowsy cows at the far end of the pasture. I hadn't realized before how small the pasture was and wondered if the cows in Normandy had been as indifferent to Rickenbacker and the great Baron as these were to me. I eased back on the stick, holding the rudder bar in equilibrium. Then we were afloat, above the slow cows, above the pines and the hickory ridge. The De Havilland was mine. I made a left turn. Blue was looking at the metropolis below.

"They ain't nothing but mites down there," Blue called through the tube.

"Termites," I added. "How you reckon we look to them up here?" I said.

"Like a big dragonfly," Blue called back. We laughed at that.

I held the De Havilland nicely in the left turn, pulled her nose up toward a bundle of clouds, and we took a long, glorious ride over the Walker Hills.

Then I swung around for a cruise over the west side of Deen, so Shelly could train his telescope on me.

From his tower, Shelly at the telescope looked like an insect blowing a horn.

Who were the others on the platform with Shelly?

No matter. Who but Uncle George would be flying Uncle George's De Havilland on Saturday afternoon?

Smiling toward the observatory like a movie star,

I flicked the tail of my white neck scarf over the edge of the cockpit and waved like crazy. I swung back east, making a straight shot between the Walker Hills and the Old Selma Road. Blue was looking down at the fleeing village. I could see the white of his eyes and his teeth.

Some stirring lines from the classroom rushed back to me:

It matters not how straight the gate,
How charged with punishment the scroll,
I am the master of my fate;
I am the captain of my soul.

I had to admit that some of the ecstasy I felt from this flight came from Shelly. At this moment, having sole control over my machine, I think I caught a tingle of the exhilaration of flying that Shelly accomplished through dreams alone. He had described one midnight excursion to me in vivid detail:

In his slumber, Shelly found himself standing alongside a misty mountain crag, overlooking a jagged crevasse of limitless scope and depth. Sensing the fatal gravity of the chasm below, he cast his vision in an elevated plane above the horizon. Then, in waves of soaring music, growing ever more and more intense and refined, to the point of transcending sound, he drew his consciousness into such sustained concentration that his whole being became infused with weightlessness. At this point in his dream, with a blast of pure faith and courage, he launched his body into space and, by attitude alone, accelerated himself to exotic speeds.

The key to Shelly's successful dream flights, as he had instructed me, was to indoctrinate myself, just before falling asleep, never to wake up in a dream crisis but to release myself completely to the exhilaration of the flight and engage my soul fearlessly in the narrative, however dreadful, to the bitter end. This was a difficult—almost impossible—commitment to keep.

So Shelly's wingless flight was not merely a contention with or a manipulation of gravity; it was a displacement of gravity altogether. I could claim no such sensation. But at least I came closer to it than Uncle George, who flew weekly over south Alabama with a slug or two of Old Raven under his belt and the worn confidence of an old hero.

I made another broad circle over the Walker Hills.

"How far's Texas?" Blue called over the hose.

"About fifteen minutes and across the Mississippi," I called back.

I wondered if Blue would recognize Jackson's Ferry when we got there. No matter. Up this high, Blue wouldn't know the Alabama or the Mississippi from Snake Creek.

I thought about Bama's Black Crow, the trouble-maker, and Old Raven, Uncle George's favorite brand of bourbon, "Golden Light." Ha! Uncle George was probably having his first snort right now in Montgomery. He always came home a little crocked. I wondered why Blue and I had never thought of taking Bama's Mr. Glumbergrumble up for an airplane ride and dumping his unhappy butt into the Alabama River.

To amaze Blue, and especially Shelly, watching us from the observatory, I put the De Havilland into a tight left bank, leveled off, and pulled her up neatly into a stall. To tickle Blue's ass, I let the bottom drop out—pushed our nose down and, at full throttle, swooped earthward, then soared up as if in the bowl of a great rainbow. Lovely Jesus, if Shelly could have felt that!

I glanced back at Blue. Yes, he was impressed. He had lost possession of the tube and was holding up something in his hand. It was the snuff can.

To kill time, I turned out of the sun and headed north up the Old Selma Road. My aeronautical performance was perfect. But I had not figured on Blue's keen sense of direction.

"The sun's in the wrong place," Blue said through the tube. The sun was to our right.

"Things up in the sky aren't always what they look like," I replied.

The seductive powers of the Gray Lady were too great for me. I imagined Sylvia in the cockpit behind me, her golden hair trailing in the wind. I flew all the way to Selma and circled the city twice. I spotted Doc Sim's huge home near the golf links. Uncle Sim was my doctor uncle who specialized in babies. Blue seemed troubled by my convoluted expedition. But I reasoned that all this flying about would make my prank more plausible. Anyway, as I had told Mother, I'd rather fly than go to Heaven. And Mother said I might as well get my flying done down here, for she doubted that I'd be granted wings in the hereafter.

"How far now?" Blue said through the tube.

"Not far," I answered.

"The sun's in the wrong place again," Blue said.

The sun was on our left.

The sun had also fallen lower in the sky than I had expected.

The fields and woods moved slowly beneath us.

Within sight of Uncle George's riverside pastures, I banked the Lady away from the sun and pulled her up over the carpet-sized cloud, hoping Blue wouldn't recognize Jackson's Ferry. Forgetting the tube, I pointed down to the Alabama River.

"The Mississippi!" I cried.

I made a broad arc around Olahatchee Swamp so I could point Blue's eyes into the sun, toward Texas. My destination was Uncle George's landing strip on Arrowhead.

Arrowhead was a triangular wedge of open pasture inscribed on one side by the river and on the other by Snake Creek. Uncle George kept a small herd of Black Angus cows there. Years ago, my grandfather had planted pecan trees around the perimeter, so from the sky you could *see* why they called it Arrowhead.

Blue was on the tube. Something about . . . corn bread?

The colorful funny-paper wrapper got away from Blue, hung for a moment on the tail fin, and fluttered away. Blue was gargling something through the tube and waving his piece of corn bread above the cockpit.

Eating now? At a time like this? How dumb can you get?

"What? What?" I cried through the tube.

"Did you . . . the Lady," Blue mumbled.

"Did I *what* the Lady?" I waited.

"Feed her! Feed her!" Blue screamed.

Blue was not talking about corn bread. He was talking about gasoline. I had forgotten to gas up the De Havilland.

We were heading straight into the sun now. *Holy crap!* I thought.

I could see Arrowhead in the distance. The landing strip was a tiny zipper down the middle.

Uncle George had said what to do if the motor stopped: Pick your landing target quickly and with care, glide to it, straighten up, check for crosswinds, fall earthward sharply to get air under your wings, pull out directly above target, drop down three-point on the ground, hold back gently on the stick, keep your tail on the ground, hold back gently on the stick (again), *keep your tail on the ground,* use brakes carefully, *don't nose over.*

The De Havilland was still purring crisply. The gasoline gauge, Uncle George had said, was stuck on Full. Or was it stuck on Empty? The gauge *always* registered . . . No matter. I didn't even look.

I was coming in. The branches of the pecan trees on Arrowhead were sweeping out to the right. There was a crosswind. I tapered into the breeze, cutting my throttle, holding the De Havilland nose-up. . . .

So now what was I supposed to do? *Fall earthward sharply to get air under my wings, pull out directly above target, drop down three-point. . .*

Wait—these were instructions for a no-power landing. My engine was still alive.

The crosswind was getting into my left wings. I held into the side of the crosswind and dropped to earth on the clay strip, hard on my right wheel. Next my tail wheel hit. Then my left wheel. The De Havilland made two huge rabbit hops off the runway and set out bouncing toward the battery of pecan trees that lined the pasture. The motor sputtered, and the prop stopped like a dead finger.

Out of gas.

Uncle George's face rose up before me.

Mercifully, the right brake didn't hold. The left brake did. It grabbed and spun us around, quite grounded now, under a pecan tree.

There was a prolonged silence. Then Blue sang out:

"Texas!"

Blue hopped to the ground.

"Wonder how all Mr. George's pecan trees got here?" he said. I had forgotten that the year before, Blue helped Uncle George shake down pecans.

"And look," Blue said. "There's Mr. George's bull." And there the bull was, the finest specimen of cow flesh in Alabama, grazing thoughtfully at the end of the pasture.

"I reckon Mr. George's bull can fly too," Blue said.

The gas gauge in the De Havilland said Full. So the gauge *was* stuck on Full.

V

Somebody was coming down the road in a pickup, its hind wheels riding at a knocked-out-of-line angle so that it looked like an old hound catagoggling down a path. It pulled up beside the De Havilland and stopped. It was Clayton Slaughter and his daddy. Clayton was driving.

"What the hell you doing down here in your uncle's airship?" Mr. Slaughter said. Clayton crawled from under the steering wheel and came around the tailgate, smoking a cigarette. He had his sleeves rolled up tight so you could see his muscles. When he pulled his cigarette up for a drag, his biceps popped up like a young melon.

Blue, like the Tar Baby, didn't say.

"We were—" I began.

"Shut up, you little pissant," Clayton said.

"We—" I started again.

"Shut up, you and ya nigger both. You gone and stole Mr. George's airplane, and there it sets to prove it. We just came from Deen. The midget at the jail-house told us all about it."

Zulu? All about *what?* I wondered.

I stuffed the white scarf inside my shirt, buttoned up tight, and jumped to the ground beside Blue. I wondered what had become of Blue's corn bread and snuff can.

Mr. Slaughter got out of the truck and adjusted his hat so low on his brow you couldn't see his eyes. Running into the devil on my side of the river was one thing. Running into him on his own territory was something else. Thank God for Blue.

Zulu? The jailhouse? What did Clayton mean, "all about it"?

Mr. Slaughter whispered into Clayton's ear, then

got a wrench from under the pickup seat and started taking the propeller off the De Havilland. He was using a crude, gapped-jawed pipe wrench. I was saying "Goddammit, stop," when Clayton backhanded me across the mouth.

Sometimes it's better not to be born. If it had not been for messing up the De Havilland or destroying Shelly's and Blue's faith in me, I would rather have gone crashing alone into the solitary earth, leaving not so much of me as a grease spot.

The pecan trees were casting oblong shadows across Arrowhead. How dumb can you get, flying over south Alabama on an empty Full tank of gas with a black smartass? It wasn't that Blue was trying to be rude by shoving my dead prank down my throat. Looking back now, I think Blue was rather kind. But at times there are just *ways* a body ought to say a thing.

Mr. Slaughter had the propeller off. It was as tall as Clayton. Goddamn, how I hated that cocky little sonofabitch, standing there, loving nothing better than to grin into my eyes, popping up his puny biceps and dragging on his goddamn cigarette.

Actually, Clayton wasn't so scrawny anymore. He was tight-muscled and dark-skinned. With his black hair slicked back, he looked a little bit like a young Rudolf Valentino.

Mr. Slaughter strong-armed Blue into the back of

the pickup and crammed the propeller and me into the cab between himself and Clayton. Mr. Slaughter drove. The propeller was too long for the cab, and Clayton had to stick half of it out the window. We went bumping down a narrow road on the swamp side of Arrowhead, with trees hanging over on both sides. Mr. Slaughter pulled the headlights on. The time. What had happened to time? Uncle George would be almost home now. Blue had his nose up against the back glass, looking in. His eyes were like moons.

At least, thank God, the De Havilland was still in one piece. Or was it? How helpless it had looked minutes ago, sitting emasculated under the pecan tree, and how pitiful was the amputated propeller here in my lap, sticking half in and half out of a grubby pickup truck.

Was Uncle George *already* home? The image of facing him, of seeing myself slink toward him answerless, made my eyes well and my bottom lip tremble.

❖

I was surprised at the Slaughters' home. It was a dog-trot house: closed hallway running between the two portions of the dwelling—kitchen, pantry, front room on one side; bedrooms on the other. But its boxiness was offset by an attractive A-shaped second-story room in the middle, a brick chimney on each wing, and a full screen porch in front, with potted plants and hanging flowers.

When Blue and I heard from Mr. Slaughter that *they* had been watching us from Judge Webster's observatory, through the telescope, and that *they* were out looking for us (*they* meaning Uncle George and Sheriff Holdster), Blue made a break for it.

Clayton dropped the propeller and tackled Blue at about the same time I tackled Clayton. Clayton was up first. In a tussle, Clayton ripped a sleeve off Blue's shirt, busted Blue in the mouth, and sent him flat to the ground. Mr. Slaughter was watching us from under the brim of his hat. I locked onto the back of Clayton, putting a half nelson on him when he let go backward with his elbow into my windbag, and over I went, sucking for air. Blue flew back into Clayton, but not for long. Clayton laid Blue flat out again, and when I straightened up, Clayton let me have one square in the nose, and out came the blood.

Blue fled. I could see the pale bottoms of his feet pumping away into the darkness behind the house.

"He ain't gone nowhere," Clayton said. Clayton again had possession of the prop. He towed me by the arm through the flowered porch. His pretty sister, Queeny, was sitting in the porch swing. His mother was in the kitchen doorway, holding a large kerosene lantern.

"Silas crashed his uncle's airplane and busted his nose open," Clayton said.

Clayton's mother went to the sink and hand pumped water into a pan. From the back she looked like Mother Hubbard. Clayton laid the propeller on the long oak kitchen table and thumped a cigarette from a pack. He held a wooden match in the stump of his fist and ignited it with his thumbnail.

Clayton was saying that Mr. Slaughter had gone to the ferry store to phone Sheriff Holdster that we were "captured," as Clayton put it. Then the awful knowledge fell upon me that not only wasn't Uncle George crocked, he hadn't even gone to Montgomery! He and Sheriff Holdster had watched us from Judge Webster's observatory. They had seen us as clearly as if we had been fish in a bowl. It hadn't been Shelly watching me through the telescope. It had been Shelly watching *them* watch us through the telescope. I went as limp as a summer stick of licorice. Mrs. Slaughter put the lantern on the table.

Where was Blue? *He ain't gone nowhere,* Clayton had said. Pray God Clayton was right.

Mrs. Slaughter was dabbing my nose with a cool wet cloth. She had a pleasant face like my mother's and jet-black hair. Straight lines formed across her forehead when she raised her eyes in interest. I could see why Queeny was so pretty. My nose had stopped bleeding. The soft wrinkles in Mrs. Slaughter's lips vanished when she smiled.

"Was it fun?" she asked. She meant the flying.

"I don't know," I said dimly. I knew at once that the potted plants and hanging flowers on the front porch were her creations.

"I taught school once in Arkansas and know how airplanes fly," she said.

"It's real easy," I said. She turned to the long oak table and ran her fingers over the smooth curvature of the propeller glistening in the lantern light.

"Amazing how so small a piece of wood can carry one above the clouds," she said.

Thank God for Mrs. Slaughter.

Queeny came in, looked at my nose, and smiled.

It wasn't long before Mr. Slaughter got back from the ferry store, and it wasn't much after that when Uncle George and Sheriff Holdster arrived. The official car, with its ominous lights and insignia, pulled up in the Slaughters' yard like an apparition. I expected Uncle George, first off, to slap me sideways. Uncle George and Sheriff Holdster had already inspected the downed De Havilland under the pecan tree. I knew Uncle George's first concern would be for me. I was the apple of his eye.

"Where's Blue?" Uncle George said.

"I don't know," I said. "Somewhere back there." I pointed behind the house into a darkness that stretched all the way to Birmingham.

Mr. Slaughter whistled up his hounds. Clayton was right. Blue had climbed a sweet gum tree in the backyard. With a sniff of Blue's torn-off sleeve, the dogs treed Blue in a jiffy. He was hugging the top of a big limb like a possum. Thank God for Mr. Slaughter's hounds.

After Mr. Slaughter shut up his dogs in the corn crib, Blue climbed out of the tree. Mr. Slaughter talked twenty-five dollars out of Uncle George for the propeller and promised to keep his trap shut about me and Blue and the De Havilland. It was too late to take the ferry. We tied the propeller to the top of the sheriff's car and went home the long way, over the longest bridge in Alabama.

No, Uncle George and Sheriff Holdster were not going to tell on us. It would have been too embarrassing for all. We stopped on the crest of the big bridge. Uncle George came up with a bottle of Old Raven, and he and the sheriff got out and had a smoke and a couple of drinks high above the river in the moonlight.

❖

"Were you scared?" I asked Blue on the way home. He held up his snuff can and smiled.

Thank God for Blue.

Before we got back to Deen, I unbuttoned my shirt and loosed the white scarf from my neck. With the moonlight coming through the window, I could see where little patches of my nose blood had stained the cloth. I rolled the window down and released the scarf into the dust behind us.

Uncle George and Sheriff Holdster were passing the bottle frequently between them. Laughter filled the car.

Thank God for Old Raven.

Chapter Six

Until death surprised her, nobody changed Aunt Rebecca. If any changing was to be done, it was Aunt Rebecca who changed you. After Mr. John Decker jilted her, she never strayed into the wild and seedy paths of the Roaring Twenties or trespassed onto the privacy of others. But anyone who came within her sphere of influence faced a fortress of puritanical fundamentalism encompassed by a moat that teemed with Calvinistic sharks. Her home was her oracle, her church, her citadel.

The exact time of her death was not hard for me to remember. When Mother came in to make the announcement, Uncle George was present in our home, thundering condemnation upon the British and Prime Minister Chamberlain. It was early October.

"Peace in our time!" Uncle George stormed to my father. "That spindly, umbrella-toting limey is feeding away Europe bite by goddamn bite to a sonofa-bitching mustached maniac."

Uncle George checked his language when Mother entered the room. She broke the news to me so all could hear. "Your Aunt Rebecca just passed away," she said.

No one in the family or the church expected Rebecca to die so suddenly. I never expected her to die at all. The announcement struck me as an improbability as enormous as a stray Arab's erasing the Great Pyramid.

"What will become of all her goldfish?" I asked. I often invited Sylvia to help me tend Aunt Rebecca's aquariums, not that I cared a poot for goldfish. Sylvia was something else.

Mother's instructions about "putting Becky properly on her way" were simpler said than done; Blue, Bama, Shelly, Zulu, and I were to drive Father's pickup over to Aunt Rebecca's in the morning and help Sadie Mae "clean up." Mother reminded me that Aunt Rebecca had often said, "If you want to make things turn out according to God's word and will, you must *prepare* for them."

Sadie Mae, coal black and as big as a bale of cotton, was Aunt Rebecca's cook. She ruled her kitchen with an iron skillet. Sadie Mae had called Mother on the telephone and said, "Send the boys over." Zulu not only had become indispensable to Sheriff Holdster at the jail; he also had become Aunt Rebecca's regular handyman. More important, he had become something of a personal possession of my aunt's, a willing ecclesiastical captive who confirmed with shrill authority Aunt Rebecca's theological imperatives.

The next day, Sadie Mae led us into the front room, where, in an open casket and in a green velvet gown, Aunt Rebecca lay beside her sunken goldfish pool. Sadie Mae had elevated the head and shoulders of Aunt Rebecca with a pink pillow so "Miss Becky can see her darlin' goldfish."

Three aquariums outlined the eastward windows. The early-morning sunlight cut like a flame into the glass tanks and made the water shimmer with the green undulating foliage and flash with the golden, darting minnows. The living room was filled with an air of old linen and cedar-chest sweetness. An unexpected lightness rushed upon me: the sweetness . . . the sun . . . the fish . . . the sun . . . the fish . . . Aunt Rebecca was surrounded by seething, goggle-eyed goldfish. There she lay and took, it seemed, one last long breath and held it beyond relief until she floated breast upward in her coffin like a hollow mannequin. I teetered, held my breath too . . . then felt tight fingers on my arm. It was Bama. "You hold on, boy," she said.

Later Zulu said Miss Rebecca was one of the "chosen," to share eternity with God and the Saints of Glory. Blue said he never saw nothing whiter than Miss Becky was and that if she got one shade whiter she would start turning black. Shelly said that in death one achieves the purest state of cosmic equilibrium and that Aunt Rebecca had a total of seventy-seven goldfish—not counting her golden slipper in the pool—and that the eight large goldfish in the rock pool with the sunken slipper outweighed all the others by at least four to one because the bigger the body of water you put goldfish in, the bigger they grew, which, Shelly explained, was the reason for the constant circulation of water in and out of the pool to assure a sufficient supply of oxygen, which the water plants alone would have been incapable of producing.

Before the jolt of seeing Aunt Rebecca dead had receded, Sadie Mae hit us with a cannonball that all but wiped me out. It was what was in Aunt Rebecca's cellar.

Summers ago, Sadie Mae had confided in Bama about this scandalous matter. Now the time had come to act swiftly. I knew something godawful was afoot when Sadie Mae and Bama shooed us into the kitchen, bolted the door, and confronted us grimly as though we were victims exposed to the plague. So on a bench against the wall we sat like convicts, facing these two determined black women: Shelly the young white giant on one end and Zulu the ageless mulatto midget on the other; Blue and I in the middle, I now as deathly white as my poor dead aunt and Blue as shiny black as hot tar. Sadie Mae flicked on the light switch to the cellar. In all my life I had not been allowed into this forbidden cavity.

Outside, the horizontal cellar doors, leading underneath the kitchen, worked by gravity. Sadie Mae and Bama unlocked them and pulled them open. Light fell down into the basement, dimming the small electric bulb hanging from the ceiling. Down we went.

Sweet Jesus, the size of it! An amber Mount Olympus of whiskey bottles! All ninety proof! All Southern Comfort bourbon! All empty! And all Aunt Rebecca's!

Beholding it all in one flash was like getting struck by lightning.

We were, the four of us, to get rid of the bottles each and all, utterly and absolutely, without fail and without breathing a word to anybody about this incredible disclosure. How were mere mortals to hide so enormous a sin? I felt like the poor fairy tale queen who, to save her firstborn, had to guess the name of the sinister little elf. But how, without divine aid, could anyone ever guess *Rumpelstiltskin?*

Zulu was delighted. He shaped his hands into a steeple and skipped around the bottles, chanting, "Vanity, vanity. We are as grass hewn down today—"

"Hush up, you little monkey," Sadie Mae scolded.

From behind, she snagged Zulu by his suspenders and hoisted him wiggling from the floor like a grasshopper. "You bes' cease all yo holy mumblin' and git deez bottles outta here fo I put you down in yo las' cellar with a flat rock on you."

Bama backed up Sadie Mae by glaring down at the tiny preacher and then at Blue and me. Shelly stood aloof. He took Zulu gently by the knob of his head and turned him around so that they both stood surveying the immensity of our task.

Yes, Bama and Sadie Mae had planned each summer to shovel the bottles up, out, and away. But how? Where? When? Already this summer was gone. It was October again. So as the years had piled up, the amber mound had grown. "Who knows when death will slam his door upon you, dressed fit to kill, or open it upon you naked?" Zulu sang.

"Ya'll do it *clean*," Sadie Mae boomed to us from the head of the brick steps.

"And quiet," Bama whispered. "Shhh." She touched her finger to her lips. "Miss Becky's friends'll be comin' round to see her direckly," and she left us with the morning light pouring down the throat of the old cellar.

The audacity of authority! What on earth had I to do with this mountain of whiskey bottles? And where, when full, had they come from? By whose hand had they entered the old Simeon home?

Shelly had already begun to calculate the

magnitude of Aunt Rebecca's sin. From his ineffable brain he established that Aunt Rebecca's drinking began the year after Mr. John Decker forsook her, in 1917. From the dimensions of the cone-shaped mound, Shelly figured that for the last twenty-one years there were 2,016 quart bottles in all, which came roughly to a consumption of 96 quarts a year or 8 quarts a month or 2 quarts a week. With 32 ounces to a quart, that came to nearly 42½ jiggers per bottle, which in the duration of her habit would amount to a lifetime total of 73,525 drinks of hard liquor—a record even Uncle George could not but admire.

What was Aunt Rebecca's slipper doing in the goldfish pool?

Sadie Mae threw down a bundle of gunnysacks and said, "Ya'll git busy *now*, you hear?"

Zulu had made a discovery. Finding that each empty whiskey bottle had a potent "corner" left in it, he set in quietly to sipping off the remaining elixir. Shelly's calculation here was instantaneous—and a bit frightening when I realized what might happen to Zulu if he got around to draining off all the bottles. Shelly figured that a remaining ¼ ounce per bottle times 2,016 came to 504 ounces, or almost 16 full quarts of liquor.

"Enough, enough, little priest," Shelly said, pulling a Southern Comfort bottle from Zulu's lips. However, he permitted Zulu to pour himself up a quart of spirits for future reference.

Zulu allowed that, excepting the alphabet and Edison's light bulb, whiskey was man's greatest invention. Dismissing the preponderance of Scripture against strong drink, Zulu went straight to the Bible for confirmation, sifting out for himself sure proof from such passages as when Jesus made the water into wine or when Timothy instructed that we should not drink water alone but wine "for our frequent ailments." Then he chimed out a verse that had upon it the very stamp of Aunt Rebecca's sin and her doctrine of predestination: " 'Drink your wine with a merry heart, for God has *already approved* of what you do.' "

No one in my memory had ever accused Aunt Rebecca of possessing a "merry heart."

From Aunt Rebecca's Sunday school class I had always yoked strong drink with mortal sin. Except for Uncle George and Mother. Reverend Grayson in an invidious lapse of good taste had once asked of his congregation that those who had "abstained from alcohol" should raise their hands. Before the congregational unrest congealed, Uncle George arose and said aloud and alone, "By God, I drink!" Then he walked out of the church, never to darken its door again. With Mother, sherry was an inspiration. Every night, from as far back as I could remember, Mother, before retiring, read her Shakespeare or wrote her poems, had a full glass of dark sherry, and smoked a pungent Picayune cigarette.

Zulu was holding open the mouths of the sacks, and Blue was inserting the bottles with care. We were all taking turns disposing of the bottles.

I said that whiskey wasn't a sin if it stayed in the bottle. Blue said that in or out of the bottle, it was still a sin—just as a snake in the grass was still a snake even if it didn't bite you.

Shelly was stacking the filled sacks in the truck. There were voices and movement above us in the room with Aunt Rebecca.

Shelly was disappointed at our philosophy of strong drink. He explained, turning the palms of his hands up, then down, that there was neither right nor wrong, neither upside nor downside, neither inside nor outside, to whiskey. He said that every outside had an inside, and every inside had an outside, so that you could never find the last inside of an outside or the last outside of an inside.

When the murmuring and shuffling of feet died away upstairs, I left Shelly in charge of sacking the bottles and went upstairs to see if Aunt Rebecca's slipper was still in the pool.

Sadie Mae had on a black robe with a large, drooping pilgrim's collar. It made her look like a giant penguin. She was standing behind the bier, with her back to the goldfish pool. I could hear Bama in the kitchen, shuffling plates. Platters of food were already laid out on card tables in the hall.

"I came up to see Aunt Rebecca again," I said.

"You best hurry up, 'cause you ain't got all day," Sadie Mae said.

I didn't look straight at Aunt Rebecca, but I could see her snowy profile from the corner of my eye. It was not easy to count the fish swimming. But Shelly was right. In the pool were eight large goldfish and Aunt Rebecca's golden slipper. The slipper was stationary on the bottom among the goldfish, a body length from the rock edge. Nobody would have noticed it but Shelly. But one thing Shelly had missed: the submerged crystal glass, still-intact, from which Aunt Rebecca had taken her last "tea."

Nor was this all. There was a poorly scrubbed rust-red splash on the rocky edge. I had gutted too many rabbits and squirrels not to know exactly what it was. I fished the slipper out of the pool with the fire poker and was pointing the toe of the slipper to the blood marks when Sadie Mae turned around. It was all too clear to me what had happened.

In a glance, the old Negress read my mind. She swept one fat arm around my chest, clamped her other hand over my mouth, and waltzed me into the kitchen. If Aunt Rebecca had been a general here, Sadie Mae was top sergeant. The four of us on the whiskey bottle detail were merely rookie buck privates.

"Looky here, Silas Simeon. Yo Aunt Becky's head

bustin' ain't none of yo business, you hear?" I was amazed at the strength of this old black mammy and knew instinctively that it would be not only rude and ungrateful to struggle against her, but futile. "Little Silas knows about Miss Becky bustin' her head open," she said to Bama. Sadie Mae's fingers smelled of snuff and smoked ham. She released my mouth and took the slipper from my hand. "I been lookin' for dis," she said. She went in the front room and put the wet slipper on Aunt Rebecca's foot, making a pair. "Yo Aunt Becky ain't never wore deez shoes 'cep in her own house," Sadie Mae said. "Now she goin' to walk in 'em to de Golden Gates."

Wouldn't it be all right, I wondered, if everybody knew Aunt Rebecca's death was an *accident?* Sadie Mae read the thought right through my skull.

"Far as you know, yo Aunt Becky ain't never tetched a drop a liquor, and she ain't *never* slipped," Sadie Mae said. "*I* slip. *You* slip. Yo Uncle George slip. But yo Aunt Becky ain't *never* slipped, you hear?"

I reckoned so. For Aunt Rebecca to have spontaneously combusted and gone up in a column of flames—okay. But for Rebecca Lee Simeon to have slipped ignominiously into a pool of placid goldfish—that was unacceptable.

Somebody was coming to look at Aunt Rebecca. I hurried out the side door, into the breakfast room. It was Reverend Grayson and Sylvia. I watched them through the windowpane and the split curtain. Standing to one side of the coffin, Reverend Gray-son was gesticulating instructions to Sadie Mae and Bama.

Making a perfect cross with the casket, angelic Sylvia, with her golden hair, stood like a supple poplar facing the bier, peering down upon rigid Aunt Rebecca. There came back to me the arresting dream of Aunt Rebecca, the giant wasp, charioting her flaming organ across the void, wielding lightning bolts from her fingers; and in the wake of her mad flight, I envisioned myself snug in the cockpit of the De Havilland, holding Sylvia gently between my knees, bathed in speeding clouds. . . .

Mother and Father appeared, Mother bearing a covered dish, which she handed to Bama. I went back to the cellar and the whiskey bottles. I decided we should bury the bottles in our woods on the river across from Arrowhead. After all, as a matter of family, this was my truck, my land, my aunt, and now, in a strange way, my bottles.

Sadie Mae and I had to turn the old barn inside out before we found a shovel. In the stall next to the old surrey shed was Aunt Rebecca's tombstone, waiting in readiness. I had seen it many times. It was a handsome stone cross with a white marble dove at the summit. Aunt Rebecca had designed and or-dered this memorial sculpted years ago.

"Now, Si, you bury them bottles sure and deep," Sadie Mae said.

It was past noontime. I wasn't hungry. Shelly was managing masterfully. He had stacked the sacked bottles in the truck as neatly as if they had been bales of hay. It had taken the drippings of almost two hundred bottles to yield Zulu a quart of booze. Zulu was already tipsy. But he had declared often that such a state for him was not dangerous, for unlike us, he had not very far to fall.

"My honored lord," Zulu said at my appearance, bowing, sweeping his arm like a court jester, "your entrance into this shadowy recess is as a shaft of light to prisoners of darkness." Blue and Shelly thought this was funny.

We all went out to the barn to confer about the disposition of the bottles. Zulu was riding high on Shelly's shoulders. Shelly explained that the best way to keep a secret was not to hide it in the first place. The bottles were nothing, *nothing*, Shelly insisted. They were just sacks of empty glass holes. He wanted to wait until night and dump the whole batch in front of the courthouse, so that *everybody* in Deen would be suspect and befuddled about the bottles and thus Aunt Rebecca's secret would be openly buried forever in public confusion.

Zulu applauded the idea, disagreeing only in that the bottles should be dumped in front of the jailhouse instead of the courthouse.

Sweet suffering Jesus.

Blue said all that dumping would make too much racket and Sheriff Holdster would catch us right off.

The main trouble was that Shelly and Zulu didn't have to worry about time, they didn't have to worry about the truck, and the bottles were not *theirs*.

"We're going to bury them on the riverbank. Right?" I said to Blue, sticking him in the side with my elbow.

"Right," said Blue.

Shelly sat on the back of the truck, with his legs dangling near the ground, and Zulu sat on Shelly's shoulder, with one arm cradling his resurrected liquor. Blue rode up front in the open cab with me.

II

I took the back road around the town but could see the east face of the courthouse clock. It was one-thirty. With all the food mounting at Aunt Rebecca's, not a one of us had thought of eating. I wondered if, as some had said of the dead, Aunt Rebecca's hair and fingernails would keep growing. The funeral was set for the next morning, Sunday, at ten-thirty. No Sunday school. No preaching. For Presbyterians of Deen, Aunt Rebecca would dominate the entire Sabbath. Good. Who would ever have guessed the golden slipper was not a goldfish?

A heavy gray mist had settled in. Blue held open

the gate to our big pasture. I drove through and stopped. It had rained heavily the night before, and the weather was thickening up again. I stepped out on the grass to see how mushy the ground was. Zulu was humming the church hymn "Work, for the Night Is Coming." Blue wanted to drive the truck. Okay. He would like to "slap her in double low," he said, "and spin off like a mule stung in the rump."

"Don't go slipping and sliding around out here," I said. Blue knew where I wanted to go with the bottles. Over at the far end of the pasture, across a wooded bottom, stood the lone chimney of a burned-out Negro shack. It was Uncle Black Cannon's old place. Blue stopped near a rise on the riverbank. This was the place. The water was almost at flood stage. From here I could see downriver to Jackson's Ferry. I got out the shovel.

"We'll take turns," I said.

Despite the softening rain, the earth was stubborn. The whole riverfront was overlaced with a network of frostbitten kudzu, honeysuckle vines, and scattered blackberry briers. It was hard to pry a single bite of dirt from the ground. If the vines on top didn't clean my shovel, the finger roots beneath the surface did. What was Zulu up to?

Zulu carefully placed his whiskey bottle on the running board of the truck and came over to squint down at my efforts. He had pinned a deputy's badge on his vest.

"Fear not," Zulu said. He took the shovel from me and jabbed it into the clotted earth. Zulu's rump was so close to the ground he had to mount the shovel as a child would a pogo stick. But even by bouncing up and down furiously on the blade, he made less than no progress at all.

"You got to dig deep," Blue said, with some knowledge of shovels. "Go straight down deep first, then eat off round the edges. Like this." He took the shovel and had a go at it.

Shelly said that at this rate Aunt Rebecca would get buried before the bottles. That the bottles would not get buried here at all became fact a moment later, when Shelly took his turn at the shovel. On his first dig, Shelly snapped the shovel handle off inches above the blade, and that was that. I never even bothered to take the spade from the ground but left it sticking up, like a little cross among the briers. I stood there looking at the broken spade and wondered what had run through Sylvia's mind when she stood over Aunt Rebecca's casket.

It had begun to drizzle.

Now what? I wondered.

III

The next few hours reeled off like a film of the Keystone Cops bogged down in slow motion.

"We'll have to pitch 'em in the river," Blue said.

"They'll float," Zulu said. "They'd hang up on snags at Jackson's Ferry," I said. "Our fingerprints are all over them," Shelly said. "Sink 'em down with rocks," Blue said. "Pull the stoppers out and sink 'em one by one," Zulu said. To which, looking at his wrist-watch, Shelly said, "That would take till one forty-five Sunday morning." Shelly still wanted to dump the bottles in front of the courthouse. "Ha—ha ha ha—haaa," Shelly laughed mechanically, to the tune of "Over the Waves."

"For cat's sake, Shelly," I said.

A patch of buzzards was circling high over Uncle Black Cannon's old chimney. Zulu waddled over to his whiskey on the running board, had a sip, and waddled back with the bottle in his arms.

"The only thing we have to feaaar," Zulu chanted in Rooseveltian tones, "is feaaar itself." Shelly plucked the bottle from the little man and set it out of reach on the hood of the truck.

"With care, with delicate care," Zulu pled on behalf of his booze. "Alas, such things in this spiritless world are too easily broken or set adrift."

Zulu was at his showman's best when Shelly was around. They were two unlikely magnets with a mysterious attraction for each other. Exactly why, I didn't understand. Blue I understood. We had been a common part of each other almost from the beginning. But Shelly, with his inward moods, was like a face encased in glass, crying out silently to passersby.

And Zulu—what strange alliance had this little toad with Aunt Rebecca?

The drizzle had thickened.

Shelly was watching with rapt concentration the ever-tightening circles of the graceful death birds over the old chimney. The rock chimney! That was it. Blue's idea came to life. In Uncle Cannon's old chimney there were rocks aplenty to crush the bottles and send them all to the bottom of the river.

I got stuck in the mud on the way to the chimney, bogged down axle deep; and Shelly was left sitting meditatively on the tailgate, both shoes in the mud.

Time was running out, and I was now most surely stuck—stuck with no shovel; stuck in my father's pickup; stuck with a complacent genius; stuck with a reeling midget preacher; stuck with Blue, who was as close to my own soul as I was but right now as far away as Africa; and stuck with the goddamn whiskey bottles.

Did Mother know about the whiskey bottles? About the bloodied rocks? About Aunt Rebecca's cracked skull?

Philosophers old and new have remarked that the only certainty in life is uncertainty, that in our best-hatched plans there is an inherent accident, a congenital calamity, that we can no more avoid than death itself.

What if I failed with the whiskey bottles?

A car was making its way across the pasture. We were stuck a hundred yards from the stone chimney and a quarter mile from the river. Zulu had crawled on top of the pickup and was sighting down with one eye into his bottle of drippings. Shelly was watching the buzzards again. Most of the birds had aligned themselves in tall trees and hung in patient relief on the background of the river forest like heavy black fruit.

It was Uncle George in his red Ford station wagon, combing the pasture with his spotlight. He came barreling down the riverside tunnel of trees like a bat out of hell and slid to a stop.

"What the sweet everlasting Jesus you doing way down here with all them goddamn bottles?" he said.

Uncle George was furious, alarmed. He had squeezed our whereabouts out of Bama and Sadie Mae. Blue crawled into the truck cab and slunk out of sight like a snail. Zulu waddled off into the woods, trailing his bottle, and squatted behind a bush to assess the intensity of Uncle George's anger. Zulu's deputy badge glinted through the foliage. Shelly was watching the last vulture enter the trees.

Yes, of course! Who else? I should have guessed. It was Uncle George who had supplied Aunt Rebecca with her own brand of "golden light." *His* fingerprints were on every bottle. But the greater burden of my secret, save for Sadie Mae and Bama, was mine alone. Uncle George could not have known about Aunt Rebecca's sunken slipper or her busted skull.

"Silas, by God, you step here," Uncle George demanded, taking me by the arm and pulling me upside the station wagon. "Now you looky here," he said. "If you dribble out one mumbling word about these goddamn bottles, I'll skin you with a dull ax, you understand?"

"Yes, sir," I said. He held me by the shoulder at arm's length, glaring into me.

"By God, I mean it, boy," he said. "Becky is root kin—booze, Bible, bottles, and all—and I just warn you, you best not forget it! I told your mama and daddy we're out hauling off Becky's trash. *Trash*, you hear?"

"Yes, sir," I said.

"So we'll jus' keep this 'tween you and me and the gatepost? Right?" he said, still looking into my eyeballs.

"Right," I said.

"Right!" he nailed in.

"We don't know what to do with the bottles," I said.

"I do," Uncle George said.

He did: dump them in the abandoned well on

Uncle Cannon's old place, not ten yards from the rock chimney.

But Uncle George could not know that the sheriff would show up, searching for Zulu. After which Uncle George led the sheriff aside and whispered vigorously in his ear. We left the pickup stuck. Then we gently loaded the whiskey bottles into both cars and on foot followed Sheriff Holdster and Uncle George to the old house site.

What the buzzards were after was a dead deer. The deer had caught its antlers in a snarled section of barbed-wire fence and had died trying to free itself. The ground was churned up around where it lay. The belly of the deer was ballooned out, its four legs were splayed unnaturally upward like an upside-down stool, and its dry agate eyes were frozen to the sky. Shelly was overcome at the sight of the unfortunate animal and hid his face in his hands. It was twilight; and being a comfortable distance from their business, the buzzards had no mind to fly away.

Our bottle dumping would have gone off in short order if it hadn't been for Zulu. We all shared in throwing the sacked evidence into the dry well hole; but on the last cast, Zulu teetered too close to the shaft and fell twenty-five feet down, upon the pillow of bottles below.

Sheriff Holdster flashed his light after his fallen deputy, who had landed sitting upright and cross-legged in the middle of the whiskey sacks, like a stunned frog. Not only had the sacked bottles cushioned Zulu's fall; they had miraculously saved his bottle of booze, which Zulu uncorked immediately to celebrate its survival.

Holdster knelt down and squalled into the well: "*Zulu!*" His voice wallowed around in the earth, repeating itself. "Another slug of that hooch, so help me God I'll bury your shriveled-up butt down there forever!" We all—except Shelly—got down on our hands and knees to peer at Zulu. Shelly wanted to climb into the well and lift Zulu out. There was a rotten, ladder-like siding lining the shaft.

When the sheriff's flashlight beam struck his eyes, Zulu cowered against the well wall, holding his arm over his face as if in self-defense. "Verily, verily," he cried, "let he who is without sin cast the first stone."

"*Sin*, my ass!" Holdster roared into the hole. "You crawl your squirrelly butt up out of there—now!" With his light beam, Sheriff Holdster indicated the rotten scaffolding on the well sides.

It had grown dark, and all our efforts to lure or fish Zulu out of the well had failed. Deaf to Holdster's enlarging demands, Zulu sat contented in the spotlight, humming "Shall We Gather at the River" and sipping his amalgamated booze.

Then, with one word, Blue fetched Zulu up and out of the well.

"*Snakes! Snakes!* There's *snakes* down there!" Blue shouted into the well. And up the wooden siding Zulu came, bottle and all. Shelly reached down and lifted the dwarf onto his shoulder.

"Wist ye not," Zulu lisped, "that I must be about my Father's business?"

Uncle George was saying to Shelly, "Now you just tell the Judge and Miss Gretta you helped *clean up* for Miss Rebecca's funeral. That's *all*, you hear?" Zulu was astride Shelly's neck, hanging on to Shelly's head with one hand and swinging his bottle in the other.

"Yes, sir," Shelly said. Holdster snapped the bottle away before Zulu could get it to his mouth.

"Croak one word about them bottles and I'll pickle your ass in formaldehyde," Holdster said to the dwarf.

Shelly stuffed Zulu tactfully into the sheriff's car and closed the door.

Blue and I were to leave the pickup stuck and ride home with Uncle George in the station wagon. Blue and Shelly rode together in the backseat. I could tell by the shape of the paper sack sitting beside me on the front seat that it was a pint of Old Raven.

❖

Except for Mother's Rose Room, Father had planted a radio in every room in the house. He was now installing one in the bathroom, on a shelf beside the toilet.

"You mean you threw away *all* Rebecca's trash?" Father said, flicking the small radio on, then off when he detected static.

"Just about," I said.

"You mean"—he held up his hand to his lips in an imbibing gesture—"all those you-know-what kind of bottles in her cellar?" I was dumbstruck. So Father knew.

"Yes, sir," I said.

"Good," Father said. "Now it's no use to go telling your mother about all this. Understand?"

"Yes, sir," I said.

❖

"*All* Becky's trash?" Mother asked later with an inquiring smile. So she knew too. "That's all right," she said, laying her light arm around my shoulder. "Your Aunt Rebecca"—Mother spoke as if my aunt were still alive—"doesn't break the Commandments; she just hides them every once in a while for her own name's sake. Best not tell your father about all this. He's got a notion Rebecca stands in well with the Lord and might be able to put in a good word for him one day. All right?"

"All right," I said.

IV

Aunt Rebecca's death produced for me three mysteries: why Aunt Rebecca willed away her wealth as she did, why Zulu crashed the funeral as he did, and why I cried for Aunt Rebecca at all.

I didn't find out until after the burial that Aunt Rebecca had left Sadie Mae the servants' house and lot, Zulu a thousand dollars cash, Uncle George her home place, and our Presbyterian church a considerable fortune of one hundred thousand dollars, to be used exclusively for a sky-high steeple, a pipe organ, stained-glass windows, and ceiling fans. That she left absolutely nothing to Mother and Father didn't seem, at the time, to be such a serious oversight; but that she dumped on me only her Moroccan-leather hand Bible and her orphaned goldfish was an insult that took me the better part of a year to absorb.

The rain clouds had vanished with the night, and it was a peppery, near-winter morning as we crunched on the gravel path to the grave site. The sun was high, and yard birds thought it early spring. I caught a faint whiff of mothballs and cedar from my father's woolen suit and could hear behind me the gentle cadence of Mother's satin dress. I had always feared that Mother would die before I could touch the secret of her serenity. I feared that, like a delicate leaf, she would become detached, severed, and slip away to earth while my head was turned or my eyes closed.

All those in Deen of any name or station were present at the cemetery. Reverend Grayson preceded the gold-scrolled casket borne by six elders, which was followed by Uncle George, Mother and Father, me, Sadie Mae, Bama, assorted family, and all the others. Blue was not present. I was seated in the family tent.

Prominent to me across the casket were Shelly, Judge Webster, his powerful wife, Gretta, Sylvia, Sylvia's peach-faced mother, and Sheriff Holdster. Reverend Grayson took his place at the head of the grave. In the background were a honeysuckled fence and a mock orange tree. When the shroud of mourners settled among the gravestones, Reverend Grayson bowed his head in prayer. Shelly was playing she-loves-me she-loves-me-not with a graveyard dandelion blossom. When the petals of his little game were gone, he broke open the womb of the flower and examined the delicate, seedlike tissues in the receptacle. Sylvia, directly across from me, nestled her breasts in her arms, her head bowed so that her hair swung in golden arcs over her cheeks. With Aunt Rebecca dead, I decided that the next time Sylvia helped me feed the goldfish, I would touch Sylvia's breasts and kiss her. The fantasy of Sylvia flying with me in the De Havilland had become an addiction, a prelude that often carried over into my dreams. Even now, with Sylvia bowed in prayer, I wondered when we would solo together. It was then, as if by magic, that Zulu appeared out of the shrubbery.

Sheriff Holdster's eyes, transcending anger, flashed in disbelief. Zulu was decked out like an admiral of the fleet—blue uniform, bright brass buttons, and a captain's cap with gold braid enough to dim the sun. It was Sunday, and Zulu had forgone his regular sermon to his jailhouse parishioners. Was he intoxicated? Was it written that Zulu in his finest hour, like the *Titanic*, was to converge on Aunt Rebecca's funeral and keep a date with destiny? Was his uniform a circus getup, or had he as cabin boy worn it on the high seas? Still in prayer, Reverend Grayson had not noticed the spectacle. Zulu marched front and center, squeezed in between the Judge and Shelly, and laid his stubby arm across his giant friend's rump.

Then, like a mole, Zulu turned and bored his way through the crowd, making his way toward the mock orange tree. Up the tree he went to the very crown, for a privileged view. There he stood, absolutely pretentious, glistening in the morning sun—Zulu the Magnificent! The little mariner swung out by one arm from the main stem like Christopher Columbus on lookout for a new world. Mother was visibly amused with the unexpected interlude, and I dearly wished

Blue had been there to see it all. Reverend Grayson, aware now of the intrusion, stopped in mid-prayer and sliced his eyes into the grandiose dwarf.

It struck me then that Zulu was as good an actor as Aunt Rebecca. Maybe this was part of the second mystery, this strange alliance between the Bishop, the once Wild Man of Zanzibar, and my undying aunt, the flying buttress of predestination: They were both superb actors, Zulu doing his damnedest to reveal his true self and Aunt Rebecca doing her damnedest to conceal hers. And both almost succeeding.

❖

Stranger than this to me was the other mystery: why I should have cried for Aunt Rebecca. There was no gentle family feeling on my part or any tender love in my heart for this inflexible puritan. When she had walked into my presence, alive or in my dreams, she cast upon me a shadow of restrained violence; and when I had walked into hers, I tiptoed uneasily on an ever-present rim of fear.

Nor could it have been that I cried for myself, even though Mother had once read me a poem of a little girl who wept bitterly at the shedding of the golden autumn leaves, never realizing that her heart had detected a like fate for herself.

Zulu was still transfixed in the tree. Who can predict such things? Who can prevent them?

The last of the Scripture that Reverend Grayson read over Aunt Rebecca had been prepicked and arranged by Aunt Rebecca herself and attached to her last will and testament. Her biblical patchwork, unlike consoling passages from the Psalms and gospels, was constructed with a concentration and design all her own. Her excerpts came alone from Saint John the Divine's startling book of Revelations. Although I retained only its ominous tone and a few phrases, Shelly remembered the whole rigmarole and later recited to me most of the lines with theatrical exaggeration. The words were frightening and foreboding:

Babylon the great, mother of harlots . . .
drunk with the blood of saints . . .

Zulu, still aloft, sat transfixed.

Fallen, fallen is Babylon the great,
the dwelling place of demons . . .
for all the nations have drunk the wine
of her impure passion . . .
Hallelujah!
for the marriage of the Lamb has come,
and his Bride has made herself ready . . .

I wondered when Sylvia and I would marry, lie naked together, and engage in glorious love. When such a union would come to pass, I could not know; but that it would, I was absolutely certain.

Reverend Grayson continued:

. . . gave up its dead . . .
Then Death . . . And they
were thrown into the lake of fire . . .
So may the grace of the Lord Jesus Christ
be with all the saints. Amen.

We all bowed for the Lord's Prayer.
I didn't cry then.
When I looked up, Zulu was gone.

V

About Aunt Rebecca, we were all unlucky. But Sadie Mae and Bama and I were unluckier than the others: we knew about the golden slipper and the bloodstained rocks. About the bottles, I was the unluckiest of all. I was the only one who knew we *all* knew.

On the way home from the funeral, I had an image of a goggle-eyed goldfish cautiously sniffing at Aunt Rebecca's golden slipper at the bottom of the stone pool and of Aunt Rebecca slipping with fading astonishment under the water, holding up her whiskey glass. I also had an image of Mother in her private rocker, reading Shakespeare, smoking a Picayune cigarette, and serenely sipping her dark sherry.

Alone in my room upstairs, I opened with disdain

the worn black leather Bible that Aunt Rebecca had willed me, hoping to find among the pages money at least equal to Zulu's. Instead, there fell open to me another secret, which I was too young to fathom but not too young to swim luxuriously in. At my touch, the book fell open as naturally to Solomon's love songs as if Aunt Rebecca had spread the pages and laid her hand upon the place. Of the pages of poetry here, not a streak of ink or pencil had marred the ancient verses, but the sure track of Aunt Rebecca's finger had worn smooth grooves between the lines and, by steady following, had dimmed the printed word. It was the first time I had read the Bible with such intensity. It was as if I had been lifted up and dropped into the Garden of Eden.

The sensuous phrases of the old poet poured upon me:

Oh, that you would kiss me with the kisses of your mouth!
For your love is better than wine,
Draw me after you, let us make haste.
My beloved is to me a bag of myrrh, that lies
Between my breasts.
I am a rose, a lily of the valleys.

Never had I tasted such words.

How graceful are your feet in sandals,
O queenly maiden!
Your rounded thighs are like fawns.
Oh, may your breasts be like clusters of the vine
And your kisses like the best wine that goes
Down smoothly, gliding over lips and teeth.
Come, my beloved,
Let us go forth into the fields
Whither the grape blossoms have opened
And the pomegranates are in bloom.
There will I give you my love.

I engorged these words, thinking lustily of Sylvia in every syllable. But I knew I had wandered upon sacred ground. I had no business here.

To make my intrusion complete, there fell from the pages an old envelope dated 1917, from Mr. John Decker. On the back were lines from a poet I—remembering Mother's voice—found familiar but whose name I could not recall. The lines were addressed to Aunt Rebecca, and they were in Aunt Rebecca's handwriting:

My Fairest Rebecca,
Shall I compare thee to a summer's day?
Thou art more lovely and more temperate.
Rough winds do shake the darling buds of May
And summer's lease hath all too short a date.

It was then I cried.

Chapter Seven

If there was anything wicked or ugly about sex, it never occurred to Queeny. Sex was to Queeny what music was to Shelly—a joy and a harmony. Sex in Queeny was not of a part; it was like hemoglobin in her blood. No pushover, Queeny. But she was God's gift to the uninitiated, a catalyst transforming whole souls from innocence to knowledge without herself altering an iota. Uncle George suggested that such natural spontaneity came from her Cherokee grandmother, Queeny Carson of Buffalo Bill's Wild West Show, who was said to have been a crack shot as good as Annie Oakley and who had a love affair with Buffalo Bill himself. I dearly hoped that this was true. As for me, going fishing with Queeny was a natural blessing, never in disguise.

Queeny and Sylvia were born opposites: Sylvia fair, blond, Presbyterian, and steeped in the consciousness of sin; Queeny bronze, black-haired, country Baptist, and unashamed. After young people's meetings on Sunday nights, I would huddle with Sylvia in the honey-sweet wisteria of our balcony, trespassing fearfully over her forbidden body until we were wild with desire, until Sylvia said stop. On the creekbank, Queeny's generosity knew no bounds.

Queeny and Shelly had something in common: neither cared a pig's poot for Sunday school morality, and yet each seemed intuitively refined to a moral plane above my own. Aunt Rebecca's notion of carnal sin, I think, would not have been nonsense to Shelly or to Queeny; it would simply have been nonexistent. It is fair to say that Queeny enjoyed sex unabashedly, and yet to use the wholesome word for it fit her too tightly and did her a rude injustice. Even today all euphemisms seem woefully inadequate, and to accuse Queeny of promiscuity would have laid an outright lie upon her willing body.

Queeny must have slipped through adolescence as we all did, but I remember her mainly as fully bloomed—Indian tan, boyish, ruddy-faced like a pumpkin, with bold green eyes, short neck like a wrestler's, and black hair cropped in back and cupped as straight across the brow as the hem of a handbasket. She was stocky, not fat, with firm, melon-round breasts. She had the legs of a budding quarterback, wore homemade knee-high khaki shorts, and played basketball with the boys barefooted. You were lucky to have her on your side.

Queeny not only loved to fish; she had a natural hand for it. To go fishing with her was a private privilege filled with great expectation. Although you might take Queeny fishing—that is, provide the transportation—the fact was, you always went fishing *with* Queeny. You didn't select her; Queeny selected you. You asked. Hers was the option, and few were the chosen. Rarely were our uptown pretties—Sylvia never—available for such excursions and then only with a chaperone and discouraging restrictions of time and place. More important, not only didn't these town gals know how to fish; that was all they expected to do. But once Queeny honored you with a fishing date, only at the intrusion of a natural disaster did she, at last, fail to give you her prize.

For weeks I had been fantasizing at night about Sylvia and Queeny. Queeny was steadily winning out. Uncle George had already said that honesty was the best policy, except with women. After spells of hesitation, I grew tolerably honest. One afternoon in Mr. Star's drugstore, I promised to take Queeny up in Uncle George's De Havilland if she'd go fishing with me. I'd meet her at the ferry store.

Queeny pulled my ear down to her lips. "When?" she asked.

II

I was not disappointed.

It was a sizzling Alabama August. France had fallen to Hitler. Uncle George at the age of forty-three had smelled the Battle of Britain coming on and flown the De Havilland to Montreal to join the Royal Canadian Air Force. I didn't blame him and would have done it myself in a second. However, at the moment, I was without an airplane.

Saturday morning I made preparation for Queeny. I tied Mother's fancy winter quilt into a bedroll. Mother was as much a poet with needle and thread as she was with pen and paper. This quilt was a work of art. I crammed my meager fishing stuff into a paper sack, dug a can of wigglers, put cane poles and all in our pickup, and took off for the ferry. Zeeb Rudd, the old black ferryman, floated me across the river for two bits. Zeeb had a double hernia that made the crotch of his overalls look as if it was filled with water. He wondered what the pretty quilt was for and allowed that the only thing he ever caught fishing with a blanket was the clap.

Queeny was at the ferry store with her little brother's red tow wagon, to buy groceries. At the front of the narrow store I could see Queeny's profile near the monumental cash register. A life-sized picture of a leggy girl in a bathing suit, drinking an

RC Cola, was in the background. Queeny had tied a short extension of rope to the little wagon handle to keep from knocking her bare heels on the wagon body and had hitched the tiny carriage to the store banister the way cowboys do their horses.

To give my presence a touch of authenticity, I looked under the hood of the pickup and frowned at the motor. Queeny appeared on the porch barefooted, wearing a big blue work shirt with the sleeves half rolled up and a too-large pair of Clayton's overalls. She paused to look at a Nehi-sign thermometer, shaped like a real woman's leg. From the pickup I could see high red in the needle all the way up to the pretty lady's knee. Queeny tipped down the steps, hugging to her bosom a bag of groceries, her body moving almost imperceptibly inside the loose hulk of denim.

"What's the matter with your truck?" Queeny said.

"Probably needs a drink," I said.

Queeny put the sack of groceries in my arms and went to the well pump at the side of the store. I put the groceries in the little wagon and lifted it into the bed of the pickup. Queeny came back with a gallon bucket of water. I poured. The radiator was already full and overflowed onto the motor. Up came a puff of steam.

"Now then," Queeny said indulgently, as if the

truck were a babe getting its thirst quenched. She pointed to the little wagon and said, "You ought to scotch the wheels so it won't thrash about and spill all the groceries out," she said.

"Right." I pulled the wagon to one side and blocked it off with my quilt roll. Then we made off down the dirt road toward the Slaughters' house.

Queeny propped her feet on the dashboard and turned up her overall legs above the knee. She smiled. "Thaaaat *feeeels* better," she said. "It's a hundred and one degrees at the ferry store." She held open the top of her big shirt and let the window breeze flutter across her breasts.

"What kind of bait?" Queeny wanted to know.

"Wigglers," I said. "I already dug them."

"Creek fishing?"

"Yes."

"Crickets or catalpa worms would be better," she said. Probably so.

I told Queeny that Uncle George, like a big fool, flew off to Canada to get in the war and she would have to wait for her airplane ride. She said that would be just all right and she would take a "rain check" on the airplane ride and that her mother would like to take a ride too, because her mother had been a teacher in Arkansas once and knew all about how planes flew, but that it was silly for Mr. George to go fight a new war in an old airplane. No, she was certainly *not* afraid to fly, but there *was* something about flying that she did not quite understand. . . .

III

When we pulled up in front of the Slaughters' place, Clayton disappeared from the porch swing. Again I was struck by the simple beauty of this country home—the broad yard oaks, the high-peaked center-front gable, twin rock chimneys, and the great screened front porch, lush with hanging plants and potted flowers.

Little brother Robin came out for his wagon and towed in the groceries. In the kitchen, Queeny's mother chipped some ice off a withered block from the wooden icebox and poured two tinkling glasses of iced tea. Robin wanted to go fishing with us, and Mrs. Slaughter said, accommodatingly, "I don't see why not."

My hopes fluttered and fell like lead. In a jiffy, the little fellow had on his straw hat and was raring to go. Queeny borrowed my pocket knife and went outside to cut Robin a fishing pole.

"If science had not been my first love," the pleasant Mrs. Slaughter said, "I would have been an aviatrix." For a moment Queeny's mother waxed poetic about the famous Amelia Earhart and the heroine's tragic disappearance into the Pacific.

How was it possible that this gentle half-Indian

lady could be yoked to such a coarse bastard as Cale Slaughter or that she could have carried the incorrigible Clayton in her belly?

"They say," Mrs. Slaughter continued, "that cannibals might have eaten her."

Queeny had put on a straw sun hat and a funny-looking pair of Clayton's high-top clodhoppers. She was standing beside the truck, working on the fishing pole, while the rambunctious Robin tugged at the seat of her overalls.

"Stop it," Queeny fumed, swatting Robin off her tail. Then, skillfully, Queeny punctured the end of her finger with the tip of my jackknife. She immediately gathered up the little boy, dabbed some blood on his big toe, and dragged him complaining back into the house. She returned without Robin. "I told Mama he stubbed his toe and ought to stay at home," Queeny said.

We headed out for my chosen fishing spot, halfway between the Slaughters' place and Uncle George's landing strip at Arrowhead. Queeny took her finger out of her mouth and mashed it with her thumb to see if it had stopped bleeding.

"That was a dumb thing to do," I said. "Has it stopped bleeding?"

"I reckon. Mama says you've got more nerves in your fingertips than anywhere else in your body, except your tongue," Queeny said.

The *something* Queeny didn't understand about

flying was air, how *air* held you up; because you couldn't see air, there was something insubstantial about it, something mysterious and unreliable.

"It's there, all right," I explained. "You don't have to see it. In a tornado, air can knock down trees and houses and blow a pine needle through a two-by-four."

"I know," Queeny said. "It can kill you."

IV

My fishing place was called the Blue Hole. It was a secluded cove on the Chickasaw Creek under the old Bankhead Bridge. With the coming of the new road and the new WPA concrete bridge, the abandoned road to the old wooden bridge had become weeded and ingrown to a narrow path, used mainly now by foxes, raccoons, and moonshiners. It was no secret on this side of the river that Cale Slaughter had a whiskey still in the backwoods here somewhere.

I drove the pickup as far as I could. We got out. Queeny unsnapped the leather scabbard on my belt, lifted out my woods hatchet, and bounced into the undergrowth. With a few swishes she hacked down a walking-stick-sized sweet gum, trimmed it clean of branches, and chopped out the top. Then she slipped the hatchet back into its sheath on my belt and snapped the lip shut.

"For snakes," Queeny said, holding out the stick.

"Right," I said.

"Not to kill 'em," she said. "Just to scoot 'em out the way."

I laughed. "Okay."

"Papa says snakes're scareder of you than you are of them."

Maybe. I never believed snakes had enough sense to be afraid like we do. Snakes were insidious meat tubes. They simply reacted. Was it possible, I wondered, for a snake, the very symbol of death, to fear death itself? As a child, I had seen a rattlesnake in the fatal coils of a constricting king snake. Was that a fear of death I read in the rattler's eyes? Or was it merely a primitive acquiescence to a timeless and wordless fate, without reflection? I didn't know.

"Right," I said. "Your daddy's as right as Sears Roebuck."

Wearing the baggy overalls and her daddy's big shirt and Clayton's clodhoppers, Queeny looked like a circus clown. She followed me, carrying my brown paper bag of fishing stuff and the rolled quilt. With cane poles and wiggler worms, I led the way, parting the undergrowth with Queeny's snake stick.

The Blue Hole wasn't big, but it wasn't called the Blue Hole for nothing. I hadn't been here since the summer Blue and I stole Uncle George's airplane. The creek body fell out flat here, like a big boot sunk down sideways in a green cradle of shady woods. The bank was trimmed with watercress, ferns, and creek canes, and draped in fox grape and muscadine vines from overhanging treetops. The heel and sole of the Blue Hole were the old bridge and the dark rocky falls on the upper side. Upstream, the Chickasaw seemed to pause at the rocks, wait, splinter white through the choppy slope, pause again, then smile into the deep blue pool. With the sun rarely getting through into this little Eden, save around noon, the water *was* blue, ink blue. The rocks were blue. The bridge was blue. The sky was blue. In contrast, a tongue of bank along our side was white with smooth sand, cleaned and curved by generations of swift high water.

Queeny kicked off Clayton's clodhoppers and was standing barefooted and straddle-legged over the can of wiggler worms.

Carefully I spread out Mother's art quilt under the butt of the old bridge. In open daylight you could see clearly that Mother had cleverly stitched into the pattern a vaguely camouflaged image of a smiling maiden holding a parasol. Looked at one way, the parasol was open, and it was raining. Looked at another, it was closed, and the sun was shining. The parasol girl reminded me of Sylvia.

Between the Blue Hole and where we parked the truck, Queeny had spotted a grub-bearing catalpa tree.

"Wheeeew," Queeny breathed, acknowledging the heat. Flicking a spot of moisture from her forehead, she unhooked her overalls and slipped out of them in one movement. Her daddy's great shirt came down to her knees.

"You reckon there're any grubs on that catalpa tree back yonder?" Queeny said.

"Could be," I said.

The idea hit me: *Queeny knows as much about fishing with boys as I know about flying in airplanes.* The thought was discomforting. But it suggested a face-saving balance of knowledge for me; if not in kind, at least in degree. I *could* fly an airplane. I could *fly* an airplane. I could fly an *airplane.* But for all the free and blessed knowledge of flying I'd received from Uncle George, I had not got one mumbling word from him on the nature or execution of my present mission. If Queeny, by comparison, was a virgin to airplanes, I was most abundantly the real innocent article down here on earth with her.

Fishing quickened Queeny's eyes and fingers, and in a jiffy she had her pole ready for business. She examined my wigglers. "These are big, frisky ones," she said, drawing a flailing worm from the can. True. I had dug them early that morning from Father's manure compost pile and had thrown some of the rich mulch in with them. I leaned over the worm can and kissed Queeny on the side of her mouth.

"Look," she said. Queeny smiled at the worm and pointed the eye of the hook at the pink band around the worm's belly. "Mama says that's where they mate," she said. Did I know that each worm was a boy and girl in one and that two worms wrap around each other to do it, then the pink rings drop off and baby worms crawl out of the dead rings? I had never heard of such a thing. Why, I wondered, if each worm was both boy and girl, did they need another worm to do it with? Mrs. Slaughter knew about more than airplanes.

"Of course I know," I said.

Queeny's fingers were sticky with compost soil. When the earthworm relaxed, Queeny set the barb of the hook into position over the worm's vital belt. "That's where you sink your hook. It's tougher there," she said. With that, she ran the barb through the pink sex band. The wiggler went wild in her fingers. She allowed the thrashing worm to slip down between her thumb and two forefingers, then clamped down tight upon him and threaded the hook tailward, leaving the barb inserted and the wiggler plenty of opportunity to perform in the water.

While I held the baited cane pole, Queeny rinsed her hands in the Chickasaw. Taking the pole again, she said, "Now . . ." with the satisfaction of a job well done, and kissed me on the mouth. My spirits improved. She slipped the fishing cork far up on the line and flung the bait and sinker into a twirl of blue water that eddied around the roots of a water oak upstream. She kissed her stuck finger and touched it to my lips.

"If you're going to catch anything in fast-running water," she said, "you've got to fish on the bottom."

V

However perfect the Blue Hole, I was beginning to sense that my amorous hopes were in danger. But then, even at best, my most vivid and well-directed nighttime fantasies had been failures. At least incomplete. My sex dreams were like little silent movies that ran up to the point where Queeny stripped off to her panties and I started to take off my pants, then the camera ran out of film. And in even my most ambitious productions, I could never get Sylvia's dress all the way off.

Queeny's first bite was immediate. The worm had hardly hit the surface before the cork went sailing away toward deep water. Queeny waited, stretched out her pole to give more line. The cork hesitated, popped under once, then fell out of sight. Queeny held her mouth tight, took a firm grip on the pole, then set the hook with a jerk. *"Now,"* she said confidentially, as if communing with the fish. The fish made a wide sweep toward the bank, broke water. Queeny hauled him in in a flutter. It was a grown sun perch, as big as a fat man's hand.

"Pretty! Pretty! Pretty!" Queeny beamed.

"Ye-e-es," I said. She was right. In full light, the translucent sun perch was like a fluttering slice of rainbow, unlike Aunt Rebecca's large goldfish, which plowed across her indoor house pond like slow gold bars. I had forgotten to bring a fish stringer. Queeny hadn't. She had one balled up in her big shirt pocket. In no time she had the perch unhooked, threaded through the gills, and flipping in the air. On the other side of the oak, she flung the fish into the creek and stuck the stringer needle in the bank.

"There's a moccasin over there," Queeny said when she got back. The big shirt fit her like a pup tent. It was unbuttoned halfway down. I went to take a look for the snake.

"He's gone," I said.

"It was a cottonmouth," Queeny said. Probably not. There were dozens of harmless water snakes a girl might take for a cottonmouth.

Queeny baited up again and with a single throw dropped the hook perfectly into the water. Spots of August sunlight flickered through the trees and across Queeny's hair. . . .

I would kiss Queeny now, right away before I faltered, and slip my hand inside her daddy's big shirt. . . . Should I do the hand first or the kiss? Or both at once? . . . Would the hand confuse the kiss? Or would the kiss confuse the hand? . . .

Queeny dropped to her haunches and stuck the butt of her cane pole between her thighs into the sand. The sinker on her hook held the bottom, and the current carried the cork out in a straight line downstream. Through the neck of Queeny's loose shirt, I could see her breasts. I took my shirt off and squatted down beside her. I decided I would touch her breasts first, one at a time. Then go in for the kiss . . .

"I've got a bite," Queeny said, jumping to her feet. So she had. Her cork made a beeline back up-stream toward the falls. She set her hook, played the fish for a while, then pulled him in. It was identical to the first perch.

"His girlfriend," she said, dangling the fish in my face.

"*Her* boyfriend," I said.

I took the perch off the hook and went to the stringer. Queeny had been right. The snake *was* a cottonmouth. The reptile was a short, thick, rusty one. As deadly as they come. He opened his jaws at me, showing his cotton-white throat, and slunk back slowly, looking at me. Then, just as slowly, he faded under the water. He had eaten the tail off the first sun perch.

"The snake ate the tail off your fish," I said.

"Papa says a snake can't bite you under water," Queeny said. Cale Slaughter was dead wrong on this one, as Uncle George, who had been bitten under water, could yea verily testify.

"I'll tell Uncle George that," I said.

Queeny said we might lie down on the quilt awhile if I'd go see if there were any grubs on the catalpa tree. Damn.

So I went, and there they were. The tree was crawling with catalpa worms. Thousands of them. It was said, and it may be true, that there are male and female catalpa trees, the male with the bloom and the female with the long, cigarlike pods full of seed. Blue and I used to smoke the catalpa beans in late summer when they got dry. It was said, too, that the catalpa grubs ate the leaves off the male tree only, two or three times a season, which would account for the male trees' being so scrawny. Queeny's enthusiasm for fishing had me troubled. I picked off three of the jumbo grubs and cupped them in my handkerchief.

When I got back, Queeny was standing ready by her pole. She had balled up her overalls and my shirt and arranged them as a pillow at the head of the quilt. She looked into my handkerchief.

"Is that all?"

"It's all I could find," I said. Queeny had completely unbuttoned her floppy shirt, which left a dark valley between her breasts, all the way down. I took Queeny by the hand and started toward the quilt.

"Let's try a catalpa worm first," Queeny said.

First? And then . . . what? How does one begin? *Exactly* how? *Being* naked wasn't the problem. The problem was *getting* naked—the ridiculous, apologetic, eyeball act of *taking my clothes off!* Harvey Johnson had said that doing it with your clothes on was like eating a candy bar with the wrapper on. My jeans. My shoes! My shoes would have to go first.

But first I'd bait Queeny's hook.

The catalpa larva is a succulent, ninety-nine-percent liquid worm that gorges itself on new catalpa leaves. Its green juice gives a little spurt when you pierce the worm's body, so you've got to be careful not to make a tear; otherwise you end up with nothing but a piece of limp velvet skin. Queeny watched me ready the hook.

"Be gentle," she said, like an attending surgeon.

With the catalpa grub, you ease the hook into the underbelly, then slide it in only *so* far, and stop.

"That's right," Queeny said, watching my insertion. The barb popped through the skin perfectly, without rupture. The worm held firm. I pushed the head of the hook forward into the main channel of the grub and stopped midway so that the curve of the shaft wedged in tightly to hold fast for the cast-out and so that a jerk might not rip the grub apart. "That's ju-u-ust right," Queeny hummed. The hook was ready.

"Here." Queeny handed me her pole. "It's your turn. You've got an unlucky pole," Queeny teased. She wiggled her big toe at my cane pole lying on the ground. "My pole's the lucky one," she said. She thrust her cane pole in my hand and took me by the wrist in a may-you-be-lucky squeeze. I was warmed by the suggestion in her fingers. I left the cork high up on the line, where Queeny had adjusted it, and flung out as far as I could, into the water boiling at the foot of the falls.

Queeny had seen Mother's quilted maiden with the parasol and was standing over the artwork, puzzled. "That's funny," she said. "It's raining, it's not raining; it's raining, it's not raining. Isn't it funny you can't see both of them at the same time?" She wanted to know if I had scared the snake off. I had. The fact is, you don't *scare* snakes off. They just disappear for a while when *they* want to. I wondered how far off in the woods Cale Slaughter's still was. I thought: *Clayton may be Cale Slaughter's son, but Queeny is her mother's daughter.*

Queeny was lying, bare breasts up, on the quilt, with her knees cocked in an A angle. Her black, cropped hair, her dark eyes, and her soft copper breasts exposed a new symmetry that arrested my breathing. Queeny's eyes were closed. I pushed the butt of my fishing pole into the sand and slipped my shoes off. Queeny, I think, was not looking at me on purpose. She asked did I reckon Uncle George would really mind taking her up in his airplane when he got back from Canada? So Queeny had forgotten that *I* was to do the flying. "No," I said, "if it's all right with your mother." No problem. Queeny said her mother was forever filled with curiosity and adventure and wanted to go up for an airplane ride herself. Standing unsteadily on one foot, I started jiggling one leg out of my jeans.

Did I reckon, Queeny wanted to know, that we'd all get sucked into the war? I didn't know but said Uncle George would get into it hell or high water and that I was going to get into it myself as a fighter pilot if the war was lucky enough to last that long. I was struggling with my pants leg. Had I ever "done it" with Sylvia? Queeny wanted to know. No, I had not. Most secretly and assuredly I had never done any such thing with anybody. Not even in my fantasies.

"The girl with the umbrella looks like Sylvia," Queeny said. So Queeny had noticed too. The thought now of doing it in broad daylight was unsettling, but doing it with Queeny *on top of Sylvia* would be scandalous. Queeny still had her eyes closed. My foot was stuck in my jeans. . . .

What had happened? Queeny was running toward me full blast and breast naked, her shirttails fluttering behind her. With my left leg half in, half out of my jeans, I was off balance when Queeny started her sprint. I was halfway into the creek when she arrived.

It was my fishing pole. A fish had bent my pole double, pulled it free of the sand, and started out across the deep. I was struggling to free my trapped leg when Queeny piled into me sideways and over we went, elbows and eyeballs, into the Blue Hole.

The collision was complete. Trapped in my jeans and bound to my underwear, I sank like iron, swallowing half the Chickasaw. Then silently, pleasantly, submerged, I saw Queeny's golden legs scissoring the quiet water, her shirttail flowing outward like the wings of a gentle manta ray, her nippled breasts like buoyant brown eyes. . . .

My feet found bottom, and up I came. The water was neck deep. I wondered where the cottonmouth was. Snakes *did* strike under water. The water was too deep and the current too swift for Queeny. Toe-tipping closer to the bank, she took my hand. Holding on, and with the good luck of being anchored to the bottom by my waterlogged jeans and my scout hatchet, I nabbed the pole and brought the fish out.

It was the biggest bass I'd ever caught, a fighting four pounds if he weighed an ounce. But as soon as the fish touched ground, he flipped free. Queeny zipped out of the water and was on the bank in a splash, darting back and forth in front of the floundering bass, blocking it from the water with both feet and bare legs. Before the fish could flip back home, Queeny shucked off naked and trapped it on the sand in her daddy's big shirt. She held up the fish with thumbs stuck in both gills and started jumping up and down.

"I told you I had a lucky pole," she cried. "Isn't he gorrrgeous!"

She was right. Absolutely right. And Queeny, glittering in the spotted August shade, was absolutely naked and didn't even know it.

The craziest thing about it was that there Queeny was, as stark and bare as a wet dolphin suspended in midair; but hard as I tried, my eyes wouldn't let me see her because she *was* naked. And there was I, transfixed, drenched, transparent in my clinging underwear.

But catching the fish had made a difference.

I shook off my jeans, straightened my soggy drawers around my loins, and took my sweet time in stringing the bass. The cottonmouth had eaten a chunk out of the second perch. The sun had dropped beyond the trees, and a cool breeze blowing down the Chickasaw made my skin prickle. Queeny was hanging up her big shirt and my jeans, hatchet and all, on a lower beam of the old bridge. I could see Queeny naked better at a distance. She returned to the quilt and stretched out again, face up. I decided to wait until the exact last moment before taking my underwear off.

Maybe doing it would be like riding a bicycle the first time—just start off coasting downhill until you get your balance and speed. . . . Or like swimming the first time—leap in over your head and come up paddling. . . . Or like Shelly in his flying dream—find the highest crag, the very summit, and, with absolute faith, launch yourself into infinite space. . . . Or like diving in the river, committing yourself, plunging out of the highest treetop into the deeps below . . .

Queeny was lying in the middle of the quilt, on top of the parasol girl.

"I don't want her to see us," Queeny said. I came over and knelt down beside her. I could see my particulars through my wet underwear.

"Is it raining or not raining?" I said, pointing at my mother's handiwork.

"Raining," Queeny said, almost sarcastically. She touched her cut finger to my nose. Her finger smelled like fresh creek bass.

"Yeah," I said. "That creek dunking you gave me

got me bone cold." It was a fact. I had started trembling inside.

"Now you lay down. I won't look," Queeny said, turning on her side. At the small of her back I could see Mother's pretty parasol girl. The quilt said it was raining.

"It's still raining," I said.

"Now it's not," Queeny said, flipping back over, chest up, covering the parasol girl. I touched one of Queeny's bronze nipples with the tip of my finger and started to kiss her.

"You reckon Sylvia's afraid to because her daddy's a preacher?" she said.

"If she did, Reverend Grayson would crucify her upside down," I said.

"You want to now?" Queeny asked.

"Yes," I said. The trees sifted spotted light on Queeny's thighs.

"Have you done it before?" Queeny asked.

"Yes," I said, "a long time ago." Which was a grievous lie, unless you believed in reincarnation or the transmigration of souls.

"With who?"

"Somebody you don't know," I said. Which, at least, was the truth.

This was it: the spin downhill . . . my launch from the summit . . . my plunge into the mysterious deep . . .

Rising on her elbows, Queeny lifted herself attentively toward me.

"He's looking at us!" she whispered with pistol-pointed seriousness.

My wet underwear froze around me.

It was true. He *was* looking at us. It was a raccoon on the other side of the Blue Hole, washing his inquisitive face and examining us through his bandit mask.

No matter. I had already committed myself, wet drawers and all. . . .

"Not now," Queeny said, "not while he's *looking* at us."

"He won't mind," I said. "He won't care a damn. . . ."

"I just don't want him *watching* us," Queeny said.

"Coons can't see good in daylight," I improvised. "They don't think about it the way we do."

If I had tried since the Stone Age to coax by ritual and luring this particular nocturnal creature to this very spot at this very hour, I would have failed. Yet, without prayer or prompting, here he was, all coon eyes, our exclusive audience and critic, washing his whiskers.

"Mother said coons are cleaner than we are and have the most sense of all the creatures in the animal kingdom," Queeny said.

I hopped up and galloped to the edge of the Blue

Hole, flapping my arms and making frantic scare-crows at the astonished animal. He was not in the least afraid and watched my performance with detached curiosity until I had finished; then he casually turned his ringed tail toward me and strolled back into the undergrowth, leaving me now more naked than with no drawers on at all.

Queeny sat foursquare in the middle of the quilt, naked and amused.

There was the sound of a truck on the other side of the Blue Hole. The sound came from the old road and pushed on, nearer and louder, through the trees. Queeny had moved now directly under the bridge, standing up, listening. So I could see, I tipped to the big oak and hid myself. At the lip of the bridge on the other side, the truck emerged and stopped. Queeny identified the truck by sound.

"It's Papa," she said.

VI

Sheriff Holdster harvested moonshine stills the way farmers do crops—except Holdster farmed on rotation the year round. He got two hundred dollars from the state for each still he busted up. There were always at least twelve dependable stills in the county, so he'd knock off his January still, convict and fine the moonshiner, and move on to his February still, and so on. By the end of the year, the January still had grown back healthy and ripe to be picked off again. And so it went year by year between law and outlaw on the perfectly reasonable and profitable principle of live and let live.

The first year Holdster busted Cale Slaughter's still was the same year the votes from Cale's side of the river ran heavily against our sheriff. Holdster took note and thereafter found his twelfth still on the town side of the river.

But votes were not all that held Sheriff Holdster to the town side of the law. There was something sinister and uncompromising about Cale Slaughter that made you walk around the block rather than meet him head-on or made you duck into the drugstore aimlessly while he passed by.

That August afternoon at the Blue Hole, Cale Slaughter stood expressionless in front of his truck on the bridge, a double-barrel shotgun tucked under one arm, a gallon of shine hanging from his other hand, and, as always, the seasonless gray felt hat pulled down low on his brow. In the gloom of this hidden cover, he looked like a gangster.

When another man appeared on the bridge, I slipped across to Queeny.

Uncle George had always had an uncanny way of showing up at times like this. Thank God he was in Canada to join the RCAF! I'd rather have been shot dead and naked by Cale Slaughter than have Uncle George or Shelly or Blue catch me alive like this.

Queeny squeezed my hand in both of hers. She was trembling too. "Papa's got ears like a fox," she whispered.

So, for an hour, until after sundown, we stood there frozen in the blue afternoon while Queeny's daddy sold the moonshine. But not before he and the other man smoked cigarettes and had a couple of drinks. It was dark when we listened to Cale Slaughter's truck groan away.

We put on our wet clothes and went to the fish stringer. The snake had eaten all of both sun perch, except for their heads. My bass had survived. Queeny released him, saying it would be a shame to eat him after all he'd been through.

On the way back to her house, Queeny said she would swap places with her mother for the airplane ride, because this might be her mother's last chance to fly, and that we could go fishing again, another time, if that would be all right. Yes, that would be all right.

"Did you mind that I turned your bass loose?" she asked.

"No," I said, remembering it was her pole I caught him on.

But I was glad, truly glad, that *I* had caught him.

VII

The airplane ride for Queeny's mother and my second fishing date with Queeny came sooner than I expected. The RCAF didn't accept Uncle George for the war, because of his age. But that wasn't the end of it. He wrote Winston Churchill a scorching rebuke, in which he said to the Prime Minister, "For Christ's sake, if you don't get some more airplanes up over London soon you're going to lose the god-damn war."

The next Saturday afternoon, Queeny and I were lying on Mother's quizzical quilt not far from where I had tried to bury Aunt Rebecca's whiskey bottles. I could see the nub of the old spade that Shelly had snapped off in the ground. We could hear Uncle George and Mrs. Slaughter in the De Havilland, high above the Alabama River, pulling into a steep climb, then leveling off. . . .

Yes, Harvey Johnson was certainly right. Doing it with one's clothes on would have been like eating the candy bar wrapper and all.

And yes, I could believe that long ago Queeny's pretty young Indian grandmother made love to Buffalo Bill.

"I'll bet Mama is having a good time up there," Queeny said, opening her eyes to the sky. I was listening.

Uncle George leveled out in a stall, then put the De Havilland into a dive. Beside Queeny's breast and in the curve of her bare arm I could see a tip of the parasol girl on Mother's quilt.

"Is it raining or not raining?" Queeny whispered.

I did not answer. But it was not raining, and afterward there was no doubt exactly when Queeny entered my Jar of Marbles.

Chapter Eight

For our junior class in high school, the Japanese attack on Pearl Harbor ushered in a time of excitement. Books and teachers became automatically taboo. Our war had arrived. The die was cast for all of us—except for Shelly.

That week Harvey Johnson got an army crew cut. Wiley Harper took to wearing his brother's old ROTC cap. I shaved twice and tried on Uncle George's World War I flying uniform. Shelly began to play the difficult concertos of Brahms and the marches of Sousa, and he designed in his notebook fantastic aircraft that would have won the admiration of Leonardo da Vinci. Before the week was out, I reread for the umpteenth time Uncle George's dog-earred manual *How to Fly*. Just as there wasn't the slightest doubt that one day I would inherit the De Havilland, there wasn't the slightest doubt I would be a fighter pilot in our great war. Clayton Slaughter showed no visible signs of being affected by Pearl Harbor or the European war one way or the other, but when school was out that spring, he joined the United States Marine Corps.

In fact, it was Clayton, Clayton home from boot camp—gorgeous Clayton tanned and toughened, wearing a crushed Douglas MacArthur–type cap and a tailored class A uniform—who inspired our junior-senior class picnic. The joint affair was Shelly's idea, reinforced by Zulu's imagination. From there our occasion bloomed. There was grand music by Shelly and his operatic mother, baseball, Zulu's disappearance, airplane rides, a hayride, hot dogs and hamburgers by the bushel, two churns of iced tea, and a pasture flowing with high school girls, plain and pretty, including Sylvia and Queeny.

But if Shelly and Zulu were the picnic conceivers and Uncle George the promoter, and if war was the spirit it all fed on, Clayton was its vital center, its uniformed star.

From ugly duckling to swan, from frog to prince, had Clayton Slaughter emerged, no longer a knotty, black-haired country clod dug out of an Alabama river bluff, but a foreign body, suave, sleek, and brown, dropped upon us like a Rudolf Valentino or a Tarzan. Clayton Slaughter's metamorphosis was complete. And Sylvia—her eyes betrayed her—was smitten.

It was July 4, 1942. Our two classes with assorted parents gathered behind Uncle George's hay barn, which sheltered the De Havilland. Uncle George had stuck up American flags all over the place and had a tall one anchored on the hood of the hayride truck. By ten in the morning we had stepped off a baseball diamond. Clayton and I chose teams. A bunch of the girls insisted on playing ball with us. Right off I chose Queeny, who, pound for pound, was better than any boy on either side. The bulge in Clayton's back pocket was a half pint of whiskey. There is no way to hide the shape of whiskey. So his sharpshooter's medal would stand out, Clayton hung his military shirt sideways on a fence post near third base and slipped the whiskey bottle into his cap on the ground. Harvey Johnson said Sylvia was afraid to play because she was too pretty and might break. Clayton took off his T-shirt and pitched the ball game bare-chested, with a dead cigarette butt in his mouth.

I struck out twice. Queeny got on base once and stole home. Clayton knocked a home run off me in the ninth, which ended the game. I got two runs, and my side lost three to five.

Mother had fixed a couple of hampers of hot dogs and hamburgers, and Mrs. Slaughter and her little son, Robin, tended the iced tea and cake. Cale Slaughter, Clayton's daddy, would sooner have been caught dead than be seen at such a gathering. Uncle

George and Blue rolled out the De Havilland. Uncle George had planted a small American flag on the top wing. To class members with written permission, Uncle George would give airplane rides.

Reverend Grayson was still adamant. "No!" he said. My heart sank. "Sylvia may not fly with George Simeon or with you *and* George Simeon." Clyde Grayson had not forgotten the Sunday Uncle George rose in indignation and stalked out of our church forever.

Queeny and her mother had already flown with Uncle George. But for more secure fishing privileges, I would make sure Queeny got another ride today.

To calm all fears, Mother took the first ride, during which Uncle George did a stall and a simple left turn and slipped the De Havilland in for a perfect three-point. Chesty Gretta Webster told the Judge that Shelly was ab-so-lute-ly not going up in that cracker box. Judge Webster had hired some colored men to haul out Shelly's baby grand piano on the flatbed of a cotton truck. Shelly played some Chopin and afterward accompanied Gretta, who sang "God Bless America" with a patriotic gusto that equaled Kate Smith's and left tears in Uncle George's eyes. Johnny Holliday, from Alabama Polytechnic Institute, who was our new assistant county agent, sang "When Irish Eyes Are Smiling." He was a soft-voiced 4F, deferred from military service, and drove a yellow Pontiac roadster. Plump-jawed and Presbyterian, he sang tenor in our church; he had the favor of Reverend Grayson and Gretta Webster. To my ire, Holliday had often outmaneuvered me and driven Sylvia home after Sunday-night young people's meetings. The only thing I liked about Johnny was the way his named sounded—*Johnny Holliday*. When Shelly got through playing our national anthem, Reverend Grayson blessed the burgers and hot dogs. Later Zulu pulled off his near-perfect disappearing act, and that night Blue drove a gang of us in Uncle George's high-bodied cattle truck for the hayride.

After the singing and eating, Clayton and I talked war and the United States Marine Corps, while Sylvia and Queeny stood by. Clayton said that after twelve weeks of advanced training he'd be knocking over Japs in the Pacific, and I said next summer I'd be taking fighter pilot training with the Army Air Corps. Sylvia tried on Clayton's military shirt and service cap and found the whiskey. Queeny said she was going to be a navy nurse and—ha, ha—marry a doctor. Clayton had a pack of cigarettes twisted up in the short sleeve of his T-shirt. Yes, I would have one, thank you. With Sylvia and Queeny looking on, I managed to muffle the first puff but nearly perished on my next inhalation.

Robin came to fetch Queeny to help their mama

with the iced tea and cake. Uncle George was revving up the De Havilland. Janis Roberts, who was in my class, appeared, waving in her hand a small paper sack bearing written permission to fly in Uncle George's airplane. Would Clayton go, too, and let her ride in his lap so she wouldn't be afraid all alone up there in the wild blue yonder? Yes, that would be okay with Clayton, but there was a flash in Sylvia's eyes. Sylvia's arms were lost in Clayton's military shirt, and her hands looked chopped off. She was not afraid to fly, but even if she had been able to wring permission out of Reverend Grayson, Janis had beaten her to the punch.

Janis was kitten cute, a little bigger than a jumbo Shirley Temple doll and full of firecracker remarks. She was president of our Beta Club and had won first prize for a short story in the *Birmingham News*. Clayton bent over, making a climb-on gesture. Janis leapt up, straddling Clayton's hips and clasping her arms around his neck.

"Don't resist the Marines," Janis said, winking at Sylvia. "Surrender!" Janis plucked the cigarette from Clayton's lips and took a knowledgeable drag. There was no doubt that once airborne, she would share a nip out of Clayton's bottle.

Before Clayton made off with Janis, he produced a four-cornered miniature parachute that he had formed out of a red bandanna handkerchief with strings attached. He unpinned his sharpshooter's medal and hung it where the strings converged, folded it all into a little bundle, and flung it in the air. As it floated down, Clayton shot a wink at Sylvia and announced that he would toss the parachute out of the airplane to see who might be the lucky one to catch it. Lopety-lope, and Clayton pranced off with Janis.

I walked Sylvia toward the creek at the far end of the pasture with the single intention of lying beside her in the long grass and kissing her. But kissing Sylvia in broad daylight was not easy. She would not stop with me in the broom sage but swished straight through it with her lithe body and made her way to the creek bank, where she flipped her shoes off, sat down on a fallen tree, and began paddling her feet in the shallow water.

"Clayton looks real nice in his uniform," Sylvia said. Uncle George was still revving up the De Havilland.

"He's the same Clayton," I said. I sat beside Sylvia and put my arm around her waist.

"He's so grown up now," she said.

"Inside he's still the same old Clayton," I said.

"But he seems to *be* somebody now, to *stand* for something," she said. *Holy Jesus,* I thought.

"It's the uniform," I said.

Uncle George had taxied around into the wind. Janis and Clayton were waving from the back cockpit.

"It's not that," Sylvia said.

"What then?"

"It's the way he acts. He's not afraid of anybody anymore, like he used to be." *Clayton afraid?* I wondered.

"They teach you not to be afraid in the Marines," I said.

"I don't mean that," Sylvia said. "I mean *of us*. He's not standoffish anymore. He just walks into the middle of everybody like he didn't care who knew where he came from—you know."

"His mother is a real somebody," I said. "She's educated. She and Queeny have *both* flown with Uncle George in the De Havilland." I pushed Sylvia's hair aside and kissed her on the cheek.

"Silas!" Sylvia said in mock surprise. "Then *that's* where it comes from," she added.

"Where what comes from?" I asked.

"Clayton's character," Sylvia said. "His mother." Wrong, I thought. Clayton was the very essence of his daddy, only now not in shadow but in broad daylight. Queeny was her mama's girl. Inside herself, Queeny always knew where she was; pitch her up and, like a cat, she'd always land on her feet.

I slipped off my shoes. Sylvia and I both stood ankle deep in the creek water, watching Uncle George take off. The little American flag was alive on the top wing.

"I can *fly* the De Havilland," I said, pointing at

the airplane. Sylvia was not listening. She stood tiptoe in the water, peering across the pasture at Uncle George gaining altitude. "I'll be flying P-40s in the war," I said. Sylvia did not hear.

On past dates, as a matter of course (or favor) Sylvia had sweetly blessed me with moist good-night kisses. Now, with Clayton at hand, new energies possessed me.

Uncle George was about to make his first pass over the picnickers.

"Let's watch Clay—" Sylvia began. I seized her in both arms. Uncle George was flying over low to buzz the crowd.

"Clayton's going to—" she began again.

I kissed Sylvia hard on the mouth and held on as long as she would allow.

"—to throw out the parachute," Sylvia finished impatiently.

We grabbed our shoes and ran through the broom sage and out into the pasture.

Everybody was rushing to the center of the runway to be ready for Clayton's toss-out. Clayton sat at attention in the back cockpit, with Janis wiggling in his lap and waving her arms like crazy. Then there it came, floating down, the red bandanna parachute, with Clayton's sharpshooter's medal hanging on like a little hero.

II

Zulu's disappearing act was near-perfection. All screwed up in the preacher's little brown body was a genius, a sadness as large as Shelly's. Somehow genius must be punished to flourish; must be squelched, crammed into a corner before it can manifest itself; or, like Shelly's, it must be let out on a plane so broad and misty that only bees and hummingbirds may detect it.

There were two things that Shelly, Blue, and I did not know. Zulu had made bets with the menfolk, excluding Reverend Grayson, of course. After drumming up a fistful of bills, he had matched it with money from his own pocket. He would lose all if, in his act, he did not disappear *completely*. What even Zulu didn't know was that, in the tool compartment behind the cattle truck cab, Uncle George always stashed away a bottle of Old Raven, secured in a rubber boot. The tool bin looked every bit a part of the truck.

The day before the picnic, Blue, Zulu, and I prepared the high-bodied cattle truck as a stage for Zulu's performance. Now we were wrapping the slatted body all around with heavy cotton bagging, including the big rear gate, which was to serve as a "curtain" to Zulu's act. The four of us were on the inside, tying on the thick burlap with pieces of hay wire.

"Houdini, the holy priest of magicians!" Zulu chanted, alluding to the deceased mystic and illusionist. "None late or soon shall be worthy to breathe even the outcasts of his farts." Zulu crawled like a squirrel along the open gaps, wiring the burlap to plank and upright. If Shelly was present, it was always he to whom Zulu addressed himself. "Alas, poor Houdini! I knew him, Shelly. A fellow of infinite agility: nimbleness of body, precision of mind, his magic all hand-woven with patterns of pure simplicity and displayed before the milky eyes of a soulless audience—this was the marrow of the master's art," Zulu praised.

Even though Zulu was clearly Negroid, Blue considered the strange little man as alien as if he had come from another planet. To Blue, Zulu was neither black nor remote kin. Bama had put out that the dwarf was a witch doctor who practiced voodoo and ate frogs. All false, of course. In fact, for many of us in Deen, Zulu was as near as we had ever been to a real intellectual.

"Just how smart you reckon you are?" Blue asked the midget.

"Many talents are mine," Zulu crowed, "not the least of which is to keep the cow-eyed out there from seeing me as I truly am. I am the essence of humility and have no zeal to show my real self beside a common rubble who care for nothing but their own gross appetites and greed."

"It ain't you so smart," Blue said. "It's just you so little."

Which was near the truth. Although our unsuspicious audience would have been an asset to any magician, Zulu's act did not require the ingenuity of a Houdini. The key to Zulu's disappearance was our newly installed sliding plank door, opening through the rear of the tool compartment. The only "infinite agility" required was nothing more than to be small enough to crawl through the slit provided and slide the plank door shut. To all of which, from the inside, we added air holes and a flashlight.

Zulu did create a few ingenious touches that cinched his act, at least for a while: He drove into the trick door four cut-off nailheads, which made the sliding plank look nailed tight, and added a latch on the inside. Then in front of the innocuous entrance he nailed a cow turd, sun-dried and crisp, as an authentic deterrent to any extended investigation. Blue was to stay in the driver's seat, glued to the steering wheel. Zulu would fit snugly into the tool cavity. The other provision was that Zulu was to enter the secret door at the exact time that Uncle George would be taking off in the De Havilland. Also, exactly at lift-off, to signal the consummation of Zulu's disappearance, I was to fire a shotgun—a distraction! Zulu vowed that the artless audience would jump at once to the notion that he had escaped in the airplane.

The act worked better that I had imagined. After

I had blasted off with the shotgun and Shelly had flung open our "curtain" gate, the big truck body, even to me, who knew, appeared surprisingly empty. The curious crowd crawled all over, up, around, under, in, and out of the truck and found no clue and no Zulu. Some fathers tried the trick plank with the fake nails, declared it soundly nailed on, and, at sight of the cow pie, abandoned their search.

Exactly as Zulu had predicted, all agreed that he was in the airplane and promptly dismissed the whole mystery. But when Uncle George flew back, no Zulu. After which the theory quickly hardened into fact that Uncle George had taxied the midget to the edge of the woods and Zulu had leapt free and was at that very moment on his way to his comfortable den in the jailhouse.

Shelly's inspired plan had been to get Blue to drive the truck under the hayloft and have Zulu materialize on top of the barn.

But it soon came embarrassingly to pass that—in the tool bin, and with the flashlight, and in the company of Uncle George's Old Raven—Zulu began to materialize prematurely. The first signs of his return were low, rhythmic groans emitted, it seemed, from the bowels of the big truck itself, then a steady hum rising by degrees to a crescendo and breaking off into a series of high me-me-me-mes, like a soloist locating the proper pitch from which to launch into song.

As if from a smothered radio activated by supernatural powers, there arose the hymnal voice of Zulu:

When the storms of life are raging
I will seek a place of refuge:
He will hide me, safely hide me
In the shadow of His hand. . . .

Then out of the secret slot, bottle in hand, Zulu emerged. Sheriff Holdster, who at this moment would joyfully have booted his imbibing deputy out of Alabama and all the way to Zanzibar, was conveniently up in the airplane with Uncle George.

❖

Across the runway, Johnny Holliday was leading Sylvia by the hand to the hamburger table. On weekdays, shade or shine, Holliday, to appear official, always wore a khaki shirt, black tie, and a brown leather jacket with his name in gold up front like a fighter pilot's. I had often seen him eat hamburgers at Grier's Café. He would stuff half a hamburger in one side of his mouth and chew and talk at the same time. For such manners, Mother would have slapped his fat jaws.

Uncle George and Sheriff Holdster had buzzed out of sight. I figured they were up there somewhere having a snort of Old Raven.

No one could have guessed what would happen next. There arose the question among the picnickers as to the nature of Zulu's disappearance and, accordingly, who, if anybody, had won the money. Had Zulu *really* disappeared, vanished in body? Or had he merely hidden himself momentarily from view?—which, they said, was another thing entirely. Time even got into the argument: How *long*, for instance, did a person have to put himself out of sight before he could declare himself *disappeared?*

"I fooled your milky eyes!" Zulu scowled from the rear of the cattle truck, swinging the whiskey bottle in one hand and with the other shaking his fistful of money at the spectators.

Shelly took to the stage behind his little friend, explaining that Zulu had not promised to become nonexistent, that he could have won the money by making them all blink their eyes for an instant or accomplished the same feat by blinking *his own* eyes for an instant, because Zulu had not specified who was to disappear from whom.

Reverend Grayson maintained politely that wheres and whens had nothing to do with whether Zulu did or did not disappear. He said that just because he, a minister, bid his congregation to close their eyes in prayer made neither him, the congregation, nor God—who is everywhere and is always unseen—disappear. Also Reverend Grayson suggested that the elements of deception, greed, mockery, and intoxication invalidated Zulu's act and that all wagered dollars be returned or applied to a worthy cause.

Judge Webster was pleased with his son's display of brains and added that the wagerers had one and all willingly entered into verbal contracts, and "all you gamblers have lost your you-know-whats with your eyes wide open!"

Mother closed the whole dispute by declaring that all arguments were as right as they were wrong, thus neutralized, and proposed patriotically that all the bets go for war bonds. To which Zulu graciously agreed and handed Mother the money.

Seeing that Uncle George was flying back with Sheriff Holdster, Shelly scooped up Zulu, tossed the whiskey out of sight into my mother's sedan, and hustled the little preacher off for safekeeping.

III

What happened next I had no more to do with than with the beating of my heart or the digestion of the egg I ate for breakfast. I was set and ready to *happen*. For just what I didn't know. At least today I can better understand a crime of passion or unpremeditated murder.

Everything was in place: Uncle George was taking a break, nursing a jar of iced tea and biting off the end of a hot dog. The De Havilland was waiting, lined up on the runway, hot and ready to fly. Queeny was within arm's reach, watching me, studying my eyes. She had not had her airplane ride today, and by word from her mother's mouth, she already had permission to fly with Uncle George.

Then it started happening. . . . I whispered to Blue. Then to Queeny. There wasn't a hesitating bone in Queeny's body. Janis and Sylvia were playing with Clayton's little red parachute, rolling it up, tossing it into the air, and watching it float down. Clayton was laughing. He took the sharpshooter's medal off the handkerchief strings and pinned it over Sylvia's breast. That did it.

I grabbed Queeny by the hand and we sped to the De Havilland, boarded her, plopped down together in the front cockpit, Queeny tight between my knees. Blue knew what to do. One flip of the prop did it. At full throttle, Queeny and I were off toward the Black Angus bull at the far end of the strip—faster, lighter. . . . I never looked back but lifted the De Havilland up and over the slow bull, and over the trees on the hickory ridge.

With Queeny between my knees, the stick between her thighs, and the De Havilland at my command, I put on a whirring, spontaneous show: turns, banks, stalls, spins, and skimming treetops high across the picnic pasture so that all we could see down there were chins and Adam's apples. Queeny was as free and uninhibited at flying as she was at fishing. Jesus! Sweet, sweet revenge!

Afterward all were still agog when Queeny and I crawled out of the cockpit. My hand that had held the stick was trembling. But for the moment, my bliss overwhelmed all fear.

As Queeny and I approached, Sylvia and Clayton were standing alone by first base. Sylvia was fondling Clayton's red bandanna handkerchief and adjusting the sharpshooter's medal over her breast.

Like Lindbergh come to Paris, I tossed my head, flipping back a wisp of hair. "I told you," I fired directly into Sylvia's eyes, "I can *fly* the sonofabitch!"

IV

However rewarding my aerial exhibition, it complicated my hopes for the rest of the evening. Father said, "For Christ's sake, have you lost your cotton-picking mind?" Mother, with a wink, cocked her head sideways and looked at me like a cat deciphering a strange noise. Uncle George's uncensored message to me would have peeled the bark off an ironwood tree.

Except for Queeny's warm body, the hayride for me was a disaster and Clayton an ever-present pain in the ass. Uniforms indeed had their privileges, and for Queeny's and Mrs. Slaughter's sake I did not want to seem unmindful of Clayton's early patriotism.

I drove the truck into the barn. Blue, Shelly, and I removed the burlap from the cattle body and pitched in a load of new hay for the ride. Clayton stood by and had a nip from his pocket bottle. Shelly informed Blue and me that the hayride would take two hours driving at 15 mph, an hour and a half at 20 mph, and an hour at 25 mph.

Although my date with Sylvia was *understood*, it was not formally spoken for, so it happened by chance and proximity that Sylvia paired off with Clayton. The hayride was crawling with goofy, giggling bodies. Horace Clark was picking his guitar and singing "Mama don't 'low no low-down hangin' 'round." Gloria Culpepper, who had torn her skirt, was whining and complaining that the cattle truck "smells like cow you-know-what." Earl Shepherd was goosing Janis in the ribs, and Janis was squirming and squawking that the hay was "ha ha—full of little pricks." Uncle George said, "Absolutely *no* smoking." Guy Gillis and Alice Adams, who were sweethearts, sat on top of the cab, holding hands. Queeny piled into me, and down we went into the hay next to Zulu's secret door. From across the hay I could see Sylvia's legs and Clayton's high-gloss military shoes. It was getting dark, and I told Blue he'd better drive twenty miles an hour. Later, after the hay had sifted over Sylvia's legs and Clayton's shoes, I told Blue to speed up to thirty miles an hour. Then back into the hay with Queeny, who was saying that the fresh grass smelled like green sunshine. Clayton's military laughter filtered through the hay. I could see only a patch of Sylvia's white calf. I tossed back onto Queeny with shameless abandon, and, an hour later, when we pulled up to the hay barn, my lips were sore.

It was the last time I saw Clayton Slaughter.

V

Father and Mother drove the pickup home and left Mother's sedan for Sylvia and me. The bottle of Old Raven was on the front seat, where Shelly had tossed it. The immaculate, quart-sized blackbird was looking squarely at me. This was my first undiluted encounter with hard liquor. I swallowed off an inch of the old bird before the flames could ignite my innards. Sylvia had not forgotten our date after all. When I saw her coming, I took another gulp and slipped the bottle under the front seat.

On the way home, I said, "What were you doing in the hay with Clayton?"

"Well, what about you and Queeny—and showing off in the airplane!"

"Did you kiss him?" I asked.

"Who?"

"You know damn well who."

"You should ask!" Sylvia said. "You and Queenie rolling around in the hay and your mouth looking like mashed strawberries."

Old Raven was lifting my spirits.

"Did you?" I insisted about the kiss.

"What if I did kiss him?" Sylvia said. "He's going to war. He may be shot or killed or something."

"Holy Jesus, I'm going to war too. *I* may be shot or killed or something."

"Silas, quit cussing and using the Lord's name in vain. You're jealous. You're even jealous of Johnny Holliday." In truth, I was not jealous of Holliday. He was too old, too puff-jawed, and too high-voiced. Shelly had more brains and talent in one fingernail than Holliday had in his whole fat head. Clayton was another matter.

"Goddammit, I ain't taking his name in vain. I *mean* it."

"You're making such a fuss," Sylvia said. "I was just being patriotic—and watch where you're going!" The solitary road was wavering, spreading into a big V ahead of me.

"You were supposed to be *my* date. Remember?"

"Silas, for goodness' sake. This was a *picnic*. You're acting just like a little bitty boy."

"And you're running around like a little tweedle twat, kissing uniforms. Suppose kissing ain't enough? How patriotic you gonna get?"

"Silas Simeon!" Sylvia flared.

When I went around to open Sylvia's door, she was already out, standing in the moonlight. Although I still had all the trimmings and towheaded edges of boyhood about me, Sylvia was exquisitely the finished feminine product. But now I would have the last kiss. I stopped her at the gate under the chinaberry tree where, among the branches years before, she had kissed me good and hard and had given me the tiny treasure chest containing the primroses and her "Forever" note.

"I've still got my primrose," I said, looking up into the green.

"Well, for goodness' sake. I've still got mine too."

"I've got mine at home, pressed in my Bible."

"I'll bet it looks a sight."

"It's flat and thin as tissue," I said. "But it's still pink."

"I declare," Sylvia said, still exasperated. The moon was capped around Sylvia's head like a silver bowl. This kiss was to be perfect—soft but firm, impassioned but restrained, long enough but not so long as to suggest that I was not master of my own desire—and it would be I, not she, who pulled away first.

I closed gently upon Sylvia. Her lips were soft and moist. She suddenly jerked away.

"Silas Simeon, you've been drinking!" The moon fell behind a cloud. "Haven't you?" she said.

I left her standing at the gate.

Was *not* noticing Clayton's breath patriotic too? Jesus.

❖

When I got home I sat in Mother's car and had another go at Old Raven and watched the moon rise.

I imagined myself flying the shark-like P-40 fighter in combat. Rolling over and bringing a German fighter into my sights, I blazed away with my fifty-calibers . . . then the thin, fatal stream of smoke . . . the pilot bailing out . . . I waved him luck . . . he waved back . . . and, at last, the disintegration of the fated plane sinking to earth like a smoldering leaf . . .

Another belt of Old Raven went down hot and solid.

Music fluttered through my brain:

O'er the ram-parts we watched
were so gal-lant-ly stream-ing . . .
And the roc-kets' red glare,
the bombs burst-ing in air . . .

The light bulb on the front porch became detached. The moon had developed a hernia. Caesar was sitting on the top step, licking his paw and combing his ears. Somewhere out there, a poem floated by:

Breathes there the man with soul so dead
Who never to himself hath said,
"This is my own, my native land . . ."

Old Raven again. This time warm and easy . . .

In my reverie, my glorious war was over. I was stepping off a Greyhound bus, my uniform pressed to perfection, my flat sleeve folded and pinned up to accentuate its solemn, philosophical emptiness. . . . Mother and Father were there, Father trying to pick up something on his portable radio. . . . Sylvia was there. . . . Sylvia did not know. . . . I had not told her. . . . she could not see the folded sleeve. . . . Her face, in silhouette against the setting sun, was draped in golden tresses. . . .

Back to Old Raven once more.

The moon had doubled. Caesar was joined by another, identical cat, grooming itself with simultaneous motions. What now? I was standing in the middle of a sea of Bermuda grass that was our front lawn. The world was tilted dangerously sideways. Suddenly I was sick, sick, on the grass; and down, down, I went on the undulating green.

"J-e-s-u-s . . ." I wailed into the grass.

When I looked up, there was Mother, gliding smoothly at right angles to the moons. She was floating down the front steps and sailing my way across the green, her white skirt flowing as calmly as a silk kerchief given to a breeze—Mother, my North Star, never changing unless I did. . . .

The world was capsizing now, upending like the *Titanic,* into the perpendicular. I dug my fingers into the kinky Bermuda sod to save myself from sliding off the face of the earth. . . .

"Silas," came Mother's worried sigh as I clung to the last of this world. "Is that *you?*"

Chapter Nine

Our graduation ceremony and junior-senior prom of June 1, 1943, was about as joyful as doomsday. My date for the evening was, of course, Sylvia. The only uplifting spirit of the celebration was the war, that scarlet glory that lay on both sides of us, two oceans away.

It's a good thing the truth seldom tiptoes up on us, tapping us cordially on the shoulder, but instead slams down like iron upon our heads, crushing us to earth before we can run away. After which, the shock that often dooms may stun and save us. First there came the opening blast that cratered open my mind; then all the other disasters teetering on the brink tumbled in after it.

The prom followed hard upon the graduation ritual. I was to deliver the valedictory address, an honor too ordinary to fit Shelly's unique talents, too easy for Clayton to have won had he chosen to remain in school and contend. Our principal sat on stage behind the podium, fingering a note. In frustration at exactly how to honor the unusual Shelly and placate his formidable parents, Mr. Winters and the high school teachers had arranged a "Special Achievement Award," after which Shelly was to play a composition of his own called "Kubla Khan," inspired by Samuel Taylor Coleridge. Sylvia, who amid many raised eyebrows had been chosen salutatorian, sat to our left, beside Reverend Grayson. In my most awful nightmares I could not have imagined why she was weeping softly into her handkerchief.

Mr. Winters's announcement came like a slammed door with the bolt shot home: "Corporal Clayton Slaughter has been killed on Guadalcanal." It was Queeny who had handed Mr. Winters the note. Clayton was Deen's first war dead.

I shivered at the image of Clayton folding under machine gun fire, then was stung to think of the painful repercussions this would surely have on the sensitive Mary Slaughter. In the dim auditorium I could see Queeny's face pressed close to her mother's. I wondered if Queeny was crying and could only guess what response Clayton's death had called forth in the irredeemable Cale Slaughter.

Clearing his throat, Reverend Grayson rose and invoked a moment of silent prayer. My memorized speech departed. I would make no effort to recover it.

"Amen," Reverend Grayson said, and sat down.

After the silence, I stood up facing the shadowed audience and, without approaching the podium, said, "Clayton Slaughter died for his country." I listened to my words soak into the walls of the auditorium. Then I walked backstage, dumped my graduation robe, and closed myself in the bathroom.

❖

I looked at myself in the mirror. Since the previous summer my face had broadened, and my cotton mop had aged to sunshine yellow. The continents of freckles on my cheeks had merged into a cloudy tan, and my jaw had thickened. It was then, as I looked into my eyes, that I felt my own disasters toppling into the crater that Clayton's shock had created in my brain.

I say *my* disasters because how could I have known anything about them unless they had passed through *me*, filtered into *my* bones? Especially now. How, after Clayton's Guadalcanal, was I ever to know exactly who Clayton was or had been? How could he have become so fixed in my Jar of Marbles or in all of us? How can we get so mixed up with each other, be so close together, yet touch each other so minutely, be so far apart?

I could feel Shelly's particular disaster coming on as sure as autumn. The boys in our senior class had already been examined and classified by the military in March; induction was deferred until after graduation. As I had rightly figured, I was slated for the Army Air Corps. With my flying skills, what else could they have done? Shelly never imagined that he might not follow me directly into flight school. Once there, beyond his mother's will, Shelly expected to fly at long last, to get his body airborne.

Beyond his night dream flights, which Shelly could evoke at will, there was but one other way to fly: by sheer concentration—"introcognitive realization," Shelly called it. He had struck upon the idea while digging through a shelf of medieval mystics in his father's library. At times, under Shelly's spell, I almost believed his theory of flight would work. Shelly imagined that by generating a pure beam of concentration, he could overcome gravity and soar on psychic energy alone. The secret, he insisted, was to summon up an uncompromising belief, a sustained and absolute faith in one's commitment to weightlessness, at which instant one could release the body freely to space and project oneself outward at astronomical speeds. However much I enjoyed indulging in Shelly's dreams, something pulled me back at the threshold of absolute commitment. I never doubted for a moment that Shelly believed in his theory or had the faith to carry it through. I was just as sure that physical flight alone would be a letdown for Shelly. Also, and sadly, Shelly refused to acknowledge that our military aircraft were instruments of destruction that violated his very soul.

Shelly's rejection by the military was firm and irreversible. He was declared 4F. Surely they could have found no flaw in his splendid body. Judge Webster later said that an army specialist cut Shelly off from the rest of us with the pat phrase "temperamentally unfit for military service." The shock must have hit Shelly like the *Dum dum dum dummm* of Beethoven's Fifth Symphony and stuck there. This was to be not the shock that stuns and saves but the one that dooms. Poor Shelly. In his nocturnal soul he could fly at speeds and altitudes that transcended anything I could accomplish in Uncle George's De Havilland.

Johnny Holliday was the only other 4F I knew in Deen. Perforated eardrums. Holliday could hear as well as the rest of us. And see better. On Saturday, when Queeny worked at Grier's Café, Johnny, in the back booth, never missed a chance to lay a hand on Queeny's honest ass. And Shelly rejected for what? Brains. More brains, by God, than the army could measure. So okay, Shelly was a strange brain and a little stuck on math, music, and super flying. But at the induction center at Fort McPherson he was the talk of the staff officers. Shelly made the highest scores ever in math and in Morse code. He exhausted all tests in numerical and algebraic abstractions and could distinguish da-ditty-dit characters with as many as thirty-two elements! And Johnny Holliday—with his mushroom cheeks, his high tenor voice, his yellow Pontiac, and his goddamn rabbit eyes—was as happy as shit with his perforated eardrums. Christ almighty.

From the moment of his humiliation, Shelly slipped deeper and deeper into himself, completely giving up his visits to Zulu. He cut short his company with me and kept our conversation tightly drawn to his musical theory of the coordination of the fluid color qualities in sound and the possibility of recovering through psychic concentration the voices and songs of those, even Jesus, who lived ages ago.

Zulu detected at once the fatal despair of his giant friend and, borrowing from Shakespeare, eulogized: "Now cracks a noble heart."

❖

Through the bathroom transom, I could hear Sylvia in broken voice struggling through her speech. I did not know that Clayton's death was not the cause of her distress.

For three hundred dollars, our class had hired an eight-piece band from Montgomery, and I could hear the musicians warming up in the gym. Sylvia had practiced for a week to perform with the band. She was to sing Judy Garland's "Over the Rainbow."

II

Another disaster that was falling painfully into being pertained to my faithful shadow, Blue Bobiden. Bama, the grand creator of Old Black Crow and Mr. Glumbergrumble, had died that winter, and Blue had swiftly vanished to Cleveland to live with his aunt. The morning that Blue left our house for the bus, I was aware that Bama's death had been an important one for our family, but I did not suspect that, for me, the real death would be part Blue's and part mine.

I went with Mother to take Blue to the bus. As was proper, he sat in the back seat. He had tied up all his belongings in a flat, suitcase-sized cardboard box. When we got to the station, Mother gave Blue five dollars and took his hand in both of hers and said, "We are important to each other, Mr. Blue Bobiden, and I trust that you will keep your mind sound enough to remember it." Blue bowed like a gentleman and, to my surprise, extended to me our rare Confederate hundred-dollar bill. I had forgotten all about it—the fragile old relic with our blood dabbed on each end. Blue wanted me to have it.

There was nothing else to do. I tore it in two. I kept Blue's half and gave Blue mine.

"We'll put them together again one of these days," I said. "Maybe after the war."

"Yeah," Blue said, and we shook hands. It was the first time we had done that to each other.

To say flatly that Blue had "gone to Cleveland" conveys none of the crippling void he left in me. Like a great whale, Yankeeland had swallowed Blue up whole and alive. His sudden absence was like waking up the next morning and finding one of my legs gone.

In an odd way—but perfectly clear to me—Blue and I were, and had been, closer than brothers, closer *because* he was black and I was white, closer because we were *not* brothers. Though we lacked the mutual blood that locks siblings in family bond, its very absence allowed us almost complete freedom from those ties that also breed jealousy, suspicion, and hate. As illogical as it may seem, the old South segregation that held us as verily apart as the poles of our planet likewise ran an invisible but single course through the center of our common being and gave our friendship a sly forbiddenness, an excitement with more vitality than from no segregation at all. So to say that I merely missed Blue would be outright disloyalty, because of all the marbles in my jar, Blue was as close to me as I was to myself.

❖

I was very much a part of another not-so-small disaster. I did not deserve to be valedictorian and knew it. In spite of his incomprehensible, often bizarre, talents, Shelly should have had this honor. Mother, who scorned "well-roundedness" as mediocrity, knew it, too, and said so to me and everybody else. Shelly accepted my valedictory joyfully. He didn't care a butter bean about the honor or the whole ceremony, and in the shock of Clayton's death he even refused to strike a note of his "Kubla Khan" creation.

Heavier on my mind was Clayton himself, who in all academic matters, when he had wished, had clearly been my superior. What if Clayton had not volunteered for the Marines but had waited, like me, to be drafted, had stayed safe in school and competed for top grades? It was a sinking trap I had walked straight into. How could I have avoided it? But a few moments before, I had spoken *for* Clayton, not *against* him, had I not? And what was I to do now? Stand inert on the stage like a fool or walk away, my own fool, on my own legs?

That Sylvia had been an unfair choice for salutatorian was acknowledged secretly and later by almost everybody, including the teachers who had chosen her. Being the preacher's daughter didn't hurt

Sylvia's chances. Sweet, shapely Sylvia, with her honest blue eyes, could not but have charmed Coach Garrett and Mr. Winters, and her Virgin Mary radiance could not have done lesss than please the others. And although Sylvia took elocution lessons, sang under Gretta's eminent instruction, studied ballet, and aspired to Hollywood stardom, it was Janis, our little firecracker, who should have won the honor on spontaneity and wit alone. So standing in the middle of a seesaw between the incomparable Shelly and our now dead Clayton, here was I, Silas O'Riley Simeon, a hypocrite. And returning to the stage, sharing dubious honors with Sylvia, I would feel like an accomplice to a crime.

Through the transom, I now heard Mr. Winters droning on about Clayton and war and the lonesome duty and deaths of our sons on the far-flung battlefields of the world. And here I was, nailed on the wall, framed squarely in a bathroom mirror! I took my comb and swept the yellow tab of hair off my brow. The image of Queeny and her mother huddled together in the auditorium returned. I wanted to rock Queeny in my arms, but in their grief I could not tell mother from daughter. I blocked a tear from my eye. The Montgomery band across the way was playing little clips of "Sentimental Journey."

I wondered if Sylvia was crying again.

III

My instincts about Johnny Holliday were right. About Sylvia I had been stone blind. I hope God to damn me to everlasting hell if I had ever dreamed of Sylvia's danger. If I had known, I would have hung Holliday by his balls from the Presbyterian steeple. Zulu quit the junior-senior play three days before I did. To begin with, the play was a butchered condensation called "*Romeo and Juliet:* For High School Production—Adapted from the Original." At the time, even to me, the editor's attempt to "modernize" Shakespeare left key scenes flat and, worse, laughable. Mrs. Crawford, our drama coach, called for assistance from Mother, Zulu, and Johnny Holliday. Holliday had once played Romeo in college. Mother was the only one in Deen who knew more about Shakespeare than Zulu did, and Zulu knew all the leading tragic roles from Romeo to Lear. Zulu didn't consider Romeo to be truly tragic because, he said, Romeo was too young to realize what was happening to him. Zulu's first scan of the mutilated drama made the dwarf explode: "Some literal cabbage brain has deflowered the glorious word, violated the bard in his holy tomb and left his sacred bones asunder and askew." Mother agreed, although less energetically. Mrs. Crawford, who knew her Cicero well, knew little Shakespeare and had only recently read the "adapted" play under her charge. She judged this play "real sweet but too sad." To Zulu's joy, Mother confided to us that dear Mrs. Crawford was too puritan and straitlaced to understand that Romeo and Juliet weren't just mouthing off "sweet nothings" but really had the "hots" for each other. At which Zulu did a back flip of approval.

From the beginning I had planned to worm out of the Romeo part and, finally, the whole play. After their scoffing at what Zulu called "that unholy script," Mother and Zulu were mainly responsible for my reneging on the play. Their disapproval of the corrupted drama gave me an out.

Sylvia—who else?—was to play Juliet. She adored the part and cried over the scene in which she must die. I myself would have perished of humiliation to have done the love stuff on the stage with her. In two of the "doctored" scenes (Shakespeare would not have recognized his play), Sylvia and I, according to Holliday, were to lock in hard embrace. Holliday, using Sylvia as a model, showed me how to do the kissing. Mrs. Crawford closed her eyes. Zulu puffed up like a toad. Mother touched my ribs with her elbow, nodding my attention to Holliday's exhibition. I could have thrown up. From the very first, when Johnny Holliday started singing in our church choir, I'd figured if you stuck a pin in his plumskin face, sweet yellow juice would ooze out. After Holliday's kissing demonstration, Shakespeare's love scenes made me sick to my stomach. Sylvia was carried away with her Juliet role and hung on Holliday's every word and gesture as if Hollywood and stardom were just around the corner.

Zulu and I quit rehearsals, and it became known that, to keep the play alive, Holliday was to play Romeo. After rehearsals he drove Sylvia home. Queeny gave up the nurse's part when she learned that she'd have to wear a black snaggletooth and a wig. Mother tolerated my withdrawal from the play with obvious relief. Shelly was prompter, and by the first rehearsal had memorized the entire script. Mrs. Grayson thought Holliday "talented." Mother thought him gross. Zulu pronounced him an insufferable ham and vowed that we would "all be struck down by pox or plague if ever such corruption sees the light of stage."

"Fortunately!" Mother sighed later, alluding to Zulu's forecast; for a flu epidemic indeed did sweep our school before final rehearsal, and the play, a month before the prom, was scratched forever.

Through the bathroom transom, I could hear Mr. Winters approaching the close of his sorrowful message. The musicians in the gym were gently trying out a few bars of Glenn Miller's "Moonlight Cocktail."

IV

After the auditorium ordeal, Queeny and Mrs. Slaughter disappeared. Sylvia had shed her graduation gown. She came backstage, and we stepped outdoors through the side entrance. There was a full moon. Across Sylvia's profile I could see up the main street all the way to the courthouse. Sylvia clung to my arm as lightly as a ghost. She was wearing a white-lace, V-neck evening dress and upon her breast a red camellia I had picked from Mother's bush. The mossy clay walkway to the gym shone like velvet in the moonlight. Sylvia had bowed her head into her handkerchief and was sobbing.

Why was she still crying? For our courageous Clayton Slaughter—the first of us to meet the enemy, who one afternoon the previous summer caught our imaginations (and Sylvia's fancy) and who had now jolted us with his ultimate sacrifice? Or was it the incomprehensible, glory-spangled war itself—so far away, so close—that now crushed Sylvia's softness to tears? Or was it the unwelcome contradiction of the rising music now gloomed after all those crimson lips were shocked from smiles to oooohs, as the silent fact of Clayton's death fell over us like a shadow?

Or was it that I, Silas Simeon, whose arm Sylvia clung to, might also make the ultimate sacrifice? Was it I for whom Sylvia cried?

The dance was getting under way. Sylvia and I walked to the big side window of the gym and looked in. I pulled Sylvia into my shoulder.

"Clayton was a rifleman," I said. "He got *his* on the ground. If I get mine, it'll be in the air. The only difference is it's cleaner up in the air, flying." I had on my summer suit, which was too small, but Mother said I wouldn't be needing civilian clothes for a while. "I'm looking forward to you singing Judy's rainbow song. You're better than Judy," I said, and kissed her on the ear. The bandleader was as owl-eyed as Eddie Cantor, and his drummer had arms and legs like a spider's. The band was finishing its version of Glenn Miller's hit "It Had to Be You."

"I'm not going to sing," Sylvia said.

This I wouldn't believe. Not after all her hopes and practice. This was *her* night. "Come on!" I said. "Clayton wouldn't like you taking on like this." I was taking pleasure in thinking of Clayton as a fallen comrade.

"I can't," Sylvia sniffed.

"Be strong," I said. "A lot more of us'll get it before this thing is over."

"I think I'm going to be sick," Sylvia said.

"Jesus, not now," I said. We watched the crowd building up inside. The band started playing "Moonlight and Shadows."

"I'm not going in," Sylvia said.

"You've got to. Your mama'd have a fit, and

everybody's expecting you to sing. You're our *star,*" I said.

Sylvia put her face back into her handkerchief. I pulled her hair aside and looked at her eyes.

"I promise," I said prophetically, "I won't get killed in the war. Okay?" and kissed her damp cheek. In the full moon I could see her wet lashes.

Shelly was following the tiny Janis, his date, onto the gym floor—a Chihuahua leading a Great Dane. Shelly had refused an invitation to play the piano for—or with—the orchestra. He didn't condemn popular music but said it was like pretty colored balloons filled with air and set loose without direction. He felt sorry for the balloons. And for all his physical grace and coordination, Shelly *never* danced. Before the evening was over, Janis would make sure she danced with every boy on the floor, twice. Shelly plopped down glumly on the coach's bench and yawned. Janis darted across the basketball court to a covey of girls ogling the city band boys. In special chairs opposite the orchestra, Mother and Father sat with Judge Webster and Gretta, Reverend and Mrs. Grayson, and Sheriff Holdster—all chaperons. Uncle George was my special guest. Visibly in communion with Old Raven, he entered with the gypsy-haired lady who sold tickets through the mousehole at Gullet's picture show.

Johnny Holliday was monkeying around with the microphone, blowing his breath into it for instrumental effect. Apparently he had arranged with the bandleader to do some vocals. When Sylvia saw him, she collapsed upon my shoulder and wept.

"Silas . . . Silas . . . I'm . . ."

"I know. You're sick," I said.

"No."

"Scared?"

"Yes."

"To sing?"

"No." Sylvia took a deep breath, as if she were about to pull herself underwater forever.

"Then what?" I asked.

Holliday had on a white coat and a black tie and looked like a Chicago gangster.

"I'm pregnant," Sylvia said.

"I'm *pregnant,*" she repeated. *"Johnny—"* she said, and clasped her hand over her mouth lest more of this crime escape.

V

Through the gym walls I could hear Johnny Holliday's tenor trying out a new ditty that went:

Mairzy doats
And dozy doats
And liddle lamzy divey
A kiddley divey too
Wouldn't you?

Sylvia was saying, ". . . What are we going to do?"

It wasn't until much later that the full irony of her words struck me. And yet at the time two things were perfectly clear. "We" was absolutely the right word; and this catastrophe of Sylvia's, though not of my doing, was *ours*. It was, after all, *my* Jar of Marbles.

I am amazed that at that very moment I did not tear the arteries from Holliday's throat. Instead, out of the explosion, a calm terror poured into me, and a decision came upon me before I had time to think. The energy to act was not mine alone. It was ours. The terror I felt was as pure and deadly as radium and acted like a drug in my blood. It was to be an action of far greater danger to Sylvia than was the tiny intruder inside her—if indeed such an intruder existed. There would be time to hate Holliday, time to dredge up from my brain pictures of his loathsome groin and the groans of this crimson joy. In my shock, I felt shrunken to a grain of sand dropped onto a beach by the roaring sea.

"Do you *know?*" I asked fearfully.

"Yes. Dr. Roundtree felt it."

"Does your mama—"

"No!"

"Reverend Grayson?"

Dr. Roundtree had given Sylvia until the next day

to speak the unspeakable to her parents. Had this disaster happened before play rehearsal? Or after our Sunday school young people's meeting? How blind had I been?

"Oh, please, God, please damn me, damn me. I'm going to kill myself!" Sylvia cried.

"Shut up," I said, tugging her back down the clay path.

"I swear I will. I swear— Where are we going?"

"To Selma," I said. I was a centipede on a thousand legs, all carrying me in one direction. "To see Uncle Sim. He's a doctor. He'll know what to do. We're going to Selma."

"How?"

"In the De Havilland."

"At night?" Sylvia looked at me in disbelief.

I pointed at the full moon.

"Silas, no!"

"Shut up. Get in the car!" It was Mother's sedan. "I can fly to Selma blindfolded." It was a lie. But with the full moon and all the old landmarks, I could fly by the river or by the Old Selma Road.

I made straight for Uncle George's barn hangar, where I filled the De Havilland's gas tank, then pulled her out into the moonlight and onto the landing strip. When Sylvia started to cry again, I slapped her so hard across the cheek I felt pins and needles in my palm.

"Get that silly dress off. You can't fly in that dangling bag." I had found an old pair of Blue's overalls. "Put these on. They're Blue's," I said.

"I'm going in my evening dress," she said, unconsciously slipping her shoes off.

"No! You've got to sit in my lap and straddle the stick. Take that dress off. Now."

"I'm not going to wear a nigger's dirty overalls."

"Now!" I shouted. I slapped Sylvia sideways, then took her by the shoulders and shook her until her hair flopped. "They're not dirty. They're Blue's. Take it off!" I shouted in her face, then snapped her around, unbuttoned her, and slipped the dress straps off her shoulders. She wiggled the long dress down around her feet. Her slip was caught up at her waist, and she stood bare-legged in the moonlight. Faintly from the gym, I could hear Holliday's voice:

Mairzy doats
And dozy doats . . .

I was sweating. I took my tie off and dropped Blue's overalls in the back cockpit. Sylvia trampled out of her evening dress, adjusted her slip, and gathered the expiring gown in her arms.

"Ball that dangling thing up so it won't get clogged up in the pulleys," I said.

Then Sylvia was asking vacantly, "What will your

Uncle Sim do? What will Daddy think? Will they be looking for us? Will the dance be over? Will it rain? What are *we* going to do?"

"No, it won't rain. It's a watermelon moon." That was one of Blue's expressions for a full moon. "It never rains on a watermelon moon," I said.

Will the dance be over? Jesus. How silly can you get? I needed Sylvia at the controls. I gave instructions. Sylvia had rolled her evening gown into a ball. I pushed her up onto the lower wing of the De Havilland. She would not part with the dress and threw it into the front cockpit. I would follow. Sylvia's energy was deepening into mine. No matter how many legs or how crooked the path, a centipede always *knows* he is headed straight and in the right direction.

I stood in front of the De Havilland with my fingers on the prop. In the cockpit, Sylvia worked the choke and ignition exactly as I ordered . . . *Contact,* and we were ready.

Up and aboard, I crammed Sylvia into my lap, the stick between our knees, and we buzzed off toward the end of the pasture where Uncle George's Angus cows lay under the oaks like lumps of night. Then we were up and over the hickory ridge, flying into the moon. Sylvia's hair was in my face. Something was fluttering and gathering around the pedals and my feet.

I would bank the De Havilland, take a left turn, then make a pass over the barn to get my bearings, head east for the Old Selma Road, then north all the way up the squirming highway, at the end of which the Selma airfield lay south of the big river bridge. I had flown the daylight route a dozen times with Uncle George.

The gathering and fluttering around my feet was Sylvia's voluminous evening gown. It had become unballed and was uncoiling slowly on the cockpit floor. While I was doing my left turn, the wayward garment crept along the base wall of the cockpit and became entangled in the pulley leading to the right aileron. This was a serious problem. I was stuck in a slow, tightening earthward arc toward the west profile of the community—the courthouse, the Presbyterian church, Judge Webster's observatory, the water tower . . .

The gown became suddenly inflated and began crawling over me like an octopus.

"Get it off! Get it off!" I screamed to Sylvia. In my frenzy, I was snatching and tearing at all the fluttering white I could lay hold on. Sylvia was struggling frantically with the bulbous gown, pulling it taut from the jammed pulley.

"I told you, I told you!" she cried. "We're going to die!" There was anger in her voice, not terror. In my assault upon the gown, I ripped away Sylvia's slip and heaved it upward; it vanished in the night, leaving Sylvia in the moonlight, snow white in her panties and bra.

Stuck in our slow arc, we might miss the village but not the water tower. The evening dress was becoming a tragedy.

My pocket knife! I held the stick rigid with our knees. Quick—my pocket knife! The blade. The jammed gown. I fingered. I cut. I was cleared. Pulley, pedals, and cable were now working. I pulled the slow De Havilland up and eyeball close around the huge bowl of the water tower. DEEN ALABAMA, it read. As we swung low over the gym, I caught a waft of trumpet and drums. They were playing "Paper Moon." Sylvia was clutching the severed evening dress to her bosom. Johnny Holliday's voice was stuck in my ear.

And liddle lamzy divey . . .

"Get the hell rid of that thing," I shouted through the wind, as if the innocent garment had been a snake.

I was on my way back to the barn to get a bearing on the Old Selma Road. When we were over the landing strip, I snatched the evening dress from Sylvia and flung it to the winds. It caught for a moment on the tail fin, then blew away. The snowy dress floating down empty in the moonlight looked as if someone had skinned an angel in flight.

VI

It would be about twenty-five minutes to Selma. There was only the faintest trace of lightning southward from Mobile. Sylvia's string of questions began floating through my mind. *What will your Uncle Sim do?* And—Jesus—*Will the dance be over?* And a question of my own: Would getting rid of this intruder be bloodless, like plucking a grape from its vine?

The stars were dimmed by the sky's light, but the old asphalt road below was as clearly defined as a blacksnake. In the moonlight, Sylvia was phosphorous white. Never had I been so close to her. Never so far away. A crude passion to ravish Sylvia in the cockpit seized me, but the thought of Holliday froze all my joints. I was infuriated by the outrageous exhilaration of being pressed so close to Sylvia's special softness where Holliday had dogged her. I could not help but think with pity of the homeless bitch dog that years before had brought Shelly to tears. "There was nothing," Shelly had blubbered, "nothing, nothing she could have done about it." Without hesitation, Shelly had then adopted the brindled bitch. Later, as a prisoner of war, I saw a similar slack-teated bitch, a war dog on her search among the ruins, with her two clumsy pups bobbing along behind her. Within a week, driven by her dry dugs, this same bitch was making her regular rounds with a single pup. How could she have avoided so great a calamity? What dog had straddled her in her period of weakness? Shelly was right about his brindled bitch. There was nothing, nothing she could have done about it.

Soooo—
Mairzy doats
And dozy doats . . .

An idea struck me: I would blame my whole crazy flight this evening on the war. What would not be pardoned on the threshold of so great a crusade? What could I, like Clayton, not do now and be forgiven? Except get killed. Or get Sylvia killed. Or perhaps smash up the De Havilland.

Sylvia's vague terror fled through me. I was numb, a zombie flying in a fog, and yet there above us was the absolute moon, with no clouds except a pink outline of thunderheads far to the south. With a slight tailwind, I made the trip to Selma in less than twenty-five minutes.

The airfield was marked by a single red bulb over the headquarters tower. Without reversing myself to get the headwind, I went straight in, set the De

Havilland down smoothly, and went at once into the main office to phone Uncle Sim. Sylvia stayed aboard. At a solitary desk sat a sleepy watchman, who looked like the straw man in *The Wizard of Oz*.

Aunt Flora answered the phone: Did I not know that Uncle Sim was at this moment in Deen, Alabama, in my own home and was going fishing with Uncle George tomorrow? No, I did not know. And wasn't this the night of our junior-senior prom? Yes. And did George, ha ha, get a date with that gypsyish-looking lady at Gullet's picture show? Yes. And what—for goodness' sake—was I doing in Selma at this unlikely hour? "Silas—good Lord! You are *not* up here in George's airplane! At night! Silas O'Riley Simeon, answer me!" she demanded.

I hung up and went back to the De Havilland.

Sylvia was sitting resolutely in the cockpit. With her thin neck and her hair now bunched up behind her head, she made me think of Amelia Earhart, who had crashed in the Pacific and was raped and eaten by cannibals.

"We've got to fly back home," I said. "That's where Uncle Sim is."

"I'll jump and kill myself," Sylvia said stiffly. "Dr. Roundtree is going to tell Mother and Daddy tomorrow if I don't tell them first."

"Uncle Sim will know what to do," I said. But I had my doubts. Uncle Sim was a positive man, dogmatic and unbending in his diagnoses. With his sharp nose and deep-socketed eyes, he looked like Sherlock Holmes on the prowl. He had estranged many of his patients by bluntly telling them the unhappy truth about themselves.

The engine was hot and kicked off with one flip. I dumped Blue's overalls into the front cockpit.

"It's going to rain," Sylvia said flatly. I was arranging Sylvia's silken buttocks between my legs. Why were silk panties more arousing than a bathing suit? Why had this crude violation of Sylvia kindled in me a passion as wicked as Holliday's? Over Sylvia's shoulder I could see the smooth cleavage between her breasts. I gagged to think of Holliday hovering over Sylvia and smothering her with his hot belly.

If the words sound queer
And funny to your ear
A little bit jumbled and jivey . . .

I gave the De Havilland full throttle and gripped the top of Sylvia's thigh to steady her. She took tight hold of my wrist. The runway was almost as short as Uncle George's pasture strip. A left turn and we were over the Selma river bridge.

It was not that I had seriously misjudged the weather; with the full moon and pursuing disasters,

I had dismissed the weather altogether. The thunderheads were in fact gathering swiftly from the south, but in twenty minutes I would be able to beat them to Deen. I decided to follow the river home. The river was more crooked than the Old Selma Road, but it was broader and would be more reliable should the clouds close in. The moon was still with us. On my right wingtip, it followed us in the river like a silver disk. If we were approaching the thunderheads at seventy miles an hour, they were approaching us at an unknown velocity all their own.

I could not have known that Aunt Flora was at this moment hooked up to our sole telephone operator in Deen and spreading the word of my whereabouts. "That crazy Silas is flying George's airplane home at night! In a *storm!*" Flora was all mouth and no brain.

"It *is* going to rain," Sylvia said above the sound of the airplane. I put my arm around her chest and could feel her heart struggling. An image flashed to me of Clayton withering under machine-gun fire and of Queeny throwing her body upon her dying brother and inserting her fingers into his wounds to stop the blood—and then another image, in Grier's Café, of Holliday, in his cockroach-leather jacket, laying his fat hand on Queeny's ass . . .

A kiddley divey too
Wouldn't you?

I would rather it had been Clayton who had got to Sylvia.

The energy of Sylvia's terror was pouring steadily into me again. In dismissing the clouds, I had also ruled out the wind and the rain. The headwind hit us first, pushing us into slowness.

The De Havilland is a lovely and graceful craft. Its lift and tight turns are thrilling, but in bad weather its wings are sluggish. We were not more than ten minutes downriver when the first threatening clouds arrived, sweeping overhead at incredible speed, so swift that to look down at the slow river was, suddenly, like watching a nickel dropped in molasses. With the De Havilland I was holding my own. The moon shuttered through the clouds, leaving the river downstream in safe view. But when the clouds stacked up and darkened, showing only stitches of lightning, I was forced down to the belly of the river. I prayed for lightning. Uncle George himself had flown by moonlight. Had he flown by lightning?

Then came the beautiful, splintered light; but then, too, the rain came, first starting down in drops as big as scuppernongs, splashing into the cap-bill, celluloid windshield. Then, in a torrent too dense for the prop wind to scoop over our heads, the flood fell down. With both hands I tightened on the stick, squeezing Sylvia in my arms. In slow succession came the lightning: the light—the river—the rain—the rumble; the light—the river—the rain—the rumble . . . A river bend was ahead—the treetops—and now a long thank-you-God stretch of straight river downstream.

The engine developed a cough. The rain was getting to the vitals of the old machine. I forced the throttle, holding it at Full, cutting down, and coming back to Full again. We were losing power, losing altitude. I should have been able to hold the De Havilland, with her double wings, up, but the rain had made her heavy in the air. I pumped the throttle, trying to clear the plugs and tubes and to drive the quenching water out. . . .

Was Sylvia humming?

My only guide now was the ruffled, green-black riverbanks.

Now what? What on earth? Whether out of melancholy or madness or from some pitiable overflow from her well of terror, Sylvia was singing:

Somewhere
Over the rainbow
Way up high . . .

Sylvia was putting her heart and lungs into the lyrics, swaying between my knees with the notes as surely as if she were singing confidently with the Montgomery orchestra back in Deen. She was in control of the song. In a flourish of lightning, she looked back at me wistfully, the wet words on her lips:

Skies are blue . . .

We were coming out from under the rain. I recognized the river bend. We were not more than thirty seconds from Jackson's Ferry. Within minutes we would be at Uncle George's landing strip. The moon flickered through the clouds. The motor resumed its rhythm. Sylvia was in full voice:

Troubles melt like lemon drops
Away above the chimney tops . . .

I could see Jackson's Ferry. But I had forgotten the deadliest trap on the river: the ferry cable that hung between the banks like a gigantic scythe. Two British cadets from Craig Field had met their deaths at the steel cable. One flier had forgotten and too late seen the sagging blade; the other had dared to fly under it and was decapitated. I should have remembered. The sinister cable hung directly before me like a spider's thread. No way but under. I dropped down to the skin of river, following the moon on the tip of my right wing.

Over the rainbow . . .

Please, Jesus— My wheels skipped river twice. The moon was still on my right wingtip. I dared not look back.

Bluebirds fly . . .

My bearings were right again. The galvanized top of Uncle George's barn would be easy to spot.

Why, then, oh why can't I?

VII

Uncle George's bright barn top was like a dime in the distance. It lay in the moonlight to the right of Deen and to the left of the river. But my path of approach would be critical. I would not be able to tell the exact angle in moonlight. Should I approach the barn obtusely across the pasture rather than broadside? A twenty-degree error, and I was certain to bash my wheels off in the drainage ditch. I could not recall, nor would I have been able to distinguish, a coordinate landmark to make an adjustment and thus fix myself in a straight shot for the runway. Holding the De Havilland on a steady line between the river and the barn, I went into a left turn.

A string of automobile lights was forming on the

outskirts of Deen, but I could not tell where they came from or in what direction they were traveling: west? northeast? or heading north on the main town street? Were the lights moving on the crooked riverside road? Why hadn't Sylvia been chilled by the wind and the rain? She was warm and relaxed, swaying from side to side between my knees. She had not seen the lights and was saying:

"I'll tell Mother and Daddy myself."

I was losing my bearings again.

"What? What? What?" I cried frantically.

I was pointed toward the barn now and descending. The engine was purring. I could hear Sylvia's words perfectly, but they made no sense. "I'll tell Daddy myself," she was saying.

Because of the river and the barn, I knew where I was, but I didn't know precisely where I was *inside* where I was. Had my left turn been too tight and would I hit the low left side of the pasture and pile into trees? Or had my turn been too broad and was I headed for the drainage trench?

The crawling auto lights below blurred and confused me. I lost all confidence. I began to tremble. Sylvia's hair had fallen loose and was in my face again.

"It was just a silly, sentimental song anyway," Sylvia was saying.

I was barely breathing now. "What? What?" I

cried, loud enough for Uncle George's cows below to hear me. I had time, maybe, to pull out, pull the De Havilland up, to make another round. . . .

In the moonlight ahead of us in the pasture was a white spot, a white glob in line with the barn. Before pulling out, I let the De Havilland down a second more, to see. . . .

It was Sylvia's fallen evening dress, in the middle of the runway.

All my bearings rushed back into place. I knew my altitude and my line of flight. I would take the De Havilland in.

"I know now," Sylvia said. Her words made no sense.

I bumped the De Havilland down on Sylvia's white evening gown, taxied to the barn, and killed the motor.

"What? What?" I said, still trembling.

"I said, I know now what I have to do."

VIII

After my blunder down the river, I remember the rest of the evening only in pantomime, as soundless as an old movie without music:

Sylvia and I are stranded in the moonlight beside the De Havilland. Sylvia, barefooted, in bra and panties, is stepping into Blue's overalls and slipping the straps over her shoulders. She is doing this all on her own. She squeezes my hand, trips tender-footed down the runway to retrieve her mangled evening gown, and comes back to me. The caravan of lighted cars is arriving as if at a funeral. I put my summer suit coat around Sylvia's shoulders. Without regret or dishonor, I think: *Thank God for the war and Clayton's death.* Sylvia slips her arms into the sleeves of my coat and clings with one arm to me and with the other to her ruined evening gown. Sheriff Holdster points his official car so that his headlights spot us, then stops. Zulu is with Sheriff Holdster. The car lights almost blind me but not so much that I can't see into the milling crowd. Sheriff Holdster and Zulu come toward us and stand between me and the spectators. Sylvia is squeezing my hand. Holdster stands with his back to us, his hands in the air like a barrier, as if a murder had been committed. How is it that Zulu always comes dressed for the occasion? He has on riding breeches, a gabardine military shirt with epaulets, a white scarf, and a child's aviator helmet, with snap-on celluloid goggles. Hopping around officially, he looks like a fancy Walt Disney bullfrog. Even through the glaring lights I can see Uncle George, who has been in deep company with Old Raven. He is pointing at his airplane and at me, gesticulating wildly. Mother is in the background, fragile, serious, serene. Father is shoving Uncle George back into the station wagon and rolling up the windows and insisting to the picture-show lady that she keep Uncle George shut up. I cannot spot Johnny Holliday in the crowd. Shelly is head and shoulders above everybody. Mother's expression unsettles me. Shelly stalks across the imaginary barrier, scoops up Zulu, plops him down in the front cockpit of the De Havilland, then crawls into the rear cockpit. This is as close as Shelly and his marvelous, doomed brain will ever get to mechanical flight. I can see little Janis's head bobbing among the crowd. There is Mother's face again—plain, direct, controlled. Mother is supporting Mrs. Grayson on one side, and Dr. Roundtree is supporting her on the other. Mrs. Grayson is crying. Reverend Grayson, tall and pale, is hovering close behind as if in conference. They start toward us. It is clear to me at this moment that Sylvia's disaster has been divulged, but so far only to the Graysons and Mother. I can see this in the shape and attitude in which they carry themselves. Sylvia is asking me, "What are we going to do?" I do not see my doctor-Uncle Sim in the crowd. Father is standing guard beside the station wagon. Through the window glass I can see Uncle George's open mouth and the distraught picture-show lady trying to calm his flailing arms. With malice toward none, I think again: *Thank God for the war and*

Clayton's death. What other evidence for forgiveness do I need? Who would now violate so sacred and bloody a sacrifice to settle blame on me? Or on Sylvia? Shelly is working the airplane pedals and stick, so that the elevators and ailerons make the De Havilland look like a fish flipping on the ground. Zulu is standing in the front cockpit, making a double thumbs-up victory sign to me. Everybody here is looking at Sylvia and me. Then Zulu throws me the camellia that was pinned to Sylvia's evening dress. I am surprised. The owl-eyed Montgomery bandleader and his spider-armed drummer are looking in at Uncle George and the picture-show lady. This is no picture show. This is no high school *Romeo and Juliet.* Sylvia is clutching her evening dress to her throat. Dr. Roundtree and his huddling group approach us. I glance through the crowd, trying again to see Johnny Holliday. He is not there. Mother's lips are firm. She looks at me with a seriousness I have never seen in her before. God! Does she suspect *me* of Sylvia's calamity? Oh, God! If, as Mother has said, poetry is like flying, then poetry is dangerous. Mother takes the camellia from my hand and gives it to Sylvia. Zulu leaps off the top wing of the airplane into Shelly's hands, and Shelly carries the dwarf away. Sylvia touches the side of my face with her lips and is asking me the same question again. The solemn confidants assist Sylvia into the

Graysons' car, leaving Mother and me alone beside the De Havilland. On the way home, I discover to my surprise that it is only intermission and that for the others the dance is not over. I can tell that Father does not know about Sylvia's disaster. He is fooling around with the car radio, trying to get the end of a Joe Louis prizefight. He is always fiddling around with radios but never seems to pick up anything. He says I've probably screwed up Doc Sim's fishing trip and that Uncle George is going to have a hunk of my ass for taking off in his airplane. Mother asks, "What did Sylvia say about Johnny Holliday?" I am silent. But I understand from her question that Mother knows all. Except for a few pink sky veins left by the thunderstorm, the moon is still full, though smaller. On the road home, I watch Judge Webster's observatory approach. It stands out like a lighthouse.

I think about what Sylvia kept saying to me: "What are we going to do?"

Chapter Ten

It had started snowing lightly.

"Verily, verily, I say unto you . . ." It was Zulu chanting—Zulu, the Bishop, the once Wild Man of Zanzibar. How could anyone predict Zulu? He had come to the funeral—so help me God—dressed as Abraham Lincoln, the Great Emancipator: black trousers, tails, black bunched tie, stovepipe hat, and all. The tall black hat was made of glued-together cardboard. During the procession to the cemetery, Zulu wiggled in between Father and me, supporting with one raised arm a mite of the weight of his giant friend Shelly. In our broken pace, an unlucky bobble sent Zulu's headpiece toppling underfoot.

I was not surprised that Judge Webster permitted the continued presence of the outlandish dwarf. One nod from the Judge put Sheriff Holdster at ease. Though worlds apart in size and sense, Shelly and

Zulu had shared a kindred soul, a bond that had not escaped the Judge's attention.

After eight months, this was my first and last military leave before going overseas. I was standing across the casket from Uncle George, Sheriff Holdster, and Principal Winters. Uncle George, wearing a neck brace, had recently crashed in the Walker Hills, destroying the De Havilland and very nearly himself. Coach Garrett, Father, and I were the other pallbearers. After Sylvia's sin, Reverend Grayson had stolen away into the navy as a chaplain, so the service today was being conducted by our Baptist preacher, Mr. Butterworth, who in eulogy was praising Shelly as "one who never hid his talent under a bushel, one who, on the wings of sound, soared to the rafters of heaven." Butterworth was launching into the Twenty-third Psalm: *though I walk though the valley of the shadow of death* . . .

II

In boot camp, I kept Sylvia's bathing-suit snapshot buried in my billfold, against a spare stick of chewing gum. The photograph showed Sylvia standing cock-hipped, glancing back seductively over her shoulder. During flight training, I pinned the picture behind my barracks calendar so, with a pivot, if I chose, I could tilt the calendar and look at her. Sylvia's left leg had turned dark where the chewing gum sweetener had squeezed out. And so for weeks the snapshot remained unseen.

One night after lights out, musing through my Jar of Marbles, thinking about Queeny and me fishing naked in the Blue Hole and about Sylvia and me and our wild flight down the river, I had a crazy dream: I am flying Uncle George's De Havilland down the Alabama River. Queeny is sitting on the tip of one wing and Sylvia on the other. Queeny is naked, and Sylvia has on an evening dress as big as a japonica bush. The huge dress is extra weight and a drag on the left wing. Sylvia cannot hear me shouting at her to take the bulging garment off, and we go counterclockwise into a tailspin straight down toward the river, where Mother is floating miraculously downstream in her mahogany rocker, writing in her Rose Book, serenely smoking a Picayune cigarette, sipping sherry, and paying no attention whatever to my plight—and all the while I feel perfectly sure that if anything ever happens to Uncle George, the De Havilland will be mine. . . .

Before the crash, I started up out of my dream, pushed the calendar aside for a reassuring glance at Sylvia, and found a succulent, chocolate-backed cockroach whiskering her. Where the chewing gum sweetener had spread, he had nibbled off part of Sylvia's leg. Before I could mash him, he lifted his wings like a dragon and scurried away.

The next night I caught the slinking lecher in the

beam of my flashlight. With my thumbnail, I popped out his yellow entrails and let him fall.

III

The first flakes of snow that fell on Shelly's church-warm coffin quickly vanished. All I could see of Zulu in the small crowd were his tiny black shoes.

As if delivering an edict from the bench, Judge Webster had decreed his son's death a tragic accident and defied anyone to differ. Everyone else, save Mother and me, was content that Shelly had simply and insanely jumped to his death. And why not? Even for those who had cared least, Shelly's last days were spooky. After being shunned by the Army Air Corps and barred from military service altogether, Shelly had shut himself away during the day in the Judge's library, composing wild runs on their grand piano and reading into the metaphysics of P. D. Ouspensky and the lore of the supernatural. At night, on his baby grand, high under the dome of the Judge's observatory, Shelly blasted out his worried music to the stars. The sound carried all the way downtown and tumbled into the Walker Hills beyond. Mother listened sadly to Shelly from our front porch.

Preacher Butterworth continued: *Let not your heart be troubled . . .*

Snow was forming like toadstools on hats all

around. Uncle George's nose was aglow with Old Raven. Behind my uncle stood pleasant, high-cheeked Mary Slaughter, who, before the procession to the graveyard, had whispered to me, "Queeny says, 'Pleeeeeze write.' She loves you so. Queeny's in the women's navy now, you know."

I thought of Queeny and me, naked, pulling the fighting bass from the Blue Hole and of Queeny's bronze hip cocked sideways on Mother's quizzical quilt. I thought of Aunt Rebecca, submerged, lying walleyed and limpid in her stone pool, being eyed by her obese goldfish. I thought of flying in the De Havilland with Sylvia, of being pressed tight in the cockpit against her ivory whiteness.

Uncle Sim had allowed his young intern to do the abortion, and, Mother confided, for an inordinate sum of money, which made the deed ever more malignant and damaging to my soul—to speak nothing of the insidious souls in Deen who had coagulated in the deep like a slumbering octopus, awaiting the first morsel of juicy gossip to drift by before going into action, then slinking back into a silence more deadly than all its tentacles. It was from this abiding silence—from the slow digestion of this lingering organism and from the cold shoulder of our Presbyterian congregation—that I now suddenly realized it was I, not Holliday, who was accused of initiating Sylvia's sin.

The second morning of my leave, only days away

from my war, Mother had rolled me out of bed, saying, "I wrote Sylvia you were coming home," and handed me a note Sylvia had addressed: "To SOS." In the inner corner of the envelope, like ashes, lay her primrose promise of old, its petals crumpled but still pink. Sylvia said we might start over again with a new primrose. So while I stood there in the falling snow, I decided that upon leaving home I'd travel back to base by way of Agnes Scott College, in hopes of finding Sylvia.

In my Father's house are many mansions . . .

I knew in my bones exactly how Shelly died:

On the balcony of Judge Webster's observatory, after blasting out his "Kubla Khan" into the night, Shelly had drawn himself into a pure beam of concentration and—like the opium poet himself—soared to where:

> *. . . the sacred river ran*
> *Through caverns measureless to man . . .*
> *that deep romantic chasm . . .*
> *A savage place! . . . holy and . . .*
> *. . . heard from far*
> *Ancestral voices prophesying war . . .*
> *A sunny pleasure dome with caves of ice! . . .*
> *And drunk the milk of Paradise.*

Then Shelly, with absolute faith in his weightlessness, had stepped off the ledge of Judge Webster's observatory and out into thin air. That was how it happened. Secretly to me, Mother agreed.

I am the way, the truth, and the life . . .

And yet I *was* involved. Shelly was a charter member of my Jar of Marbles. Would he have taken his fatal step if it had not been for me? For my fascination with his weightlessness and astro flights? For the De Havilland, forbidden him, which I had flown with permission and impunity?

Despite all my skills as a single-engine pilot, the Army Air Corps with its infallible logic had made me a bombardier. Compared to the fingertip lightness of the De Havilland, the B-17 was like flying a cow.

So now here stood I, Second Lieutenant Silas Simeon, over Shelly with my *wings*—bombardier's wings, wings hinged onto the belly of a dropping bomb!

Verily, verily, I say unto you, Butterworth read.

A breeze quickened the snow, which had begun to show on the crossarm of Aunt Rebecca's monument. Dear Aunt Rebecca, bound to earth and heaven by a doctrine as rigid as the stone cross she had designed, which pointed her down, and the marble dove that pointed her up; and dear, dear Mother, standing beside this imposing tombstone, serene, as much at peace on the pages of Genesis and Job as with Hamlet's soliloquies or Brer Rabbit's Tar Baby. Aunt Rebecca with her pet goldfish, Bible, and "tea";

Mother with her garden of roses and snapdragons, her Caesar and Miss Gingersnap—as lean as her Picayune cigarette, as inspirited as her dark sherry; while my ineradicable Aunt Rebecca, for all her puritanical virginity, had fallen sadly from her taking of "tea" into her preposterous pool of fat goldfish and cracked her skull. . . .

The hurried snowflakes were sticking now to the lid of Shelly's casket.

To everything there is a season . . .

A breeze had rolled Zulu's pathetic cardboard hat to the foot of Shelly's grave, where it was coming unglued, uncoiling slowly in the afternoon snow. Beneath the canvas of the family tent, Gretta Webster was bent in grief. Upon hearing a single Presbyterian rumor that her son had taken his life, Gretta had sworn never again to sing in a Protestant church. Except for her and the Judge, Zulu and I had been the only ones allowed to see Shelly before Gretta closed the casket. I lifted Zulu up so together we could see the last of our great friend, blond Shelly, with his powdered smile and his plastic hands folded in silence. Gretta then cried aloud and screamed out against Heaven and Almighty God. Zulu swore to rejoin the philistines of the circus and to remove his suffering soul from Deen, Alabama, forevermore.

. . . a time of war, and a time of peace.

Now why, pray, had the preacher broken away

from Shelly Webster to praise Corporal Clayton Slaughter, who "had given his all for God and country"? And to even *mention* me? "Silas Simeon, who stands among us, with wings and uniform, ready to make the selfsame sacrifice . . ." Heavenly Jesus!

Furious at Butterworth's impropriety, Zulu stepped forward through the legs of the mourners, slapped the snow from his whiskers, and marched away.

In benediction, we droned in unison:

Ourfatherwhichartinheaven
Hallowedbethyname . . .

IV

Time, Shelly once explained to a bewildered me, is the cosmic enigma of trying to measure in uncertain space the speeds and distances of objects or entities as they approach or depart from each other, a calculation that is performed in the fragile hope that the objects or entities, if indeed they do exist and are capable of detection, are not themselves destroyed—which would be the end of time.

The night before I left for the war, just for the hell of it I made a sketch of my Jar of Marbles and discovered it was not as easy as I thought, even though it is hard to imagine anything simpler than drawing a rectangle with circles in it and letters in the circles. It was more apparent than ever not only that the jar was itself of a very fragile nature but that in time it would be too small—unless, of course, I got killed in the war. It was also now more alarmingly clear that if I played my game fairly, I could not cast out any of those who had already entered, even those I hated. Nevertheless, even though I'm the world's worst artist and cannot even draw a dog without getting all the legs on one side, I attempted a graphic inventory of my jar, an open-ended rectangle, half full of encircled letters: a big (X) for me, an (M) for Mother, (S) for Sylvia, (SH) for Shelly, (B) for Blue, (Z) for Zulu, (AR) for Aunt Rebecca, (G) for Uncle George, (Q) for Queeny, (C) for Clayton. . . . There was no way really to complete the drawing on paper. There were other faces, other souls, of course; but it was impossible to tell the exact population of my jar. Some members, especially the older ones and those who had entered suddenly or had dropped in uninvited, were clearly colored, distinct, and initialed; others, like the folks downtown or the airmen in my training squadron, were embryonic half-moons floating in a misty background. Also—as the De Havilland and Mother's Rose Book, the cockroach and the deadly moccasin at the Blue Hole proved—not all my marbles were human.

Later that night, like a shadow, Mother tipped

into my room, tucked me in, kissed me on the forehead, and promised she had not the slightest doubt I would prevail. In prospect of my return she bequeathed to me her Rose Book and placed in my hand a copy of Shakespeare's sonnets.

"Goddammit! Goddammit!" I cried into Mother's shoulder. "They blame me—*me*—for what Johnny Holliday did!"

"I know. I know," Mother said. "Let it be. All wars aren't won by bombs and bullets. When you return, my poems shall be yours." She released her light fingers across my brow. "Pleasant dreams," she whispered. I recalled what Mother once said about truth: If knowing it made you free, it didn't promise to make you happy.

I was startled at Mother's fragility, her sticklike elbows, her glazed cheeks, but inspired by her invisible strength. Uncle George would never fly again. The De Havilland, lost now to this world, was secure within my sphere of memories; and Mother's poems, still closed to me in secrecy, would one day be mine.

V

So arrived the last morning of my military leave.

I had by now about wearied out all my goddamns on Johnny Holliday, who had disappeared from Alabama. It had been eight months since my stormy flight down the river and Sylvia's abortion. Although the mortal horde of Deen—excepting Mother—still supposed I was guilty of Johnny's crime, it no longer mattered to me. Even Father never bothered now to tune his brain in to such static; and at its mention Uncle George only winked at me.

I put Holliday to rest and took the snapshot from my billfold. I now looked directly at Sylvia. The roach had inflicted a jagged amputation. But Sylvia's best parts remained: her hips, her smile, her eyes.

Mother and Father were seeing me off on the bus, headed for Agnes Scott College to see Sylvia. Zulu, although crushed by Shelly's death, was present, dressed in vest and black bowler hat and smoking a huge cigar. He was Winston Churchill. Would he, Zulu the magician, Zulu the artist, be swallowed up again by the bastard circus whence he came? Who would dare predict? In grim seriousness, he forked up to me two stubby fingers in a V for victory and slipped a little cardboard square in the pocket of my military blouse. Uncle George, inflexible in his neck brace, gave me a bear hug and pointed to the silver bomb in the center of my wings. "You can cram one of these up Hitler's ass," he said. There was a faint aroma of bourbon about him. I walked over and shook hands with Father, who was fiddling with the car radio, trying to get some war news. On the little cardboard square, Zulu had painted a small brown man riding a tiger. In the jungle background was a white giant. The white giant was Shelly. The square's back bore an ink-drawn swastika cut in two with a broadsword. I placed the tiny painting in my billfold between Sylvia's snapshot and Blue's half of the Confederate bill. Mother stood on tiptoes to kiss me on the chin. "Take care," she said. "Write. When you get to Agnes Scott, kiss Sylvia on the mouth and tell her she's not perfect enough to be all wrong."

For me it was now bye bye Alabama and hello bombsight.

Good-bye Shelly. Good-bye all.

Dear, poor Shelly. Well, time, or whatever time is or was, had also become a part of my Jar of Marbles.

Would Sylvia be at Agnes Scott?

Would she avoid me because of her shame?

Sylvia and I, on identical buses in broad daylight, trying to meet, in fact passed each other. We were on the same route, not ten feet apart at a rest station, she pulling in for a stop and I pulling out, when our eyes met. Sylvia coming to me. I going to her. To say exactly what to each other, I could not imagine.

❖

Outside my bus window familiar road signs flicked by.

It had started to rain.

"Sylvia—" Her name came to my lips.

I sighed and, from a fresh pack, tapped out a smoke.

"Now," I said to the surprised cigarette, "what are we going to do?"